DEATHBLOW
By Joan Sween

The Encore Killer always returns
to the crime scene and kills again.

For Doug

Chapter 1: Evening, Sunday, July 4

Five minutes from the end of his life, Michael Maguire paused at the gate for a last look to make sure the yard of Building #3 was clean. Beer cans and trash had been bagged and carried out. The demonstrators had taken their protest signs away. All that was left of the UFCW rally, as usual, was the severed chain hanging from Blue Ribbon's gate.

Just as he turned to leave, his eye passed over the loading dock one last time, and picked out the top edges of signs that had been tossed in a corner. Clifford must have already passed on his rounds or he would have picked them up, Michael thought. He went back to clear them out.

Walking toward the loading dock, he checked his watch. He didn't want to be late for the fireworks. Annette would have given the kids long naps and have them ready in their pajamas and slippers. After the fireworks, their warm sleepy little bodies could be tucked straight into bed. They were good kids. Stevie, at five, would be starting kindergarten this fall and was antsy to make new friends. The kid was quite a talker; Michael hoped he got a teacher who could deal kindly with boundless enthusiasm. Lizzie, one year younger, would feel the loss when her big brother was at school. He and Annette would have to make sure she had games and pals of her own.

He smiled to himself thinking of next weekend. Annette's birthday was on the Fourth, but when Stevie came, they agreed to start celebrating her birthday a week later. Make sure one occasion didn't rob from the other.

She would be surprised this year. For months he had an expensive cookware set on lay-by at the Ultimate Gourmet. He knew she wanted these in a big way. She would cry. She always cried when he hit the nail on the head with a perfect present.

He retrieved six colored signs on wood handles from the corner of the loading dock. He'd throw them in the trunk and get rid of them later. Walking back, his thoughts touched on a promotion to line foreman that he was hoping for--if the company could weather the current economic crisis. It would mean, finally, a better car for them.

"Mr. Maguire?"

He had been so wrapped up in his thoughts he hadn't seen anyone approach. The man held out a card and said, "Chicago Regional UFCW; interested in how the rally went. I have an evaluation form here I want you to look at." He pulled a folded paper from a pocket and stepped away a few feet from Maguire to catch the light with it.

"I can't stay," said Maguire. "I have two kids waiting to see the fireworks."

#   #   #   #   #   #   #

Chapter 2: Before dawn, Monday, July 5

"Dead on the Fourth of July," said Middleton. "Lucky for the family. Easy date to remember."

"Leave it to you," said Stangler. "When shit happens, you'll have something funny to say."

Lit by security lights, the body sprawled on the macadam lot of Blue Ribbon Building #3.

Wiley Middleton pulled out a small notebook and started drawing the scene.

The dead man lay face down, one leg bent at the knee. Splayed under him in a fan shape, brightly-colored signs on wood handles demanded higher wages. One arm was caught under the body, the other bent up at the elbow, maybe in surprise or maybe in an attempt to break his fall. He wore work boots, cotton shirt, jeans, and a small neat bullet hole in the back of his head.

Blood made a trail down the back of his neck and continued in a trickle across the surface of the lot, but not far. Death must have been close to instantaneous; the heart ceased pumping, the blood went into stasis.

One hundred feet away, two uniformed officers guarded a gate in the ten-foot chain link fence enclosing the Blue Ribbon meat-packing plant. Their car slanted in to the curb, roof lights flashing.

"We supposed to leave the flashers going?" asked Simonson.

"Yeah," said Lavorski. "Until someone says turn 'em off."

"Man, I never worked a homicide before. I couldn't remember if us or Dispatch was supposed to do the Car 21 call."

"Ya learn as ya go. Keep an eye on Wiley; you'll be okay."

"Which one's Wiley?"

"The big black one. He's real smart, but he's okay anyway." Lavorski glanced up to where the two detectives stood. "Just remember, don't piss off Lobo."

"Are those cowboy boots that he's---"

"And *never* mention the boots!"

"Why do they call him 'Lobo?'"

"His real name's Lovar Boris."

Stangler checked his watch and looked up the street. Two-oh-five a.m., technically Monday, July 5th, now. The County Medical Examiner had come and gone. The State Crime Lab should show up soon. At this time of night there was almost no traffic. One lone dark van passed by slowly. He pointed to one of the men at the gate and made a come-here gesture. Simonson trotted over.

"When more uniforms show up, get them to canvassing the neighborhood. We're looking for anyone who heard a shot or saw anything."

Simonson turned a questioning look at Middleton.

"What?" said Stangler. "You need permission from Middleton?"

"Uh... no, sir... just... yessir! Right away!" Simonson stumbled over his own feet, got straightened out, and moved off smartly.

"What was that all about?" said Stangler.

"Beats me."

A white van marked "State of Minnesota, Crime Scene Unit" pulled through the gates. Door slams announced the four-man team as they got out. Actually, three men, one woman.

"Got a gunshot case for you," called Middleton before he noticed who was in the lead.

"We'll decide that, Detective," said Bradford C. Holmes, as he approached. Lean, with a gray brush cut, piercing stare, and an aversion to social skills, Holmes was respected for his forensic skills, but called "Surecock Holmes" behind his back.

"Moron," muttered Middleton.

"Touch anything?" snapped Holmes.

"No."

"Trample all around the body destroying evidence?"

"I checked for life," said Middleton.

"Jesus! How many times do I have to tell you people to stay away from the body!"

"We do that," said Stangler, "right after we determine if it's a body or an injured person. How would you like me to trample some of your teeth down your throat?"

"Just get out of the way," said Holmes.

"One of these days I'm going to let him have it," said Stangler as they walked toward the night watchman sitting on the edge of a loading dock.

Stangler had grown up in the heart of gang territory in Minneapolis, saved from getting into serious trouble by a mother whose heavy hand he feared worse than the Lords and the Dons. He went into police work the same way some men go into the army, as a discipline for violence. He found he liked the work, was good at it, and once he got a rein on his temper, moved rapidly up to detective status. The move to Riverbend meant more pay and less mindless bloodshed.

William Edward Middleton was the only son of university professors who were dumbfounded when he set aside his liberal arts education and became a policeman. Marriage to an Amazon who taught in the

Riverbend public schools took him out of Minneapolis and down river.

Bets were numerous on their partnership not lasting, but that was three years ago, and the pools had long since disbanded.

The night watchman, a short, skinny, old guy in patched work clothes, spat on the blacktop as they neared.

"I'm Detective Middleton," he said, showing his badge, "and this is Detective Stangler."

"Yeah. You said that before." He looked up at Middleton, who was six-four with a 25-inch shoulder span. "You useta play for the Vikings?"

"Nahh. Buncha sissies."

"Say that again." He spat. Sliding his eyes toward Stangler's long hair, he looked as though he might venture another comment.

Stangler eyed him with a challenging smile.

Spitting again, the night watchman decided against it.

At five-nine with glossy brunette hair that he combed back from his face and let fall to his shoulders, Stangler was a magnet for comments from the unwise. Some wondered if that's exactly why he grew it. It happened so gradually that by the time the department higher-ups realized they should have said something about his hair a long time ago, he had become their best detective and near irreplaceable.

"You're the night watchman?" said Middleton.

"Yeah."

"The regular night watchman?" said Stangler, frowning slightly at the codger.

"I ain't the night strongman, okay? I'm the night *watch* man. I check the doors, check the gates, walk around. I see or hear anythin' funny, I call in. Most action we ever get is pizza-face morons with spray cans tryin' ta climb the fence."

"Who do you call?" said Middleton.

"Blue Ribbon security guy."

"They have security?"

"Durin' the day. They need'm to break up fights, throw shitheads out, bust heads when uh monkey wrench gets thrown inta the ham-bagger, that sorta stuff."

"But not at night?"

"At night they got me. Night watchman for 17 years and nuthin's ever happened." He spat. "Till tonight."

"Tell us about finding the body."

"Nuthin' ta tell. I was walkin' the yards, came around the corner 'a Buildin' 3, and there he was. I called 911; called Security."

"Did you hear a shot?" said Stangler.

"Naw. I coulda been way out at Buildin' 6 when he got it."

"Anything else unusual tonight?" said Middleton.

"Naw. Nothin' outa the ordinary." He spat again. "'Cept a dead body. Lester Jerglens. Good riddance."

"You didn't like him?"

"Blue Ribbon suits di'n like him. Security di'n like him. Mosta the guys on t'line di'n like him. I di'n like him. Hell, we're all suspects." He spat. "Only mystery is why no one did it sooner."

Stangler looked at Middleton with raised eyebrows. "Looks like we've got motive covered."

"A plethora of suspects," said Middleton, shaking his head. "What did Mr. Jerglens do to win the Congeniality award?"

"Huh?"

"Why did everybody dislike him?"

The night watchman spat. "Stupid asshole always insisted on his rights." Seeing the blank looks on the detectives, he said, "Say Jerglens is standin' on the sidewalk and a runaway truck jumped the curb and is headin' right for him. You could holler, 'Watch out! Move! Get off the sidewalk!' and he'd stand right there and scream, 'This's a public sidewalk! I got a right t'be here, n' you can't tell me t'move!' Stupid asshole. Brains of a cockroach."

"So what's with the signs he was carrying?"

"Musta been left over after the rally."

"What rally?"

"Union had a big rally here earlier. Four-five hundred of 'em screamin' 'bout their wages, wavin' signs, lookin' like morons."

Both detectives looked at him in astonishment. "You said nothing else happened tonight," said Middleton.

"I said nothin' outa t'ordinary happened t'night. Union has this rally every Fourth a July, same ol', same ol'. Contracts are up on the 15th; they have a rally on the Fourth, screamin' 'bout how they needa be paid more next contract."

"So he could have been killed during the rally? No one would hear a shot over all the noise," said Middleton.

"Coulda, but wasn't. Rally starts 'round six 'n everybody clears out by eight ta go see the fireworks. I passed here right after that 'n there was no body then."

Middleton's cell phone rang. He answered it and looked toward the gate where the two uniforms talked to a wildly gesturing bearded man in a gray sweat suit.

"Hang on." He turned to Stangler. "Some guy kicking up a fuss. Says if something happened at the rally, he should have been notified. What do you think?"

Stangler looked toward the gate. "Might be their security."

"Let him come." Middleton clipped the phone back to his belt.

"What happened?" the man called as he covered the distance at a run. He pointed at the night watchman. "Don't say anything, Clifford." Fat and out of shape, he leaned forward, hands on knees, sucking in air.

Stangler studied his face. The man was wearing an honest-to-god Van Dyke beard, the goatee portion waxed to a curling point and the mustache curled into a handlebar.

"I'm Ray Harrington," the man said as soon as he could breathe easier. "Vice-president of the UFCW local. If there's trouble, the Union should have been notified immediately. What happened? What do those police cars mean? There was no trouble at the---"

"Shut up and quit running off at the mouth," said Stangler.

Harrington opened and closed his mouth several times, looked at Middleton, looked at Stangler, shut his mouth, and waited.

"Detective Stangler," he said, showing his badge, "and Detective Middleton. This is a crime scene. We don't consult with citizens."

"I'm not an ordinary citizen! I'm Vice-president of the Union!"

"You're an officious asshole," said Stangler, turning away. "Go home."

Harrington didn't move. After a moment and using a conciliatory tone, he asked, "What kind of a crime scene? Was there a break in?"

Middleton and Stangler exchanged a look, with the senior detective giving a slight chin drop of a nod.

Middleton turned to Harrington. "I'm sorry to say someone, probably a co-worker, was shot here tonight."

Stangler could see the blood leave Harrington's face. "Shot? Like shot dead?"

Middleton nodded.

"That's terrible," said Harrington, shaking his head. "One of the guys? Dead?" He rubbed his eyes with two fingers of one hand, and drew in a deep breath. "Tempers were hot at the rally, but... shot? Wh... who?"

"Lester Jerglens," said the night watchman, and spat.

"Oh," said Harrington, looking surprised, but not shocked. "Oh," he said again.

"Was he a friend of yours?" said Middleton.

"He was a dues-paying union member in good standing."

"Answer the damn question," said Stangler. "Was he a friend of yours?"

"Uh. Well, no."

"But you knew him fairly well."

"Well, yeah. We worked the same shift."

"You didn't like him," said Stangler.

"Terrible thing to say, him being dead and all, but I don't know anyone who did like him."

"*Un embarras de la richesse,*" muttered Middleton, who had taken French in college and liked to show off.

"What?" said Harrington.

"Too many suspects," said Middleton.

"Never mind," said Stangler, turning back toward the crime scene. "Mr. Harrington if you would remain right here, as soon as we---"

"Oh, no," said Harrington, straightening and jutting his goatee. "As the only union representative on site, I should be given the courtesy of all the facts. I want to see where Lester was shot." He cocked his fists on his hips.

"No," said Stangler, looking steely-eyed.

"I might notice details that you wouldn't realize are significant," Harrington shot back. He bounced on his toes belligerently.

Middleton raised questioning eyebrows at Stangler, who stared thoughtfully at Harrington for a moment. "All right, come with me," he said.

As Stangler and Harrington moved toward the scene of the crime, Middleton gestured at the officers near the gate. The night watchman's statement would need to be taken. Lavorski hurried over.

"What was that business with Simonson?" said Middleton.

Lavorski wasn't surprised Middleton remembered their names. The big detective's retentive memory was well known in the Law Enforcement Center.

"Uh, nothing. Murder scene, you know. He's just afraid of screwing up."

After giving instructions, Middleton caught up with Stangler and the union rep as they approached the crime scene, now lit with portable flood lights, all three stopping 20 feet away.

"Was he shot during the rally?" Harrington asked.

Holmes looked up. "Stop. That's far enough," he commanded.

"You notice we're already stopped, you self-important pissant?" said Stangler.

"Oh, very professional," sniffed Holmes, going back to his procedures.

"See anything?" Stangler asked Harrington.

"I'm looking," he said.

The Crime Lab techs got into position to turn the body over. With two of them rolling and two bracing so as not to dislodge anything, they turned the body.

"Ohmigod!" squeaked Harrington from a swelling throat. "Ohmigod! Oh, noooo!"

Stangler and Middleton leaped to catch him as his knees buckled and he pitched forward.

"That's not Lester Jerglens!"

* * * * * * * * * *

"Lemme go! I didn't faint," growled Harrington, jerking his arm free of Middleton's steadying hand. "I just felt a little unsteady."

"Sure," said Middleton, understanding Harrington's embarrassment and stepping back.

Middleton watched the Crime Lab people carefully pick up a half sheet of paper from under the body, slip it into a clear plastic evidence bag, seal it, and label it.

"May I see that?" he said.

"It's evidence," said Holmes, dropping it into a box of other bagged items.

"Come on, Holmes, don't be such a horse's hind end. You've got it bagged and tagged."

Holmes emitted a sigh of deep long-suffering, pulled the bag out of the box and handed it to one of his assistants who made a wide circuit of the area to hand it to Middleton.

Stangler came back with the night watchman. When Harrington took a breath, the senior detective's hand shot out toward him, finger pointed in an unmistakable admonition to be quiet.

The night watchman looked to the white-faced union rep for a clue to what was going on. Receiving nothing, he turned to view the crime scene.

"Ah, crap!" he said. "Goddammit to hell!" He walked a few steps away and spat. Turning back, he glared at the detectives as though they had done something wrong. "Ah, man," he said, with tears running down his wrinkled cheeks, "That ain't Lester Jerglens." He hauked twice, trying to clear his throat. "Ah, crap," he said softly. "It's Mike Maguire." He pulled a wrinkled handkerchief from his back pocket and blew his nose. "Jeez, Mikey Maguire. Who in hell would want to shoot Mikey Maguire?"

"Why did you think it was Jerglens?" said Stangler.

"Ah, jeez. All them rally signs, you know. 'N Jerglens pissed everyone off, one time er another."

"He's right," said Harrington. "From the back, it could have been Lester, and Jerglens was... is... the kind of jerk who was asking for it. You announce to the guys on the line, 'A Blue Ribbon worker got shot last night,' and everyone would say, 'Good. Someone finally shut that piece-a-shit Jerglens up.'"

While the two Blue Ribbon employees stood in mute mourning, Middleton held the plastic bag up to Stangler, turned to catch the light. Half a sheet of plain paper, hand printing, black ink.

"OUR SACRED DUTY
DEATH TO ABUSERS AND USURPERS
DEATH TO THE HOUNDS
OF ABSOLUTE DESPOTS
NEW GUARDS FOR FUTURE SECURITY"

* * * * * * * * * *

The State Crime Lab van was gone, the body was on its quiet unmarked way to the Riverbend morgue in the basement of Our Lady of Hope. All that could be done that night was in progress.

"Okay, Mr. Haugen, lock it up," Middleton called to the night watchman. "Keep anyone out of the yellow tape area till our people get here tomorrow."

The night watchman spat, but offered no comment.

"We got people canvassing?" Wiley said to Lavorski as the two detectives neared the gate.

"Yessir."

"Where's Simonson?"

"He wasn't here when I was done with that statement. I figured you guys sent him somewhere."

"No, we didn't." Middleton pulled his phone off his belt. "Dispatch? Ask Luke Simonson to check in, give us his 10-20. Radio it in."

Several moments passed before Lavorski's radio crackled. "Simonson not responding."

"Have her check with people canvassing."

Middleton drew a scowling Stangler aside while Lavorski talked to Dispatch. "He's new. Probably accidentally keyed his radio off."

Lavorski's radio cracked with negative responses, then suddenly, "Code 30! Code 30! 1565 NW 43rd Street! Code 30!"

"Stay here! Close the gates!" Stangler shouted at Lavorski as he and Middleton ran up the street, guns drawn, in response to the "Officer Down" call.

#   #   #   #   #   #

Chapter 3: Noon, Monday, July 5

(Theme Music:)
(Voiceover:)
THIS IS KRBM-TV, NEWS AT NOON. UP TO THE
MINUTE REPORTING ON WHAT'S HAPPENING IN
THE RIVER LAND WITH NOON NEWS ANCHOR
SALLY FELDNER.

(Anchor:)
GOOD NOON TO YOU, MONDAY, JULY 5.

TWO HOMICIDES HAVE LEFT A BLACK MARK ON
RIVERBEND'S FOURTH OF JULY FESTIVITIES.

LATE LAST NIGHT THE BODY OF MICHAEL
PATRICK MAGUIRE WAS DISCOVERED ON THE
GROUNDS OF BLUE RIBBON FOODS, DEAD FROM
GUNSHOT WOUNDS. MAGUIRE WAS WELL KNOWN
AND RESPECTED AS THE PRESIDENT OF THE
LOCAL CHAPTER OF UNITED FOOD AND
COMMERCIAL WORKERS, ACCORDING TO OTHER
MEMBERS. THE 32-YEAR-OLD VICTIM LEAVES A
WIFE AND TWO CHILDREN.

EARLIER IN THE EVENING UFCW MEMBERS HAD
STAGED A RALLY DEMANDING PAY HIKES AND
INCREASED INSURANCE BENEFITS FOR THE
COMING YEAR. LOCAL ECONOMIC SOURCES SAY
BLUE RIBBON IS ON THE ROPES AND EITHER AN
INCREASE IN WAGES OR A MASSIVE WALK-OUT
WILL DEAL THE COMPANY A DEATH BLOW.

HOURS AFTER THE DISCOVERY OF MAGUIRE'S
BODY, AND ONLY TWO BLOCKS FROM THE SCENE,
POLICE OFFICER LUKE SIMONSON WAS SHOT AND
KILLED, APPARENTLY WHILE CANVASSING THE

NEIGHBORHOOD FOR POSSIBLE WITNESSES. SIMONSON, 26, WAS UNMARRIED, THE ONLY SON OF JACOB AND ALBERTA SIMONSON OF RURAL RIVERBEND.

ACCORDING TO A LAW ENFORCEMENT CENTER SPOKESMAN, DETECTIVES HAVE NO SUSPECTS IN EITHER MURDER AT THIS TIME, NOR WOULD THEY CONFIRM THAT OFFICER SIMONSON MAY HAVE ATTEMPTED TO APPREHEND THE FLEEING KILLER.

WATCH KRBM NEWS AT SIX WHEN WE WILL HAVE INTERVIEWS WITH UNION MEMBERS AND POLICE OFFICERS CLOSE TO THE TWO VICTIMS.
....
ON A SOMEWHAT HAPPIER NOTE, LITTLE EIGHT-YEAR-OLD ANTHONY HAGEN, WHO HAD A FIRECRACKER EXPLODE IN HIS HAND YESTERDAY, WILL NOT LOSE THE SIGHT IN HIS INJURED RIGHT EYE, ACCORDING TO INFORMATION RECEIVED BY HIS PARENTS.

TAKEN BY HELICOPTER TO ROCHESTER'S MAYO CLINIC, ANTHONY UNDERWENT SIX-HOURS OF SURGERY ON HIS FACE AND RIGHT HAND. A CLINIC SPOKESMAN ANNOUNCED THAT DOCTORS ARE OPTIMISTIC THE EYE WILL RECOVER, AND THEY FEEL HOPEFUL THAT ANTHONY'S RE-ATTACHED FINGERS WILL EVENTUALLY REACH 80% OF NORMAL FUNCTION.
....
UNDER THE HEADING OF GOOD DEEDS, YESTERDAY EVENING, ALMA MICKLESON, WIDOWED FOR FIVE YEARS AND BADLY AFFLICTED BY ARTHRITIS, RETURNED TO HER HOME TO FIND A VERY PLEASANT SURPRISE. UNABLE TO DO YARD WORK OR AFFORD LAWN CARE AND TRASH PICKUP, MS MICKLESON HAD REGRETFULLY WATCHED HER HOME OF 50 YEARS

BECOME AN EYESORE, WITH NEIGHBORS PETITIONING THE CITY TO CONDEMN THE PROPERTY.

WHILE SHE WAS ON A SALVATION ARMY BUS TRIP TO SEE THE FIREWORKS, HER PROPERTY WAS MOWED, CLEANED, PICKED UP, AND BEAUTIFIED. ON HER RETURN, SHE FOUND A REJUVENATED HOME. A GREEN BERET WAS LEFT ON HER FRONT PORCH, WITH A NOTE SAYING SIMPLY, 'HELPING MAKE OUR WORLD BETTER.'

WATCH KRBM NEWS AT SIX WHEN WE WILL HAVE INTERVIEWS WITH HER NEIGHBORS, WHO, IN A DRAMATIC TURN-AROUND, NOW WONDER WHY THEY DIDN'T "PITCH IN" INSTEAD OF PETITIONING.
....
THE TEACHERS' STRIKE CONTINUES TO GENERATE HEATED TEMPERS. KRBM NEWS AT SIX WILL HAVE A COMPLETE UPDATE.
....
WE'LL BE RIGHT BACK WITH "WINDY" WINDHORST AND THE WEATHER. "WINDY" WILL TELL US HOW LONG WE CAN EXPECT THIS BALMY WEATHER TO STICK AROUND.

# # # # #

Chapter 4: Early afternoon, Monday, July 5

Middleton hunched at his desk in the cluttered detectives' room, thoughtfully re-reading his notes while Stangler paced behind his own desk. The clear plastic evidence bag lay on its surface.

"OUR SACRED DUTY
DEATH TO ABUSERS AND USURPERS
DEATH TO THE HOUNDS
OF ABSOLUTE DESPOTS
NEW GUARDS FOR FUTURE SECURITY"

Stangler looked at his notes again. "Dammit, Wiley, I get pie-eyed reading what I've got from these Blue Ribbon people at the fireworks! A remembers seeing B standing near the keg talking to C and D after the big blue burst with squiggly stars. C can't remember talking to B, but he's sure he saw E and F sitting on lawn chairs with their wives just before the bunch of red bursts that were so loud. It's a damned crossword puzzle!" He sat down and tossed his notepad on the desk. "We'll give our notes to Emily, have her make some sort of chart. Maybe something will stand out."

Four uniformed officers walked into the room. Stangler recognized them as all men with double-digit years of experience with RPD. They looked grim.

Knowing Stangler wasn't good with names, Middleton helped him out by nodding a greeting at each man. "Klindworth. Tufte. Harders. Kaminski."

They nodded back. "Middleton."

There was an awkward silence, then Kaminski, a respected cop who kept himself in shape, said, "Lavorski's pretty torn up."

"Yeah," said Stangler. "We all are."

"Simonson was a rookie."

"Yeah, that sucks."

"Lavorski thinks it's his fault," said Kaminski.

"It's not his fault," said Stangler.

"Someone should have made sure the kid understood his orders," said Kaminski, looking uncomfortable but determined. The other three shifted uneasily but kept unapologetic eye contact with the senior detective.

Stangler and Middleton both slowly stood up. Without looking at him, Stangler motioned Middleton back in his chair.

"Yes," said Stangler, looking straight back at the challenging cops. "Knowing he was a rookie, I should have made him repeat the order back to me and asked if he understood it. I should have cautioned him to keep a head's-up at a crime scene. I feel like shit because it's my fault, and I can't go back and fix it."

"Yeah, well...." said Kaminski, dropping his gaze and easing up on his tone. "We'd like to know exactly what you did tell him."

"He and Lavorski were on the gate. I called him over and told him when more uniforms showed up to tell them to start canvassing the neighborhood."

"Could he have thought you meant him, too?"

"Ah man, I don't see how, Kaminski. I've been over it a hundred times in my mind, but there was nothing special about it. It was just a routine request."

Middleton shifted uneasily in his chair, wanting to back up Stangler, but understanding that anything that smacked of defensiveness would be the wrong thing.

Kaminski nodded, relaxed his stance and hooked a thumb in his belt. The others nodded and looked mollified.

"So he misunderstood and was canvassing," said Kaminski.

"We don't think so," said Stangler, looking over at Middleton to bring him into the conversation.

"Simonson passed the instruction on to the next uniforms," said Middleton. "He was at the gate when they left to canvass. Something else drew him away."

Captain Harlow Pickett walked in and looked at the uniformed officers in surprise.

Kaminski nodded at the two detectives, and all four cops walked out.

"What was that all about?" said Pickett.

"Lavorski feels guilty. They're worried about it." said Stangler.

"You guys want to talk more about Simonson?"

"No," said Stangler.

"Okay," said Pickett, "let's talk about the citizen you have in Interrogation Two. I've gotten complaints; suggesting you either calm him down or shoot him."

"That's our boy, Lester Jerglens," said Middleton, getting up. "When I called, he said he had his rights, he didn't need to talk to us, and we couldn't make him."

Standing beside each other, Middleton and Pickett were a contrast. Both were 6'4" and the same color, but where Pickett was a lean marathon runner with muscles like cello strings, Middleton had a linebacker's build.

"And so...?" said Pickett.

"So I asked Rask and Stummer to go get him," said Middleton.

Pickett pulled a chair over and sank into it laughing.

"I am not laughing!" said Pickett. "You have to be careful with those two; they're going to land us in a lawsuit one of these days."

"I thought the handcuffs might have been a bit excessive," said Middleton, "but I didn't want to criticize my fellow detectives."

"Ah, shit!" said Pickett. "One of these days I'm going to have to kill all four of you. His squealing is upsetting the whole floor."

"We'll talk to him," said Stangler. "Irritating asshole. I was hoping he'd burst a blood vessel. He's the only guy not nominating the victim for sainthood. We'll have to nail down where he was and see if he owns any firearms."

"You going to call him a suspect?" asked Pickett.

"Have to," said Stangler, "he's all we've got until we find anything about any New Guards. This note could be misdirection."

Pickett stood up. "You guys get anything to go on, come tell me what it looks like. We're keeping the note under wraps, right?"

"Yes."

"Lavorski remember anything else?"

"No, dammit. He and the night watchman had their backs turned, using the loading dock to write on. They thought Simonson was watching the gate."

Assistant Chief Roger Jevne walked into the room. The other three waited in silence as Jevne made his way to Stangler's desk. Stangler tried for a professional attitude of acceptance. Of course the higher-ups would be checking on the circumstances of Simonson's murder, and here was Jevne doing just that. Again.

"Harlow," Jevne said, nodding at Pickett.

"Roger."

"Detective Stangler," said Jevne, the formality of the address ominous, "you've had some time to go over this in your mind. You're sure Officer Simonson was not carrying out any instruction from you?"

"I'm sure."

"Could either of you offer any explanation as to why Officer Simonson was found dead two blocks away?"

"Dammit, no!" said Stangler, leaping up. "You think this isn't killing us? You think we aren't asking ourselves what the hell happened? We don't know why the hell the kid left the gate!"

"Okay, okay," said Jevne, holding his hands up in a placating gesture. "This has got the whole department shook up. I'm sorry the questions have to be asked. And probably asked again. Just keep your cool and we'll get through it." He turned to go. "Sorry, Harlow," he said as he left the room.

"Hang in there," said Pickett as Stangler dropped back into his chair. Then he, too, left the room.

#   #   #   #   #

Chapter 5: Monday, June 14
THREE WEEKS BEFORE
THE MAGUIRE MURDER

Martin Driver stepped out of the warehouse and heard the automatic lock thunk behind him.

He was now completely "less." Homeless. Emotionless. Purposeless. Since his wife and daughter--all that meant "home" to him--had died in a car crash a year ago, he had ceased to care. His loved ones gone, he had divested himself of everything he previously thought he valued. It took him the time since the accident to accomplish his "divestment," but now he had nothing. He didn't care if the sun came up tomorrow, if he was hot or cold, hungry or full, lived or died.

Hands in pockets, the 45-year-old man hung his head and walked aimlessly in the direction of downtown. He wore blue jeans, soft athletic-style shoes, and a short-sleeved cotton plaid shirt. He didn't notice the pleasant air of the mid-June morning or the warm sun on his dark brown skin. The passing scene interested him little. His direction was whatever; his destination wherever. He moved for no particular reason.

Reaching a small park on the downtown periphery, he sat on a bench. The ascending sun behind him made moving shadow patterns on the sides of the tall downtown buildings. For hours, his eyes noted the patterns. His heart didn't notice, didn't care.

* * * * * * * * * *

Sunset came and went. Darkness settled in.
Monday was now passing the midnight mark, becoming
Tuesday.

Excepting a couple trips to a restroom in the
nearby library, Martin Driver had not left the park
bench. City lights obscured the stars, leaving the
moon's silver crescent to reign alone. Martin didn't
notice the sunset or the moon. It was enough to sit with
an empty mind.

"Yeee hah!" suddenly rang through the quiet
night. Tires squealed. Something broke with a shatter
somewhere. "Nailed that sucker!" was shouted.

Martin didn't care enough to wonder what it was
all about.

Some minutes later, a jacked-up pickup roared
past. "Hey! Hey! Turn around!" a raucous voice
shouted. His attention caught by the noise, Martin's
eyes listlessly followed the truck, saw it squeal into a
U-turn two blocks down the street and head back in his
direction.

He turned away, insufficiently curious to see
where it was going.

A hand grabbed the back of his shirt collar,
pulling him off the bench onto his knees in the grass.

"Are you suicidal or just stupid?" a voice snarled
close to his ear. "Come on! Follow me!"

Martin looked around to see a solitary woman's
figure, bent double, scrabbling through the grass toward
the darker reaches of the park. She stopped and looked
back. "Move it! Move it! Before they see us!"

Unsure what the hurry was, Martin got his feet
under him, running and stumbling after her.

She led across the park, along a bike path, over an
iron railing, down a steep rock-piled slope that was
treacherous in the dark, and finally stopped on an area
of flat packed earth punctuated by weedy hummocks

beneath a small bridge. She sat on a grassy tangle and gestured for him to do the same.

"What were you doing out there? Her voice was rough and demanding.

"Nothing."

"Oh, sure, and roadkill isn't flat!"

It took him a moment to get his mind on top of what she meant. By then she was at him again. "Hell, were you waiting for someone?"

"No."

Short and small-boned, she rubbed her hands through a tangle of curly auburn hair, produced a cigarette from the pocket of belt-cinched jeans too big for her, lit it, and studied him. Ambient light from the streetlights on the bridge dispelled the deeper shadows around them. Martin guessed she was in her early 30's.

"What were you doing on the park bench?" she asked again.

"Nothing."

"Ah, just shoot me!" she said in disgust.

"I'm homeless."

"Yeah, and I'm Miss Minnesota!" She started to laugh, sucked in a breath of smoke, coughed, smacked her chest, tipped sideways, made some more "huk, huk" sounds that may have been laughing, then finally sat up again.

"What's funny?" he said.

"Look at you. You're not street people."

"I'm just starting out."

"Now we've got entry level?" Laughing and coughing, she flopped on her back in the weeds, kicking her feet gleefully. "We're going to need a bigger boat!"

Martin felt a tiny bubble of irritation rise to the smooth surface of his apathy.

She sat up. "What's your name?"

"Martin."

"Okay, Martin. You can call me Muggs. You're not homeless, you're clueless. I saved your ass once, I guess like the Chinese say, I'm responsible for you. But only so far. Stick with me tonight, and tomorrow I'll help you get home."

"I don't have a home. I'm homeless."

She regarded him thoughtfully, snuffing her cigarette out on the dirt, dropping the butt into a nearby tin can. "Yes, you have a home. Don't be a jerk. Something pissed you off and you came out here to pout and make them sorry you're gone."

"No," he said, shaking his head.

"You've accomplished your mission. By tomorrow morning, your family's probably going to be worried sick about you."

"I don't have a family."

"Martin, I'm running out of buttons for you to push. Why don't you have a family?"

"They're gone."

"They'll come back."

"No."

"Okay. Whatever," she said with exasperation. "Tomorrow we'll get you back wherever you came from. I'm beginning to think it might be a psychiatric ward."

"Where I came from is not there any more."

Muggs lit another cigarette and smoked it thoughtfully, glancing over at Martin from time to time. His responses were not self-pitying, they had the flat, unemotional ring of truth. She snuffed out the cigarette, dropped it into the can, and stood up suddenly, a decision made.

"Okay, we'll do it your way and see how long you last," she said irritably. "Understand this. Street people do not have a walk in the park. You cannot take courtesy or fairness for granted any more. There is no security, only abuse. You have to develop a whole new set of safeguards or you won't live long. Do you understand that? Are you taking me seriously?"

"I comprehend what you're saying," said Martin, not looking up.

"Comprehend, but don't believe."

He could hear the frustration in her voice. *She's a strong woman*, he thought. At another time, he and Sara might have made friends with her, invited her over for barbecue on the patio. Laughed together. No, he corrected himself, at another time he would not have met a homeless person. But the time was now, Sara was gone and he was sitting on a clump of grass under a bridge in the middle of the night. "I will listen to you," he said. It was the best he could offer.

She scuffed a toe of her shoe in the dirt for a few moments, head bend, thumbs hooked in her back pockets. "I don't think you're going to make it. You'll live longer if you just get rid of that stiff neck and go home."

"I don't have a home."

"All right," she said, looking at him with fierceness. "Safeguard number one: Get off the streets when the bars close. Drunken rednecks, especially the ones that come out of Brewster's, prove they've got balls by beating street people,. When you're black, they don't stop with just a beating."

She made her way up the slope under the bridge where it was darkest, pulled two blankets from a plastic trash bag, and gestured for him to move into the shadows.

"Tomorrow, I'll start teaching you how to stay alive on the streets."

#   #   #   #   #   #

Chapter 6: Monday evening, June 14
THREE WEEKS BEFORE
THE MAGUIRE MURDER

The conference room in the office suite of
Burkhalter Developments, Inc. might have
overwhelmed most small groups, but not the five
confident people presently cushioned in the soft leather
padding of the chairs.

Dark reddish-brown cherry paneling gleamed in
the soft light cast by Tiffany-style sconces. The glow
was picked up on the surface of a conference table so
intensely finished that those around it might have been
tempted to thrust a finger at it to test its depth.

At the head of the table, Wilfred Burkhalter
carefully placed his Cartier fountain pen in front of him
and folded his manicured hands. He had no papers with
him, nor did the other four.

In his 60s, with an unremarkable physique and
thinning white hair, Burkhalter did not immediately
present himself as a man of power. His firm
dispassionate voice gave him away. He was
accustomed to having his opinions taken as commands.

"I think we should begin by defining our
commitment."

He looked at the others, one by one. Audra
Cantrell, a 40-ish, petite, dark-haired fashion buyer who
still looked somewhat girlish. Chris Frahdley, in his
30s, the large heavily muscled public relations
chairman for Our Lady of Hope Hospital. Gregory
Turner, 40s, small, bald, vice-president of First
Midwest American Bank. Lawrence Madden, 50s, a
tall distinguished-looking orthopedic surgeon with

startlingly vivid blue eyes under heavy brows and long blond hair worn in a peruke style.

"We will be assuming the right to do away with outrageous situations that others either cannot or will not rectify," Burkhalter said. "There will be those who will cheer us on; those who accuse us of overstepping."

Heads nodded.

"We will do what needs to be done. It will be difficult work for people of our status--dirty, disgusting and not of our choosing--but we will persevere."

Nods of agreement.

"We will publicize our mutual goal, but seek no personal recognition."

More nods.

"Once started, we cannot go back. No matter how repulsed we are by the tasks, we are committed to wiping out filth until none remains."

"Yes, yes, don't be such a melodramatic old maid," said Madden, drumming his fingers on the table. "We all know what we're doing."

Cantrell sat forward, tugged her linen tunic more smoothly across a still-firm bust line and flicked a thread from a sleeve. "We've talked enough," she said. "Let's get on with it."

"All right, then. Think about specific targets," said Burkhalter. "Get your suggestions to me personally. I'll make a list. When we meet next Monday, we'll discuss it and do some final planning."

"We may have to change the list as time goes on," said Turner.

"Yes, I imagine so. Some situations may clear up; new ones may arise."

"We have to have a name," said Frahdley, patting his pockets for something to make notes on. "And code names. We should all have code names, just in case."

"We already have a name."

"Discussed. We discussed a name, but it won't hurt to run it though again alongside some new ideas."

Burkhalter gave him a look of assessment.

"Don't look at me that way. There's nothing wrong in being enthusiastic. You'll appreciate my enthusiasm once we get to the tough stuff."

"I certainly hope so," said Burkhalter, standing.

"That's it?" said Cantrell as the other three rose. "'It's going to be a tough job, make a list.' That's what we came down here for?"

"Don't criticize Wilfred," said Frahdley. "It's a basic public relations strategy. Results are always better if you get your entire project team together for a facial assessment before beginning."

"Well fine," said Cantrell as she stood and smoothed her skirt with jerky pats. "Here's my face. The lady behind it does not like to have her time wasted."

#   #   #   #   #   #

Chapter 7: Friday, July 9

Stangler glared at the white board in the detectives' room. It was full of notations in red and blue and arrows from one place to another, but nothing was making any logical connection. Days of interviewing had produced nothing. He was furious with himself for not asking the right questions, not seeing what might be right in front of his face, not doing whatever it was that he wasn't doing. Why was Maguire killed? It was eating him up inside. No. The case would get solved; it always did. What was eating him up was Simonson. What could he have said that caused Simonson to leave his post? What was the rookie officer doing two blocks away?

"Why did the kid leave the gate, Wiley?"

"I don't know," said Middleton, patiently answering the question yet again.

"Shot in the back of the head right in someone's front lawn, Wiley!"

Stangler sat down, glared at his wastebasket and kicked it over.

Middleton allowed a short silence while looking at his notes. "How's Emily doing on the Internet search?"

"She's looking a little bleary-eyed."

When he had asked for an Internet search of "New Guards," the detective department's secretary had stared at Stangler through her overlarge glasses and said, "Who's going to do all my other work for the next month?"

"New Guards" having produced 23 billion hits, Emily was currently wading through sites with training programs for new school crossing guards, looking for anything that might yield something helpful.

A young woman wearing a white lab coat and red hair pulled into two ponytails, one over each ear, walked into the detectives' room. She stopped in front of Stangler's desk, and smiled shyly at him.

After an extended moment, Stangler said, "What?"

"I'm Amy," she breathed, trembling with her own daring.

Stangler's face turned deep red and creased into a ferocious scowl. "And?"

She giggled.

"Amy? Do you have something for us?" said Middleton.

"Oh, yes," she said, not looking at Middleton, closely watching Stangler's hand reach forward. She hesitantly handed him two large clear plastic sacks. "These are what the State Crime Lab gathered. Contents of your victim's pockets. Contents of Officer Simonson's pockets. We've got all the prints and other little stuff, so you can keep them." She handed him another bunch of papers. "And this is the autopsy report."

"Thank you very much," Stangler said.

She stood and smiled at him adoringly.

"You can go back to the lab now."

"Amy," she breathed.

"You can go back to the lab now, Amy."

"Hold on," said Middleton. "The prints belong to anyone?"

"They're all from the two victims," she said, finally seeming to notice Middleton. "No prints of any sort on the note found under the first one."

"Anything else from the scene?"

"Hairs, human and animal; cigarette butts, leaves, excrement, we'll catalog it all, for future match," she said.

"Excrement?" said Middleton.

"Mostly squirrel," she said. "We pulled Mr. Maguire's car in. Still going over it."

She directed one last melting look at Stangler. "I'd better go back to the lab now." She didn't move. "Unless you need something else?"

"That should be all for now. Thanks Amy," said Middleton.

She didn't move.

"That should be all for now. Thanks Amy," said Stangler.

She left.

"Damn, I hate that," said Stangler. "What is wrong with women?"

"Must be your cologne."

"I don't wear any damn cologne."

"Well, then, it's just pure pheromones."

"Huh! Let 'em go after your damn pheromones for a change."

"I do not emit any pheromones. Amarantha put it in the small print of the marriage contract. I give off so much as one pheromone and she has clearance to kill me. Let's see that autopsy report." Stangler passed it over. "Says here both were shot in the back of the head at close range with a .25 caliber handgun, probably a Beretta automatic. Bullet entered low in the head, traveled at an upward angle and did not exit. Doc guesses Maguire was hit between 8:30 and 9:00; Simonson between 3:00 and 3:30, which jibes with our estimate.

"Why would the killer hang around?" said Stangler. "To watch what we were doing? What could he see from two blocks away? And if he saw someone coming, why didn't he just leave?"

"Beats me," said Middleton.

"Why did the kid leave the gate, Wiley?"

"I don't know," said Middleton, patiently answering the question yet again.

Pedersen and Nguyen walked in, reached for two more chairs and dragged them over. "Well, guys, I'm telling you that was no fun at all," said Pedersen, sitting down, his face flushed solid red.

Stangler used to worry about the pair. Pedersen looked like a wuss with lank blond floppy hair and a habit of ducking his head to one side when he talked. Nguyen looked as though a strong wind would blow him away. After one memorable brawl, however, when the two put the lights out on four contentious bikers, he learned they both practiced Vovinam, a form of Vietnamese martial arts that was part of Vo Thuat, a discipline that emphasized force and calculated yielding as combat techniques.

"Talked to the wife?" said Stangler.

"Yes."

"Pretty cut up?"

"Ah, man," said Pedersen. "She's the all-American girl-next-door with a good head on her shoulders. You can tell she's hurting bad, but she held it in and answered questions without hysterics. Husband's dead, but the house is neat, the two kids are clean. She's dealing with it."

"Nice kids," said Lu.

"She give you any help?" said Middleton.

"Maguire left a little early for the rally. She expected him home around 8:30 to go to the fireworks, but he didn't come. Jeez, what a sweetie. Instead of getting all bent out of shape because he's late, she assumes it must be something important that he couldn't avoid, and she feels bad for him missing the fireworks."

"Did she say important like how?" said Stangler.

"Yes. If Blue Ribbon gave the pay raises UFCW was demanding, they would have to either lay off half the work force to stay afloat or fold the company. There were fighting opinions on both sides, and as president of the Union, Maguire was handling a lot of unusual pressure."

"Which brings us right to our next stop--talking to Blue Ribbon execs," said Stangler, standing and heading for the door. "Good work, guys," he said over his shoulder.

* * * * * * * * * *

Alerted by the sound of boot heels, Pickett caught up with Stangler and Middleton halfway down the hall. "Something break?" he asked, matching strides with them.

"Heading out to talk to Blue Ribbon people," said Stangler, moving at his usual fast pace past the elevator and down the stairs.

Pickett watched them enviously. Promotion to a desk job brought a bigger salary but less personal satisfaction--and sometimes more grief. He was due in a meeting with the police chief and the mayor. Chief James Boucher was an embarrassment who had risen to his position partly by dumb luck, partly by political toadying. His idiotic confusions were the butt of countless jokes. Mayor Ronald Duponte, handsome and charismatic to his constituents, was an evil-tempered bane to underlings. Any event that might be used to further his political ambitions brought him into the Law Enforcement Center, intent on being first to associate with success or to denounce failure. No doubt, thought Pickett, he wanted to know chapter and verse why they didn't have the cop killer in custody. Asshole would probably use the funeral for a photo op.

At the other end of the hall, three incident input clerks watched Stangler and Middleton take the stairs.

"It's the cowboy boots that light my fire," said Laura.

"All he's got to do is give me one of those scowling bad boy looks and my underwires melt," breathed Sandi.

"You know what Middleton says about the boots?" asked Jessica. "He says Stangler's so short he has to wear cowboy boots with lots of heel so he won't be mistaken for Middleton's pet dog."

They giggled and continued to the break room.

* * * * * * * * * *

Charles L. Petrovich's office at Blue Ribbon Foods was nice enough, but not ostentatious. Stangler and Middleton each held a mug of coffee fetched by the CEO himself.

Stangler's hair was tied back in a knot low on his neck, a concession Middleton had seen him make whenever they were dealing with bureaucrats, Republicans, and little old ladies.

Petrovich was tall and well-built with craggy features. He had never heard of a New Guards but was comfortable answering questions about the company.

"Oh, yes, what you hear on the news is true," he said. "We're in the same economic boat as many others."

A woman in a floral print dress whisked through the open door of the office, laid a sheaf of papers on his desk and left.

"Thank you Janine," he called after her.

"Shall I close the door?" said Middleton, starting to rise.

"No, no," said Petrovich, gesturing him back down. "We've been experimenting with a new company dynamic based on a Chinese system that was in the news about a year ago. It eliminates artificial boundaries, while encouraging individuality, accessibility and open communication. I'm doing well with accessibility, but I still sometimes sound like a stuffed shirt. Where was I? Oh, yes. We have cut and trimmed to the bone, but it's only a drop in the bucket. Frankly, if we don't do something drastic, we'll have to close the doors."

A young woman in blue jeans with bright orange hair spikes and a nose ring stepped in, holding up a glass coffee pot. "Refills, anyone? I'm trying to kill the pot."

Stangler and Middleton shook their heads. Petrovich held his mug up. "Thank you LaShonda, top me off," he said. She poured his mug full and left.

"We have two options," he said with a rueful grimace, "one would be to pull production back a bit and lay off 10 percent of the work force."

"How many does the company employ?" said Stangler

"A thousand, give or take."

Middleton whistled softly. "That would mean pulling the rug out from under a hundred people."

"Yes. Although not out of the question, layoffs are the last choice we want to make."

Out in the hall, a metallic rattle and a squeaky wheel had underscored Petrovich's remarks. The noise stopped. A young man with his pants crotch down to his knees and waistband low enough to show a good stretch of underwear, walked in. "Thank you, Spider," Petrovich said as the kid plopped a small stack of mail on the desk, and left, his departure accompanied by the squeaky wheel.

Petrovich gazed after the mail boy with a wistful expression. "Sometimes I also have difficulty with the individuality part."

"Option Two?" said Middleton.

"Is what we hope to make happen. We are asking every employee, from top management all the way down to the night scrubbers, to take a voluntary ten percent pay cut. The dollar result would be the same as laying off one hundred workers, but no one would lose his job, either by layoffs or by the company going under."

"So about this rally last night," said Stangler.

"United Food and Commercial Workers stages a rally every Fourth of July. Blue Ribbon has been giving cost-of-living raises as a matter of course, and we work at improving the insurance plan, so the rally has gotten to be more of a social event than anything. Every year UFCW workers cut the chain on the gate to get into Yard #3, wave signs, make speeches, do a little rough-housing, and then go home. They've made themselves heard, the Union is happy. No harm, no fault. Total cost, one chain."

"But this year someone got killed," said Stangler.

"Yes," said Petrovich. He stared at his hands clasped on his desk for a long moment. "I simply can't believe it."

"Bad feelings about the pay cut?" said Stangler.

"Yes. There is a contingent of hot heads in the union who are opposing the cut. Their position is they get the pay raise or they walk out."

"What would a walkout do?" asked Middleton.

"I'm not sure," said Petrovich. "It depends on how many walk out. The company could go down and everyone would lose his job. Ironically, if around 100 walk out, it would give the company a fighting chance."

"So the walkout could hurt the union members more than Blue Ribbon?" said Middleton.

"Hurt the Union members, definitely. Hurt Blue Ribbon? Maybe. Maybe not. We'd have to see."

"And as president of the Union, Maguire was the spearhead of the walkout?" said Stangler.

"Mikey?" said Petrovich. "My god, no! Mikey was working *with* us! He was trying to convince the militant ones they would only hurt themselves."

* * * * * * * * * *

Back at the LEC, coming down the hall, Stangler and Middleton ran into Chief Boucher, accompanying an older weeping woman and a red-eyed man.

"Ah," said Boucher in a voice sounding much like a drowning man who has just been thrown a life preserver, "here's Detective Stangler now. Detective, these are Officer Simonson's parents."

Stangler cleared his throat. "I'm very sorry for your loss."

Mrs. Simonson dabbed at her eyes with a soggy tissue. In a voice that sounded as though she had no hope of hearing what she wanted, she asked, "We're just looking for answers, Detective. Can you tell us why our Luke was blocks away from everyone else, in the dark?"

"No, Ma'am, I'm sorry, I can't," said Stangler.

Mrs. Simonson nodded dejectedly.

"Come now," said Mr. Simonson, in a voice too loud for the hallway, "he was a good soldier and a good soldier follows orders! You must have sent him there!"

"No, Sir," said Stangler. "He had no orders to be where he was."

" Not your fault, hey? He just wandered off on his own, is that it? You're telling his mother that it's all his fault he's dead?"

"I didn't say that. All I'm saying is that we don't know why he---"

"Never mind! It's a cover-up. We get that message loud and clear. We've lost our only son, but to you he was only one expendable cop! Come on, Mother; we shouldn't have come."

* * * * * * * * * *

"You ran into the parents," said Pickett, as Stangler and Middleton walked into his office.

"Yeah," said Stangler, slumping into a chair.

"It's going to get worse. Hizzoner Duponte has been chewing the carpet and pointing fingers. Boucher is making the rounds trying to get morale off the ground with hot air and jolly clichés."

"Ignorant cretin," said Middleton.

"Which one?"

"Take your pick."

"Yeah," said Pickett. "All right, what did you get? Any lead on New Guards?"

"No," said Stangler, the corners of his mouth turning down in disgust. "Petrovich drew a blank. Emily's wading through sites on entry level salaries for new security guards."

"Basically, we've got nothing," said Middleton.

Stangler shook his head, folded his hands in his lap, and slouched lower in his chair.

"Well, let's run through the nothing," Pickett said, elbows propped on the arms of his chair; fingers steepled.

"Lab's running the slugs through NBIN. Maguire's car yielded prints and half-eaten animal crackers. Non-matches will be run through AFIS. No defensive wounds in either case."

"How did they let someone with a gun walk behind them?" said Pickett.

"How did they get Simonson two blocks away from where he was supposed to be!" Stangler's outburst was a near shout. "Sorry."

"Suspects?" said Pickett.

"Not good," said Middleton, "everyone or Jerglens. With Simonson, we're assuming the poor kid went off for some unknown reason, ran into the perp and was killed simply because he was in the wrong place at the wrong time. With Maguire, everyone on both sides of the wage fight says he was a candidate for sainthood. They say Lester Jerglens was ripe for a *coup de grace*, but not Maguire."

"What about that?" said Pickett.

"Jerglens can't or won't give us an alibi; he may be our man. On the other hand, maybe our killer was actually gunning for Jerglens."

"The night watchman mistook one for the other," said Stangler. "Trouble is, Jerglens is such a minor pissant, no one would consider it worth a slug to put him away."

"How about the wife?" said Pickett.

"His wife," said Middleton, "thought he could walk on water."

"So, what's next?" said Pickett.

Stangler straightened up, with his hands on the arms of his chair. "Now we do it all again. Everyone else's case loads are clearing up, so Rask and Stummer can take the Union workers, Pedersen and Nguyen will talk to Blue Ribbon people, Rivera and Olson will talk to the wife and work up a list of non-work associates."

"And you two?" said Pickett.

"We'll talk to Jerglens again. He's like a damn mule, resisting any efforts to lead him." said Stangler, standing up. "Maybe if we go in soft and nicey, he'll tell us where he was. Might as well see Harrington while we're at it."

"A mule and a billy goat," said Middleton. "I think I feel my blood pressure rising."

* * * * * * * * * *

Petrovich appeared at the Blue Ribbon conference room door in rolled-up shirt sleeves, gesturing to an accompanying Jerglens to precede him.

Jerglens, wearing a heavy oilskin apron and an expression much like a Rottweiler who's just been told he's going to have a bath, looked around truculently, glared furiously when he saw Stangler and Middleton, but finally pulled out a chair and sat down. He placed his chain mesh cutter's glove on the conference table, looked quickly at Petrovich, and moved it to his lap. "I got rights," he growled, "I don't hafta answer nuthin'."

"Don't act like a moron, Les," said Petrovich. "They're not going to infringe your rights. The company is just as eager to get this settled as the cops are. Try to cooperate." He pointed to the telephone at the end of the table. "I'm extension two. Call if you need anything." He left.

Jerglens smirked. "How can I help you dickheads?" he said.

Stangler put his arms on the table, and leaned forward. "Mr. Jerglens, if you could tell us where you were for the rest of the evening after the rally, it would be helpful."

"I don't hafta tell you nuthin'. Where I was is none a' your business."

"We'll find out eventually. Why not make it easy for yourself?"

"Don't make me laugh. Easy for you, ya mean. Findin' out where I was should keep you dickheads busy for a while."

Stangler controlled his face, not letting his expression reveal how much he wanted to smack Jerglens right across his stupid smirk. "Mr. Jerglens, is it possible that Maguire was shot by mistake, the killer thinking it was you?"

"What!" said Jerglens. "I don't look like Maguire!"

"From the front, no; but from the back, yes. Several other Blue Ribbon employees looked at the face-down body and thought it was you lying there."

"But he must not'a been layin' down when he was shot," said Jerglens, starting to be shook a little.

"He was shot from behind. I'm not saying for sure that a mistake was made, because as you've just pointed out, we're dickheads; but we have to consider all possibilities. Do you have any enemies, Mr. Jerglens?"

"Hell, no! I'm a real popular fellow. Ask anybody."

"No one you've had an argument with? No one who resents your work?"

"Nah, none'a that. We're all good buddies on the line."

"How about the union? There were a lot of hot tempers at the rally."

"And why not? Company suits linin' their pockets with gold parachutes, and askin' the common man to take a pay cut! You bet there was hot tempers, but I ain't the one people was hot at."

"A walkout was threatened," said Stangler.

"You damn betcha!"

"Was everyone in favor of a walkout, or were there some who opposed it?"

"We was a solid front." Jerglens jerked his chin up as though a thought had occurred to him. "Except Maguire. That ass-kisser was goin' around sayin'--he adopted a prissy tone--'we gotta be reasonable.'" He dragged the word out. "'Let's not cut off our noses to spite our faces,' he said. 'Look at the long-term picture,' he said." He struck the table with a fist. "Didja ever hear anythin' so stupid? Nah, it was Maguire asking to have his mouth shut, not me."

"If he was opposing what you wanted, you realize that looks like motivation? Are you sure you don't want to tell us where you were?"

"Oooo," laughed Jerglens, pretending to shiver. "I'm a suspect? Hot shit!"

Stangler thanked the prince of a fellow who had no enemies--and no alibi--and let him go.

"One more question," he said, as Jerglens headed for the door. "Do you belong to New Guards?"

"Nahh, I'm a Moose," said Jerglens.

"Can you tell us how to contact New Guards?"

"They must be new; I ain't never heard a' them," said Jerglens, and left.

Stangler turned to Middleton with a disgusted look. "You know why he's a Moose? Because there's no organization called Jackasses." He buzzed Petrovich and asked if they could see Harrington.

A few minutes later, Harrington bustled in, wearing a white lab-type coat, an elasticized blue netting over his hair, another over his mustache, with ties that passed over his ears, and a third over his goatee.

"Good," he said, pulling vinyl gloves off his hands. "I was on the verge of calling you. What have

you got to report?" The net over his goatee wagged
coquettishly with every word.

Somewhere it must be written, thought Stangler,
*that it's a sin to kill a man with a hairnet on his beard,
even if he is an unbearable asshole.*

"You do realize," said Harrington, "that with
Mikey's death, I am now the president of UFCW?"

"You do realize," said Stangler, "that we don't
give a good goddamn if you're president of the union or
queen of the fairies."

"We have a few questions to ask you, Mr.
Harrington," said Middleton quickly.

"Fine, fine; you follow your procedures," said
Harrington in a tone that preserved his dignity. "After
that, a report."

Middleton took Harrington back and forth through
the same territory, looking for anyone who might have
reason enough to kill Maguire or Jerglens, but got
nowhere. No one had anything to gain by killing the
universally popular Maguire. No one had anything to
gain by killing Jerglens--unless it was to silence a
constant irritation. Middleton finally gave up.

"Do you belong to New Guards?" asked Stangler.

"No," said Harrington. "What's that? It's not one
of our union committees."

"Does the name bring up anything in your mind?"

"Right Guard?" ventured Harrington. "Oh, no,
that's a deodorant. Sorry, can't think of a thing. Why
do you ask?"

"Just a random thought."

Harrington waited a moment to see no other
questions were coming. "Now," he said, "what do you
have to report?"

Letting loose with an exasperated sigh, Stangler
said, "We don't have a damn thing to report!"

"You know what we know, Mr. Harrington," said Middleton. "Mr. Maguire was universally respected, and yet he was shot." He scrubbed a hand across the top of his close-clipped hair. "Maybe it was aliens."

"That's not funny," said Harrington, standing up.

"No, it's not," said Middleton as he and Stangler stood. "The remark was born of frustration; I shouldn't have said it. *Je regrette.*"

As the three men walked toward the door, Harrington in the lead, Stangler asked, "When will the walkout happen?"

Harrington stopped and turned to him, looking incredulous. "Walkout! Do you think we're crazy? There won't be any walkout."

* * * * * * * * * *

Stepping into his kitchen from the garage, Stangler stopped for what he thought must be the millionth time to frown at the old cabinets, counter, appliances. A year after his move to Riverbend, he had bought the house. It had been built in the late 40's, and never updated, which was fine with him; he was slowly making it his home. His first change had been the big bedroom on the second floor. Spreading magazine photos in front of a contractor, he had said, "Make it look just like that." The result was a room elegant in the broad strokes but with no detail. The small touches that gave a room personality would come with time, he assumed, and would be his, not some decorator's. The bathroom had come into being in the same way, waiting until he found a look that appealed to him. The kitchen would be next. He wanted everything modern and convenient, but looking cozy--a room for serious cooking but lazy breakfasts with the newspaper. So far, inspiration had yet to come. And so far he had managed to keep the "decorator" side of his personality from all but Middleton.

He left his kitchen thoughts and took the stairs two at a time. He pulled his dress uniform from the back of the closet and started changing. The line-up at the LEC would make parking difficult, so he was leaving his six-year-old Mustang Cobra in the garage. Amarantha was dropping him and Wiley off.

A horn beeped out front.

* * * * * * * * * *

Standing at attention in the cemetery, Stangler was aware of Wiley beside him, of being part of the police presence in dress blues, visored hats, white gloves, and black mourning strips across their badges. He let his lower jaw drop a little to ease off some of the tension by breathing through his mouth.

He had managed to hold it together through the sight of the weeping family, the flag-draped coffin passing from the church, the slow motorcade with bar lights flashing.

The mournful wail of bagpipes were background to his recollection of snapping at the young officer when the kid looked at Wiley to confirm his order.

The crack of the rifle salute under the cloudless blue sky jarred a thought.

We never even heard the shot that killed Simonson.

He lost it at "Taps," still rigidly at attention, tears rolling down his face.

\#   \#   \#   \#   \#   \#

Chapter 8: Before dawn, Monday, July 12

The phone brought Middleton awake on the first ring. Twisting up on an elbow to see the clock on his bedside table, he discovered he was on Amarantha's side of the bed. It had been a satisfying evening and they had fallen asleep where they ended up. His cell phone, sitting on the opposite table, rang again. Lunging over Amarantha to reach the phone, he heard her say, "Mwoof!" as her face was weighted farther into her pillow. The clock said 2:15 a.m. "Middleton," he snapped, working at sounding alert. He listened a few moments and said, "Okay, on my way. Maybe 25 minutes."

"What?" said his wife as she straightened the sheet over her shoulder.

"Homicide downtown," said Middleton, pulling on clothes.

"On a Sunday?"

"When we catch the bad guy, Honey, I'll have a talk with him about his timing."

"Good," she murmured, falling back asleep.

* * * * * * * * * *

Outside the three open decorative arches that formed the entrance wall of the Lindstrom Hotel's second floor ballroom, stood a chrome easel with a large printed sign:

DEALING WITH SUBPRIME MORTGAGES
Sandra J. Goetzman
EVP: Consumer Lending
Coastal Banking Systems, San Francisco.

Middleton walked through the arches into the ballroom and looked around. A dinner function had occurred earlier in the evening. Round tables, some still with tablecloths, some not, were spaced randomly, chairs stacked along one side wall. Centered against a long wall was a speaker's rostrum on a raised platform. Stangler and a uniformed officer stood on the platform, staring at something behind the rostrum. Just to one side, down on the ballroom floor, another officer stood between two tables--a small man in a suit and a comb-over seated at one, a young man in a sky blue tunic at the other. The small man sat stiffly upright and looked pained. The young man rolled crumbs around with his fingertips, hung his head forward and flicked uneasy looks at the others in the room.

Middleton threaded his way through the tables and stepped up on the platform.

Lying behind the rostrum was a woman. Her face was liver-colored, her mouth hung open, her tongue, which appeared to have been bitten several times, protruded. A cord, leading from somewhere behind the raised platform up to the microphone on the podium, was wrapped around her neck. If she was once pretty, thought Middleton, she wasn't any more.

He guessed she was in her late 40's, and kept her appearance up. Her short sandy-colored hair showed several shades of blonde streaking; the fingernails he could see had little jewels pasted on each one. She was wearing a draped cream silk blouse with full gathered sleeves, pulled out in places from a slender dark plum-colored skirt that had rucked up a little, panty hose, and soft fuzzy elasticized pull-on footlets, one of which was halfway off.

"How long have you been here?" said Middleton.

"Not very long," said Stangler. "I came down to make sure what we had before waking you. M.E. was fast, been and gone. He called the Crime Lab."

"Do we know who she is?"

Stangler jerked a thumb at the nearby officer, who consulted a note pad and said, "The night manager says she's Sandra Goetzman, some sort of mucky-muck for Coastal Banking Systems. She was the speaker at a dinner here tonight, planning to catch a plane tomorrow morning."

Middleton stared at the officer. "Did he actually say 'mucky-muck?'"

"Uh... no, Sir... uh, he gave her title, but I can't write that fast."

"Most of us can't write that fast, Reichel. Just ask people to repeat what they said."

"Yessir."

"Tell Middleton what we know," said Stangler.

"Yessir, Lo...uh...Detective Stangler."

Turning to Middleton, Reichel said, "That guy over there," he pointed to the young man in the sky blue tunic---

"Whose name is...?" said Middleton.

"Yeah, uh, Trevor Redding. He says things went until about 10:00. Then most of the people cleared out, except for a few standing around talking to Ms Goetzman. When they all finally left about 10:30 or a little after, he rolled a cart in here and cleared leftover stuff on the tables."

"He see anything unusual at this time?" said Middleton.

"He says not."

"How long did it take him to go get his cart after he saw Ms Goetzman leave?

"He didn't go anywhere. He was standing with the cart over in the corner, waiting for the last of them to clear out."

"All right, keep going."

"At these dinners, he says, it's pretty common for there to be untouched desserts left on the tables. When he wheeled the dirty dishes out to the kitchen, he had half a dozen pieces of chocolate cake, which he sat down and ate, along with a cup of coffee."

"Don't the servers usually clear the dishes?" said Middleton.

"Yeah, most of the time, he said, but there was something about if the waitresses worked over a certain number of hours, the hotel would have to pay benefits, so they were told to go home. When he came back to get the linen---"

"How long was he out in the kitchen?"

"He guesses from about 11:00 to midnight. When he came back---"

"Can he see into the ballroom from the kitchen?"

"There are small windows in the top of the doors, but it's a sharp left into the kitchen. No direct line of sight." He paused for another question. None coming, he continued. "When he came back, he didn't see her right away, and started collecting tablecloths and napkins into a laundry cart, but when he got closer to this stage thing, he did."

"Did he see anyone else in the room?"

"He says he didn't notice anyone, but he didn't check under the tablecloths."

"Did he touch anything up on the platform?"

"He says not. He says he let out a yip and ran for the night manager. That's the other guy over there in the suit. Night manager came up---"

"Name?"

"Got that. Edison Fulbright. Night manager took one look, had the desk call 911, and stayed right here with the kid, and waited."

Elevator doors could be heard opening, and then the sound of equipment dollies.

"Let's move off here," said Stangler, stepping off the temporary staging.

"Hey Lobo!" said a husky voice. "Have you stayed true to me?"

Three Crime Lab technicians walked through the entrance arches, led by a wrinkled four-foot-eleven-inch 60-ish female with a frizzy pouf of orange hair and a cigarette squint. The cigarette was long gone; the squint remained.

"I've saved it all for you, Marlene. What did you do? Fly?"

"Nah," she said in a rasp that tattled on her previous habit. "We'd just wound up a job in Red Wing, so we were only up the road a piece."

"Nice to see you," said Middleton. "I was afraid we might be in for yet another lecture on our ineptitude from Dr. Holmes."

"He's busy with something nasty up north," she said.

"Nastier than him, I hope."

Coming closer, she lifted her chin to sight up the 17-inch height difference. "How's Wiley?"

"Same as ever, Dr. Liebowitz."

"And Amarantha?"

"I had to mash her some, getting to the phone tonight, but she'll bounce back."

"Outside of mashed, how is she?"

"Happy as a mouse in a cracker box. Teachers' strike has cancelled summer classes, so she's doing research on her book."

"Tell her hi for me." She turned her attention to the room. "Well, what have you got for us?"

"Up behind the rostrum."

Crime Lab people headed for the small stage. Middleton gestured for the two uniforms to step to one side. The department had recently acquired six new officers, all with four-year law enforcement degrees, but no experience. *Just like Simonson*, thought Middleton.

"That was good collection of information, Reichel," he said. "You, too, Hanson. Hanging on to those two hotel people and keeping them separated was good procedural work."

They nodded, poker faced. When you were new, you worked at keeping your cool.

"While Crime Lab does its thing, Hanson, you go back and stay with the hotel people. Don't let them talk. Sorry, you know that. Reichel, get yourself just outside of here, in the hall. Don't let anyone in without checking with us. Got that?"

"Yeah."

Middleton started to walk away from them, stopped, turned. "Reichel? Stay right there. Do not leave without checking with us. Okay?"

"Yes, Sir." A hint of impatience.

Middleton paused, hated himself for it, but said, "Repeat your instructions."

A look of outraged incredulity filled Reichel's face. He glared at Middleton in tight-lipped insubordination. Finally, he said tersely, "Stay here in the hall. Don't leave without checking with you."

Middleton shifted his gaze to Hanson, who said easily, "Stick with the hotel people; don't let 'em talk."

Middleton nodded and walked away.

"That ain't right," said Reichel in a furious undertone. "He can't treat us that way."

"Forget it," said Hanson. "They're just jumpy about Simonson. Middleton'll tell Munson that we did okay. Everyone says he's good that way. It's Stangler that we don't want to piss off."

"Jeez," said Reichel, "I almost called Stangler 'Lobo.' Right to his face."

"Did he give you one of those looks?"

"What look?"

"You know. One of those looks that say, 'If you don't drop dead right now, I'm going to help you do it?'"

"No. He acted like he didn't notice."

From across the room Middleton called, "Now, Officers." They moved.

Middleton went back to Stangler, standing off the stage, watching the Crime Lab.

"What have they got?"

"So far, nothing we didn't already assume. Indications of a small struggle. No purse and indoor footwear mean she came back from her room. Let's take a look at it."

When they were halfway across the ballroom, Dr. Liebowitz called, "Yo! Guys! You might want to look at this."

They walked back and leaned forward to look where the Crime Lab chief was using a tongue depressor to hold aside a voluminous fold of blouse sleeve.

"Oh crud," said Middleton, "this isn't good."

A half sheet of paper with black printing lay underneath.

"OUR SACRED DUTY
DEATH TO ABUSERS AND USURPERS
DEATH TO THE HOUNDS
OF ABSOLUTE DESPOTS
NEW GUARDS FOR FUTURE SECURITY"

* * * * * * * * * *

Holding guns, Stangler and Middleton stood on either side of the door to Sandra Goetzman's room, one flight up and almost directly over the ballroom. The night manager peered cautiously from around a corner down the hall.

Middleton zipped the manager's master pass card through the slot, dropped it, turned the door knob with a handkerchief, and pushed it open a fraction of an inch.

Weapon extended, Stangler smacked the door with his left shoulder, panning the room. He stepped inside the bathroom and pulled the shower curtain aside. Coming back, he knelt, lifted the spread, and peered under the bed. "Clear," he said.

Middleton picked up the key card, handing it to the night manager who had scuttled forward in time to see Stangler rise. Firm hand holding the small man's elbow, Middleton edged him a few feet into the room. "Do not touch anything, Mr. Fulbright, not even the walls or the woodwork."

"Do real detectives really look under beds and shout 'clear,'" said the night manager, hovering on a laugh.

"I'm afraid so. Everyone understands 'clear,' and it's a lot quicker than shouting, 'Okay guys, I've checked everything out and there's no one here.' We feel idiotic looking under beds, but sometimes bad guys hide under beds."

"What's your definition of a 'real' detective?" said Stangler, scowling.

"Um... oh, my... no offense intended."

They stood just past the bathroom door. The carpet was plushy and would show footprints.

Earrings and a necklace on the bureau top. High-heeled shoes on the floor beside the bed. A black leather purse, a small open overnight case, and a dark plum-colored ladies suit jacket on the top of the bed. What looked to be the usual cosmetics and grooming items littered the bathroom countertop. From what they could see, the overnight case appeared to contain nothing more than spare underwear and a new packet of pantyhose.

"Look around carefully, Mr. Fulbright," said Middleton. "From a hotel standpoint, do you see anything unusual or out-of-place? Even anything merely interesting?"

The night manager took his time. "She was very neat," he finally said, "but other than that, I don't see anything missing or out of place."

* * * * * * * * * *

On the way back to the elevator, Middleton made notes. "Who arranged for tonight's event?"

"The Banker's Association of Riverbend," said Fulbright.

"Must have cost serious money to get her from the West Coast. She a popular speaker?"

Fulbright stopped and turned, his eyes wide in surprise. "Don't you know who she is?"

Blank looks.

"For pity sakes! She was heavily involved in the whole bailout scandal--the poster lady for greed and stupidity. She's the most hated woman in the country. We had a riot out front tonight, protestors damaging hotel property and blocking the street for an hour. How can you not know about that? Don't you cops talk to each other?

* * * * * * * * * *

Back at the ballroom, Middleton looked around.
Rookies! It's worse than herding cats.
"Hanson! Where's Reichel?"
Stangler stopped and stared at Middleton
questioningly.
"Isn't he out there in the hall?" called Hanson.
"Did he tell you where he was going?"
"No. Isn't he out there?" Hanson strode rapidly
across the ballroom.
"Did you see which way he went?"
"No. I couldn't see him from where I was," said
Hanson, now in the hall, looking left and right.
Middleton pulled his cell and called Dispatch.
"Get Paul Reichel's 10-20, please. I'll hold."
Stangler focused on the phone Middleton was
holding.
*Don't get excited. Kid ran to the can, is all. Too
green to tell anyone where he was going.*
Middleton held up a finger. He was listening. He
looked at Stangler and shook his head.
"Okay, go to Code 2, Dispatch, possible 11-99.
Get all units to seal off the Lindstrom Hotel. Hold
anyone trying to leave."
"Goddammit, Wiley, where did he go!" shouted
Stangler. "I'll start here and work up. Get down to the
desk. See if they have a PA system. Hanson, go back
by the hotel people and do not leave. You got me? Do.
Not. Leave!"
* * * * * * * * * *
Officer Reichel lay on the loading dock at the
back of the hotel, just off the alley. He looked peaceful,
except for his unfired gun, partially fallen from his
hand. A bullet had pierced the back of his skull.
* * * * * * * * * *

Still before dawn, having spent the intervening hours questioning hotel staff and getting preliminaries from Dr. Liebowitz at the loading dock scene, Stangler and Middleton waited on the front stoop of Judson Lundquist, president of the Bankers Association of Riverbend. In his mid-60s and bald, but still looking trim, he answered wearing pajamas and a light cotton bathrobe.

"Are you sure?" he snapped, glaring at them. Then, "No. Foolish thing to say. Of course you're sure. You're the police." He gestured they should follow him from the good-sized foyer into a spacious living room.

Before they could be seated, Mrs. Lundquist appeared. Her silver pageboy was newly combed, and she wore a full-length quilted satin housecoat. "Jud?" she said.

"Someone killed Sandra Goetzman," he said, irritated by her intrusion.

"Oh, no!" she said.

"And a police officer," said Stangler.

"Yes, of course. And a police officer. Sorry, to be abrupt, my dear, it's shock talking. Lucy, this is... uh... Detective...."

"Stangler. This is Detective Middleton. Sorry about the early hour, but it can't wait."

"Of course." she said. "Why don't you men come into the kitchen and I'll make coffee."

"Oh, for pity sakes, Lucy---"

"We won't be here long," said Stangler.

"Then don't drink all of it. At this hour you need coffee."

The kitchen was ultra-modern in its appointments, but decorated in yellow and white 1950s collectibles. Center was a chrome and yellow Formica table with matching chairs.

Stangler looked around slowly.

This is it!

"*Combien beau*," said Middleton under his breath.

"*Merci!*" said Mrs. Lundquist.

"No French!" said Stangler.

"Lucy!" said Mr. Lundquist.

Mrs. Lundquist quickly turned to making coffee.

"How was she killed?" asked the banker.

Stangler wanted to smash the banker and his one-sided concern, but held his temper. *There's nothing he can tell us about Reichel's murder, so let's just get on with it.*

"She was on the stage, behind the rostrum, strangled with the microphone cord."

"How horrible!" gasped Mrs. Lundquist.

"What was she doing there?" The banker's voice conveyed criticism--she was to be censured for being in the wrong place. "Everyone left. She had gone to her room."

"We don't know."

Mrs. Lundquist placed cups on the table.

"Do you know any person or organization called the New Guards?" said Stangler.

The banker frowned and thought. "New Guards. New Guards. They're not members of the Downtown Business Association." And clearly therefore not important.

"No one I've heard of, either," said his wife.

Lundquist glared at his wife.

"Don't be such a curmudgeon, Jud. There are more organizations in town besides the Downtown Business Association." She turned to Stangler. "What is it?"

"Nothing," he said. "A minor point."

"Can you explain why Ms Goetzman was known as the most hated woman in America, and yet your association asked her to speak?" said Middleton.

"That requires an explanation of the whole bailout mess," said Lundquist peevishly.

"We'll have someone in our office research that area," said Middleton. "You tell us about Ms Goetzman being hated."

"That's complicated, too," said Lundquist.

"Go for 50 words or less," said Stangler.

"Impossible!"

"Give it a try," said Stangler in an unyielding tone, beginning to tire of the banker's attitude.

Mrs. Lundquist placed a plate full of homemade peanut cookies on the table, sliding them close to Stangler, who didn't notice. When she turned her back, Middleton slid the plate in front of himself and took one.

Lundquist cleared his throat and began, pausing officiously between sentences to compose his thoughts. "Sandra Goetzman showed banks how to package and sell their risky subprime loans in what was called 'mortgage-backed securities.' This maneuver allowed financial institutions on the brink of failure to sail under the federal oversight radar, while hoping for a turnaround in time to pull them out. Instead they slid deeper into debt. If fewer banks had followed her idea, if the subprime loan problem had been discovered sooner, a federal bailout might have been avoided. She is... was... the mother of the bailout crisis."

Mrs. Lundquist poured coffee into four cups, put the pot back on its burner, and sat down. Smiling sweetly at Stangler, she slid the sugar, cream, and cookie plate close to him.

"I can see why people hated her," said Middleton.

"Professionally, yes," said Lundquist. "What she was doing personally, however, made her reputation most unsavory." He wrinkled his nose as if smelling a bad odor.

"What was that?" said Stangler.

"She was holding notoriously lavish parties in high-end California homes that she, herself, had given subprime loans and then foreclosed on."

"So why does a reputable bankers' group in the Midwest pay a nationally hated person to come and speak?" said Middleton, as he reached for the sugar, cream and cookies.

"Humph!," said Lundquist. "It was only business, I assure you. She made lemonade of lemons, selling herself on the talk circuit as an expert on qualifying mortgages and securities packages. In that respect, what she has... had... to say was valuable."

"Somewhat like hiring a reformed bank robber to help you catch bank robbers?" asked Mrs. Lundquist.

He huffed a sigh of irritation at her. "Like that, yes."

Another hour was filled with questions regarding who attended the speech, when people left, who lingered, and Ms Goetzman's movements during and after the dinner. Another pot was brewed and the cookie plate refilled, before they were finished.

* * * * * * * * * *

When morning moved along to 7:30, Stangler and Middleton sat in the detectives' room, waiting for the others. Stangler alternately drummed his fingers, looked at the door, looked at his watch, opened and closed the folder in front of him. Middleton read through his notes.

One by one, six detectives walked in, carrying coffee. Last was Steve Wishink, the department's undercover drug investigator, wearing dirty sweatpants, a stained T-shirt reading, "Life's A Bitch," no socks and three-day whiskers. He treated the room to an evil squint. "This is a pain in the butt," he said. "You assholes ever think of having a meeting in the afternoon?"

"That's 'Ms Asshole' to you," said Carmen Rivera, one of two female detectives on the force.

Pickett strode into the room, closing the door behind him. "Okay, Lobo, get us going."

Middleton rose, walked over to the white board and picked up a felt-tip marker. Stangler moved up beside him and cleared his throat. "As you know, last night an executive from Coastal Banking Systems in San Francisco, Sandra Goetzman, was strangled in the Lindstrom Hotel ballroom."

"Fuck the banker," said Rask, "what happened to Reichel?"

"Ah man...." said Stangler. "One small-caliber bullet to the back of the head... his gun was in his hand when he fell."

"He sees the perp, draws his gun, then lets the perp walk around behind him and shoot him?" said Rivera.

"No way of knowing," said Stangler. "Maybe he saw the perp but there was an accomplice behind him. Maybe he drew his gun because he thought he was in an iffy situation but the perp was hiding behind him."

"Yeah?" said Rask. "And maybe he's so wet behind the ears he tells the perp to get behind him where it's safe."

"He had orders to stay put?" said Pedersen.

"Yes," said Middleton quietly. "He repeated it back to me."

Rask slammed a fist on his desk. "Why the fuck did Munson have two rookies ridin' together? That's what I want to know!"

"I can't question another captain, but you can be sure someone will," said Pickett. "And you can bet money it won't happen again. But so what? Simonson was paired with an old-timer like Lavorski and they still got him. Our experienced people can't be expected to baby-sit."

"When's the funeral?" said Pedersen.

"Don't know. Reichel's family is in Wyoming. Munson's having someone out there break the news."

Silence. There were no more questions, only angry faces.

"All right," said Pickett, "let's move along."

Stangler pulled a clear plastic evidence bag from the folder he was holding, handing it to Nguyen, who was closest. "Pass this around," he said. Lu glanced at it and handed it to Pedersen. It was the paper reading:

"OUR SACRED DUTY
DEATH TO ABUSERS AND USURPERS
DEATH TO THE HOUNDS
OF ABSOLUTE DESPOTS
NEW GUARDS FOR FUTURE SECURITY"

"You've all seen this," said Stangler. "It's the note that was found under Michael Maguire's body. An identical note was found under Ms Goetzman's body."

Pickett made hold-it-down gestures as the questions started again. "We'll get to everything! But first, let's all understand, we sit on these notes as long as we can, okay? We don't want a media clusterfuck screaming 'serial killer.' I'll warn all departments. Are we all agreed on this?"

"Okay, no one says anything," said Brittany Olson, a tall short-haired blonde who looked as though she should be on a high-fashion runway, except for the gun, "but we've got two homicides a week apart with a cop killed each time, and you think no one's going to think serial killer?"

"Oh, god, I hope not," said Pickett. "I'm hoping we can make serious progress before public reaction gets crazy. Let's let Stangler and Middleton get us up to speed on this new one; then we'll talk."

Looking at his notes from time to time, Middleton described the crime scene in the ballroom, the victim's room, the crime scene on the loading dock and their interviews with hotel staff and the bankers association president.

Questions were raised. Why had Sandra Goetzman gone back to the ballroom? Why had Reichel left his post after being specifically told not to?

"Ah, man, we just don't know," said Stangler. "Two cops ignored their instructions and we don't have a goddamn clue. I mean, we can say 'rookie' all we want, but these men were trained, they wouldn't just wander off."

"It's a real bitch," said Stummer.

Stangler stared at the papers in his hand for several beats, then went on. "We've got preliminary reports from Dr. Liebowitz." He scanned pages and passed them on. "With Goetzman, strangulation appears to be the cause of death, pending examination by the forensic pathologist. Crime Lab people are pretty sure she was killed where she was found. What little struggle there was produced no bruising. Maybe vasovagal reflex."

The detectives were familiar with the quirkiness of the vagus nerve in the neck, which could cause quick loss of consciousness in response to shock, sudden surprise, unpleasant odors, and sometimes even the sight of a phobic object--such as a mouse or a snake.

"Key card was tucked in a skirt pocket. There's a lot here about other bits and pieces they collected-- hairs, food crumbs, chalk crumbs, dirt, paper punch-hole dots.... Doesn't look like anything immediately helpful. Smudges on the mike cord look like gloves were used." He passed the papers on and selected two more from the folder. "Here's a list of detritus collected from the loading dock, including a peach pit and a condom. Then Liebowitz gets into what they found in Room 306. I'm skipping the detailed list; nothing of seeming importance that we haven't mentioned. Okay, this is interesting."

"What's interesting?" said Stummer, looking up from the page he was reading.

"They found three sets of footprints in the carpet pile, other than ours. Prints of high heels and soft footlets matching Ms Goetzman's, and prints of high heels in a larger size. The night manager said the room was vacuumed shortly prior to Goetzman's check-in."

"So another woman was in there while Goetzman had the room," said Olson.

"Lady banker greeting her before the dinner?" said Pedersen.

"There are ladies in the bankers association, but none attended the dinner," said Middleton.

"Nothing in there about you mucking up the carpet with your big feet?" asked Stummer.

"Somewhere in there she has it," said Stangler. "Something about the detectives entering X number of feet in the course of their investigation."

"She was obliged to mention it," said Pickett.

"No problem there," said Stangler. "I was just imagining if it had been that asshole Holmes. The perp could have been sitting in the room with an Uzi, and Holmes would go ballistic if anyone went in before him. Why hasn't someone shot him by now?"

"They've tried," said Nguyen deadpan, "but it takes a silver bullet to kill him."

"One of these days, I'm going to goad him into jumping me," said Stangler.

"Injured while assaultin' an officer?" said Rask.

"Damn near killed while assaulting an officer," said Stangler, grinning wolfishly. "Man, it's my dream."

"Are we supposed to assume that Maguire and Goetzman were abusers and usurpers, and cops are the hounds of despots?" said Pedersen. "Simonson and Reichel were killed simply because they work for the establishment?"

"It looks that way," said Pickett. "Anyone have any other ideas?"

"I've still got my question," said Olson. "We do have a serial killer, don't we?"

Pedersen leaned forward on his elbows, hands clasped. "Different victims, different weapons. Two cops, yes, but I don't see a pattern that fits a serial killer profile."

"So you don't think we've got a psychopath?" said Pickett.

"No," said Pedersen. "Not from the evidence we have so far. Do you?"

"I don't either," said Rivera. "Feels more like someone on a mission."

"Or two of them," said Wishink.

"Ya mean two different killers?" said Rask.

"The same pair of killers each time."

"Makes sense. It says 'guards' with a 's,' for crisakes. When I went to school, that meant more than one."

"One perp trying to sound like a group is an old trick," said Pickett.

"Yeah," said Stummer, grinning, "Rask claiming he went to school is an old trick, too."

"Ah shaddup," said Rask.

"Someone on a mission should be easier to find than a psychopath," said Pickett.

"I agree with Carmen," said Pedersen. These notes look like someone with a plan. He doesn't *have* to kill, he *chooses* to kill. He strikes me as more like a vigilante, making a better world by getting rid of bad people."

"Hits me that way, too," said Stangler.

"Yeah," said Stummer.

"I'll buy that," said Rask. "This guy isn't nuts; he has a good reason for wiping people out."

"Okay, there's a place to start," said Pickett. Let's concentrate on finding what sort of badness Maguire and Goetzman had in common."

Middleton rotated the white board toward the wall so what faced the room was its cork side, with photos of the crime scenes pinned up.

"Pedersen and Nguyen, you ride herd on the Maguire work," said Pickett. "Rivera and Olson will back you up. Stangler and Middleton, stay with Goetzman and have Rask and Stummer check out the protestors."

"Hey!" said Rask, ready to protest Pedersen and Nguyen getting a lead assignment before him.

"We've gotta have you two," Stangler said to him. "Finding those protestors and getting anything out of them will take experience and superior interrogation techniques."

"Gotcha," said Rask with a smirk.

"Ah, shit!" said Pickett. "One of these days I'm going to have to kill all four of you."

As the detectives were leaving, Assistant Chief Roger Jevne entered. Pickett, Stangler and Middleton stayed put, knowing what was coming.

"Detectives, I guess you know why I'm here," said Jevne.

"Ah, man!" said Stangler, kicking his dented waste basket over again.

"Let me get right to it, Sir," said Middleton. "I'm the one who gave Reichel his instructions. I told him to stay at the entrance to the ballroom and under no circumstance to leave without checking with Lobo or me."

"You were that specific?"

"Yes Sir, I wanted to make sure there was no room for misunderstanding."

"Who heard you say this?"

"Officer Hanson."

"Then why did Reichel leave?"

"I don't know."

"Ah, man!" said Stangler. "What the hell could have been so important that he took off without saying anything?"

#   #   #   #   #   #

Chapter 9: Noon, Monday, July 12

(Theme Music:)
(Voiceover:)
THIS IS KRBM-TV, NEWS AT NOON. UP TO THE MINUTE REPORTING ON WHAT'S HAPPENING IN THE RIVER LAND WITH NOON NEWS ANCHOR SALLY FELDNER.
(Anchor:)
GOOD NOON TO YOU, MONDAY, JULY 12.

LATE LAST NIGHT RIVERBEND WAS ROCKED WITH TWO MORE HOMICIDES, MAKING IT FOUR DEATHS IN ONE WEEK.

THE BODY OF SANDRA J. GOETZMAN, EXECUTIVE VICE PRESIDENT OF COASTAL BANKING SYSTEMS' CONSUMER LENDING DIVISION, WAS FOUND IN THE BANQUET ROOM OF THE LINDSTROM HOTEL. UNCONFIRMED SOURCES SAY SHE WAS STRANGLED WITH A MICROPHONE CORD. MS GOETZMAN, A KEY PLAYER IN THE SUBPRIME LOAN BANKING FAILURE, WAS OFTEN DESCRIBED BY PEOPLE WHOSE HOMES WERE AT RISK AS "THE MOST HATED WOMAN IN AMERICA."

LESS THAN AN HOUR LATER, POLICE OFFICER PAUL REICHEL WAS FOUND ON THE LOADING DOCK OF THE HOTEL, DEAD FROM A BULLET WOUND. POLICE SPOKESMAN A. F. BRODHEAD SAID INVESTIGATIONS ARE ONGOING; NO DETAILS CAN BE RELEASED AT THIS TIME. QUESTIONED ABOUT THE SIMILARITIES IN THESE MURDERS AND THE TWO THAT OCCURRED ONE WEEK AGO, HE OFFERED NO COMMENT.

A HOTEL EMPLOYEE WHO DID NOT WISH TO BE IDENTIFIED WAS OF THE OPINION THAT IT WAS THE SAME KILLER, MURDERING ONE CITIZEN, AND THEN ONE POLICE OFFICER AS AN "ENCORE."

WATCH KRBM NEWS AT SIX WHEN WE WILL HAVE MORE DETAILS ON THE FAMILIES OF THE VICTIMS AND AN INTERVIEW WITH JUDSON LUNDQUIST, PRESIDENT OF THE BANKERS ASSOCIATION OF RIVERBEND, THE ORGANIZATION SPONSORING MS GOETZMAN'S APPEARANCE IN OUR CITY.

....

IN A RELATED STORY, APPROXIMATELY 80 PEOPLE GATHERED IN FRONT OF THE LINDSTROM HOTEL LAST NIGHT, PROTESTING THE PRESENCE OF SANDRA GOETZMAN. THE CROWD BLOCKED THE STREET, THROWING ROCKS AND EGGS, AND SETTING FIRE TO TOPIARY PIECES. NO ATTEMPT WAS MADE TO ENTER THE HOTEL, ALTHOUGH A WINDOW WAS BROKEN. HOTEL PERSONNEL ESTIMATED $9,000.00 OF PROPERTY DAMAGE WAS DONE.

THE PROTEST LASTED FOR ABOUT AN HOUR UNTIL POLICE RESTORED ORDER. NO ARRESTS WERE MADE, ALTHOUGH SEVERAL PERSONS WERE HELD FOR A "COOLING OFF" PERIOD, ACCORDING TO POLICE SPOKESMAN BRODHEAD.

....

RENE STORLEY, PRESIDENT OF THE RIVERBEND EDUCATION ASSOCIATION, INFORMED KRBM THERE HAS BEEN NO PROGRESS IN THAT GROUP'S NEGOTIATIONS WITH THE SCHOOL DISTRICT FOR SALARY AND INSURANCE CONCESSIONS.

STORLEY WAS QUOTED AS SAYING THAT IF NO PROGRESS IS MADE, THE STRIKE PRESENTLY AFFECTING SUMMER AND SPECIAL EDUCATION

CLASSES WILL CONTINUE INTO THIS FALL'S REGULAR CLASS SCHEDULE.

....

AN UNSIGHTLY GARBAGE-DUMP IN THE SOUTHERN REACHES OF THE CITY EXISTS NO MORE.

THE AREA ALONG BADGER CREEK BETWEEN EAST HAMILTON AND EAST KLINGER HAS BEEN USED THIS SUMMER AS A DISPOSAL SITE BY CARELESS CITIZENS, UNTIL IT BECAME "A DISEASE-RIDDEN EYESORE," ACCORDING TO A NEARBY RESIDENT. LAST NIGHT THE AREA WAS RESTORED TO AN UNSPOILED CONDITION.

A GREEN BERET WAS LEFT HANGING FROM A TREE LIMB WITH A NOTE SAYING, "HELPING MAKE OUR WORLD BETTER." LOCAL RESIDENTS ARE REFERRING TO THIS ANONYMOUS GROUP AS "THE GREEN BERETS," AFTER THE WELL KNOWN MILITARY SPECIAL FORCES UNIT, BUT IN THIS CASE, THE "GREEN" REFERS TO PRESERVING A GREEN EARTH.

....

THE DEPARTMENT OF PUBLIC HEALTH REPORTS THAT THE INCIDENCE OF POISON IVY CASES REPORTED OVER THE HOLIDAY WEEKEND WAS DOUBLE LAST YEAR'S FIGURES.

THE INCREASE, SAYS THEIR OFFICE OF STATISTICS, WAS DUE TO THE MEMBERS OF A TEEN CAMPING PARTY PICKING LARGE AMOUNTS OF THE POISONOUS VINE, MISTAKING IT FOR MARIJUANA.

....

WE'LL BE RIGHT BACK WITH "WINDY" WINDHORST AND THE WEATHER. "WINDY" WILL TELL US IF THE RAIN WILL HOLD OFF THROUGH THE COMING WEEKEND.

Chapter 10: Monday morning, June 21
TWO WEEKS BEFORE
THE MAGUIRE MURDER

Martin and Muggs leaned against the side of a building a few feet down an alley. The sun of the clear June morning warmed the bricks, creating a pleasant radiation of heat. Muggs took a quick look around the corner to the nearby City Hall building.

"Okay, Newbie, take a look. See that woman coming? Watch her."

The woman tossed a Starbucks coffee container into the trash receptacle at the foot of the steps, hurried up, and disappeared through the doors.

"For the next half hour, people will be coming for work. Watch what they throw away. They're in a big hurry; they buy a drive-through breakfast; they don't eat it all."

"Like that last woman," said Martin.

"Yeah, except that was just coffee. Leave the pop and coffee alone; you don't want too much liquid."

"Why?"

"Give me a break! I expected inexperience, but not stupidity."

"Oh. Bathrooms?"

She didn't bother to answer.

A man strode past the alley entrance, carrying a McDonald's sack and drinks container. He tossed the sack in the trash as he charged up the steps.

"Watch me," said Muggs.

She left the alley, walking at a business-like pace--not fast, but as though she had something to do. She approached the trash receptacle, pulled out the McDonald's sack, turned and with a purposeful air, returned. Martin noticed that the navy blue blouse hanging over the waist of her cinched-in too-large jeans, created an acceptable floppy-style look and hid the fanny pack she was wearing.

She opened the sack, extending it for Martin to see into.

Inside was a crumpled ball of logo-printed wax paper. Beside it was another wax paper bundle, unopened and warm.

"Take it," she said, suddenly thrusting it against his chest while watching a young woman pass and discard a sack in the trash.

After a repeat performance of her retrieval style, Muggs and Martin sat on their haunches, backs against the sunny side of the alley, and explored their sacks. Martin found an untouched sausage and egg biscuit; Muggs had half an order of hash brown nuggets and a large pastry with one bite taken off the end.

"You know," said Muggs, as she nibbled her pastry and licked her fingers. "Someone should do a study of personalities based on their eating habits. Like, your guy." She gestured at his sack. "Every morning he gets two breakfast biscuits, eats one, and tosses the other. Why doesn't he order just one? Does he hope someday the time will stretch to two biscuits? Is it a compulsive thing? Two being a necessary number? Did he once have a girlfriend who rode with him, and even though she's gone, he's still ordering a love-biscuit for her? Or is he into denial, ever hoping that his ulcer won't kick in immediately after the first biscuit?"

"You don't talk like a homeless person," Martin said.

"I'm not, really."

He stared at her. "I guess that one lost me."

"I'm not homeless, I'm houseless. By choice."

Martin continued to stare, blankly.

"You're like a lot of people, Bubbelah, thinking the 'homeless' covers everything."

"What doesn't it cover?"

"There are two types of homeless people," she said. "Actually, there are more than two types if you do a serious study, but for the purposes of Educating Martin 101, there are two. First type is the truly homeless who had life roll over them and they couldn't cope. Most of them can't cope on the streets, either. They lose connection with all but a very few rational thoughts and become the crazies."

She nibbled a potato nugget.

"The other type are those who choose not to deal with the impedimenta of life, preferring to have as few possessions and expectations as possible. These people are not 'homeless,' so much as they're merely 'houseless.' 'Street people' is a better word for them than 'homeless.'"

Martin picked crumbs from the wax paper cupped in his hand and regarded her thoughtfully.

"Take yourself," she said. "For some reason, you're running away from your previous life, and my guess is that your previous life included a college education. If you become a street person, do you intend to start talking like a fourth-grade drop-out?"

"I'm not running away," he said. "I just don't care anymore."

"Sure, and the Pope's a Unitarian. Fool yourself if you want to, but I think you care so very much about something that the only way you could handle it was by running away."

* * * * * * * * * *

Martin was footsore. He had never walked so much in his life. He grinned ruefully, thinking how he used to believe that his once-weekly racquetball games kept him in shape. When night fell, the folded blanket under the bridge was pure heaven.

He hadn't been back to the warehouse for a week now. No reason to. Following Muggs, he had learned where to eat, wash up, do laundry, and how to earn a little money. He had seen parts of the city he never knew existed. Too many parts of the city, according to the muscles in his legs.

The activity provided a diversion from his aching heart. More than that, he had to admit it was interesting. Surviving as a street person wasn't totally unlike the tactics of rising up the corporate ladder.

His biggest surprise happened the day Muggs took him to the Salvation Army Thrift Store and bought him a used, but still good, fanny pack.

"What do I need this for?" he asked.

"Because you need to carry some essentials with you at all times--moist wipes, spoon, jackknife, a little money, and your cell phone."

"Cell phone!" He looked to see if she was teasing. "Seriously?"

"Do cats like milk? A phone you buy in a store and plug with minutes every two months or so is best. We recharge at the library. Read a book while sucking in power."

Martin looked bleak. "No one's going to call me."

"Right on the nail!" said Muggs, "No one to call you means there's no one checking to make sure you're okay. If you get in trouble, you need that phone to call for help."

"If someone had told me this before, I wouldn't have believed it."

"Yeah, well, even free range chickens know enough to squawk when they're in trouble."

Another trip to the Salvation Army bought him two additional changes of clothing for four dollars-- everything with a yellow tag one dollar that day. Socks and shorts in the right size were found at the Dollar Store.

"I can't let you go on paying for things for me," said Martin quietly.

"You'll pay me back," she said.

After that, they scrounged for a sack that Muggs insisted he needed. She was finally happy with a large clean white plastic bag with a Shopko logo and a good-sized new-looking box that once had held an inexpensive desk lamp. She nestled the box inside the sack. The picture of the lamp could clearly be read through the white plastic.

"I suppose there's a good reason and I'm about to learn it, but why didn't we take the first sack and box we saw three hours ago?" asked Martin, respectful as a novice monk.

"You're not in Kansas any more, Doofus! You've got to blend. Right now you look like a middle-aged janitor walking around on his day off with a cheap lamp in his sack. If you carried a Marshall Fields sack with some sort of high-end box inside, it would blow your cover. People would stop and take a second look, thinking, 'what's wrong with this picture?' You don't want people to take a second look. You want them to pass you by unthinkingly because nothing stands out."

"I knew there would be a good reason."

They had spent all of Saturday picking up aluminum cans, starting at the edge of the downtown commercial district, going up one side of a street and down the other. Each time they found a can, they stamped it flat, Martin putting his inside the lamp box,

Muggs' in a K-Mart shopping bag. When their sacks were full, they walked to the recycling center, sold their booty, and came back.

"This isn't logical," Martin said. "It's taking too long. We need to get bigger sacks and make fewer trips."

"Well kiss my cheeks and call me Fannie! You've got another gear besides neutral." She patted his forearm; the proud teacher. "Right. You're absolutely right. You figure out how we can do it without blowing our cover, okay? Meanwhile, we have all the time in the world."

"We could make three times as much in the same amount of time. We don't have all the *money* in the world," argued Martin.

"It has to do with blending in. You can't lug around a big trash sack without calling attention to yourself."

"How about one of those nice little shopping thingies. You know, they're wire and have two wheels and you pull them behind you?"

"Like that?" She grasped his arm and turned him to look back down the street.

A woman with snarled gray hair, bright pink knee-high socks, black high-top tennis shoes, and a plastic rain coat was making her way haltingly down the street. One of her dirty hands clutched the handle of a two-wheeled wire shopping cart stuffed with an assortment of sacks and fabric. She was mumbling to herself, "Can't do that, can't do that, no sir, no sir, not my fault, didn't do it, won't do it, can't do that, take it off, gotta take it off...."

When she got to them, she turned her head away, and hunched a defensive shoulder. "Got a dollar?"

"Here," said Muggs, reaching in her jeans pocket and extending a crumpled bill.

The woman's claw-like hand darted out, grabbed the dollar, and shoved it down the neckline of her dirty blouse. Without looking at them, she began walking away. "Can't do that, can't do that, no sir, no sir, not my fault, didn't do it...."

"That's terrible," said Martin, after clearing his throat. "Can't something be done to help her?"

"Did Mary Ann get anywhere sifting sand?"

Martin frowned. He knew the song, but couldn't see the point.

"Lots of people have tried," she said in a voice that reminded him of his third grade teacher when he still didn't understand multiplication, "but trying to help the crazies is like helping feral cats. First you have to literally catch them. Then, no matter how much cozy living and kibble you give them, they're desperately unhappy and keep trying to escape."

"Okay," said Martin, accepting what she said for the time being. He would think more about the plight of the crazies later on. "I see the trash bags and wheelie carts send the wrong message, but there has to be a way to do more cans at a time."

"Uh... well...," said Muggs, surprised at this new attitude she was seeing. "You work on that, Martin."

"I will," he said, and then started to walk down an alley, as though looking for cans. He needed a few minutes to collect himself. The old Martin Driver had just intruded into the new Martin Driver's life. Was that a good thing or a bad thing?

#   #   #   #   #   #

Chapter 11: Monday evening, June 21
TWO WEEKS BEFORE
THE MAGUIRE MURDER

"Whoof!" said Frahdley, dropping into a leather chair and nodding at his four colleagues. "It's hot out there for June." To Cantrell, "How do you manage to stay looking so cool?"

She swiveled her chair to face away from him. "The skyways are air-conditioned," she said in the same tone she would have used informing him the earth was not flat.

"Just like a woman, taking the cushy way. I braved the elements for two blocks. Sundown, and you can still do eggs on the sidewalk."

"Let's get down to business," said Burkhalter. "I have compiled a list of suggestions---"

"Before we get to the nitty-gritty, Wilf, let's settle some basic things," said Frahdley.

"Such as?"

"A name. I've got some suggestions here---"

"We already have a name, Chris."

"It won't hurt to hear a few other suggestions. It's a good marketing practice. We hear some other suggestions, we say nope, nope, we like the first one better, then we've proven that our first decision was good. If not...."

"All right. Go ahead," said Burkhalter.

"Some of these are just top of the head, you understand, but who knows? All right. 'Wrong Righters Regiment.'"

He looked up to see blank stares. "You know, like making wrongs right? It's neat alliteration. And 'regiment' sounds like a military operation. Sort of like special ops?"

He looked around again. "All right, not that one. Try this on for size. 'Cavalry To The Rescue.' You know, like... well, you know."

He looked for comment. "Tough Group, huh? All right, here's a slightly newer twist. 'Guardian Angels.'"

"Chris," said Burkhalter, "we appreciate your enthusiasm for the project, but as this is a very serious venture, I think we want to avoid anything light or upbeat."

"No cutesy crap," said Madden. "Notice my alliteration."

"Take a damn vote and settle it," said Turner in a grumble that almost couldn't be heard.

"I'll have a show of hands," said Burkhalter. "All those who want to keep the name as we originally discussed?"

Three hands in addition to Burkhalter's rose from the table surface.

"Okay, okay, no new name for the group," said Frahdley, "but we definitely need code names. There may be times when we might be overheard and we want to keep something secret, and we wouldn't want to say, 'Tell Greg this or that,' you know, so we don't want to use real names."

"It's Gregory," said Turner.

Burkhalter cleared his throat.

"No, no, just bear with me a few minutes," said Frahdley. "Now take Audra."

Burkhalter looked over at Ms Cantrell. From what he knew of her, she was bitchy, critical, uncompromising, and had been known to lash out with sudden fury at slacking employees. Her insistence on high standards made her an ideal addition to the team.

"Her code name is 'Falcon,'" said Frahdley.

The other three men in the room concealed smiles. Cantrell puckered her lips in indecision, as though trying to decide if the name was flattering or not.

"Larry's code name will be 'Wolf.'"

"Lawrence," said Madden, but appearing not entirely displeased with being known as Wolf.

Frahdley looked toward Turner. Burkhalter tried to second guess what was coming. Turner was soft spoken and devious. He was good for their project because he stopped at nothing to accomplish what he decided was right, never mind if his methods involved a certain amount of double dealing. *Weasel*, thought Burkhalter. *He's going to call him Weasel.*

"Greg," said Frahdley while Turner rolled his eyes at the repeated familiarity, "your code name will be 'Snake.'"

Even better, thought Burkhalter.

"Wilf," you'll be 'Owl,'" said Frahdley.

Burkhalter nodded in acceptance of the name. "And yourself, Chris?"

"I'll be 'Bear.'"

Burkhalter could see smiles of agreement. The man had accurately tagged himself. Although Frahdley viewed their mission more as a game than a somber purpose, they needed him in the group. Large and strong, he could handle any of the more strenuous problems they encountered. Madden was physically fit, but protective of his surgeon's hands.

"All right, we now have code names," said Burkhalter. "Thank you for thinking of that, Chris; those are good names. Moving on to our target list---"

"Wait," said Frahdley. "We have to decide on a pin design."

"What?" said Cantrell.

"You know," said Frahdley, "a lapel pin in a secret design that only we understand. I was thinking of a torch crossed with---"

"No pins," said Madden.

"Definitely no pins," said Cantrell.

"Right." said Turner.

"Listen, I'm getting a little bummed out with all this negativity," said Frahdley. "You don't like lapel pins, fine. But we have to talk about uniforms next, and I don't want to hear any knee-jerk vetoes without some consideration. We definitely will need uniforms so our regular clothes don't get seen or stained."

"I know exactly what you're talking about, Chris," said Burkhalter, reaching out and patting the table in front of Frahdley, "and I have an idea for the perfect uniform. Will you give me until next week to show you?"

"Something that will hide who we are?"

"Absolutely."

"Keep our own clothes from getting messy?"

"Yes."

Lawrence Madden sat forward in his chair, and Burkhalter threw him a quick look, then turned back to Frahdley.

"We will have uniforms, but you understand, of course, that there will be times when it will be wiser to appear in our normal clothes?"

"Oh sure, like when we're scouting a situation."

"That, yes, of course. So, if there are no objections, we will get on with our target list." Burkhalter referred to a note card. "Audra, I've got your suggestion noted first. Let's hear your thinking."

As Ms Cantrell began talking, Burkhalter leaned back in his chair and considered the group. He was still somewhat surprised that five people who were so dissimilar could be so united in their commitment to an altruistic goal for which they had no previous skills.

#   #   #   #   #   #

Chapter 12: Afternoon, Tuesday, July 13

"A week of everybody on the Maguire case full press," said Pickett, "and we've got bupkis!" He glared at Pedersen and Nguyen, not so much in criticism as hoping for new news.

"Yessir," said Pedersen, brushing his hair out of his eyes. "but with two homicides we've got new angles to look for... not that... I mean... I don't mean that more homicides is a *good* thing." He blushed fiercely. "And I don't mean *two* homicides, I mean four... I didn't mean to...."

Pickett shook his head, and said, "How did a Norwegian Lutheran farm boy with a conscience ever decide to be a cop? Never mind. You're right, the two civilian homicides do give us more direction than one, and unfortunately, it would appear that cops were simply collateral damage. Collateral damage. What an ugly concept." He pulled himself out of the mood. "No walkout, huh? Never was going to be one?"

Pedersen flipped through the notebook Middleton had passed on to him. "This is Harrington. 'Oh, hell no. We're not stupid, you know. Better to take a 10% pay cut than have no job at all. Come the 15th, we'll all make a big show of pledging our support to the company and then everyone will keep on working.'"

"How long did they all know that?" asked Pickett.

"Apparently Maguire and Harrington quietly went through the membership during the week before the rally and got a consensus."

"So why the damn rally?" said Pickett.

"As I understand it," said Pedersen, "it's an excuse for a rowdy party, and if they get coverage in the newspapers, it looks good to the National UFCW."

"So neither Blue Ribbon people or the union members were unhappy with Maguire."

"That's it."

"And he's tops with wife, kids, friends, and every dog in the neighborhood."

"He was a nice guy."

"So what are his 'egregious abuses and usurpations?'"

"Darned if I know."

"Got an alibi from Jerglens yet?"

"No, he's having fun being obstructive, and we can't find anyone who knows where he was."

"Well, keep on him," said Pickett. He glanced at Nguyen, whose stoicism was sometimes a little unnerving. "You okay on this case assignment switch-over, Lu?"

"Yes," said Detective Nguyen.

"Mind if I join the party?"

Chief of Police James Boucher stood in the doorway.

Boucher was short, rotund, styled, manicured, and reeked of cologne. "Oily" came to mind. Right after "buffoon." Everyone knew Duponte had been on Boucher's case since the Maguire homicide. Now with a second murder, Duponte, often called "Mayor Viper" behind his back, was ramping up the criticism.

Pedersen jumped up, leaving his chair for Boucher, and moved over to lean on a filing cabinet.

"Thank you Detective Pedersen," said Boucher. He gave a polite nod to Nguyen. "Detective Nigooyen." And sat down.

Nguyen smiled. "Good afternoon, Chief Bowcher."

"That's 'boo-shay,'" said the chief. "It's French."

"That's 'nuh-wen,'" said the detective. "It's Vietnamese."

"Of course, of course," said Boucher.

"What can we do for you, Chief?" said Pickett.

"I thought I'd join this bull session and see if I could be a little help. Another viewpoint, even from an old fuddy-duddy who's been kicked upstairs, might shed some fresh air on things."

A glance of agreement flashed from captain to detectives and back. Nothing would be said about the notes.

Leading with "I'm just asking..." and "Have you boys thought of..." and "I assume you've checked..." and "This is probably too simple an idea, but..." Boucher talked them through the entire Maguire investigation to date.

Pedersen could tell Lu was becoming increasingly irritated. Not because Lu was doing anything, but because he was not doing anything in spades.

Having experienced times in an investigation when a simple remark by an inexperienced person had struck a loud clang of enlightenment, however, Pedersen stayed calm. He was content to go along with Boucher's clueless interference, just in case.

"There must be something I don't understand here," said Boucher, smiling disingenuously. "For over a week we've had eight detectives doing interviews? A whole week?"

"There were quite a few people to interview," said Pedersen.

"Or," said Boucher, widening his eyes in all innocence of any criticism, "maybe you're asking too many questions? Interviews could be cut much shorter, hmmm? I'm just asking, of course; you boys are the ones on the front line. But you may want to think about it."

No one responded. Two notes on two dead bodies created more, rather than fewer, questions to be asked.

"Well!" said Boucher, adopting a let's-get-to-work tone and slapping his hands on the armrests of his chair. "If you were to ask me, I'd say we quit all this questioning and simply get everyone's fingerprints over at Blue Ribbon. When we compare them to the unknown ones in the car, that should narrow things down nicely! What do you think?"

Pedersen and Pickett didn't know how to respond. In the first place, there was no guarantee the killer was ever in Maguire's car. "Excellent idea!" said Nguyen. "Do we have your permission to do so, Sir?"

"Absolutely! Let's get right on it." Boucher stood to go, his hands checking the smoothness of his hair. "Yes, excellent idea, if I do say so myself. Although I'm only a mere desk jockey now, I can still carry my weight in an investigation."

He stopped at the door. "Two premeditated murders so close together, one of them a national figure. These are exciting times for Riverbend. Do you suppose I should prepare a statement for the media?"

Pedersen straightened from his lean on the filing cabinet, face flushed a bright red. "*Four* murders, Sir."

"Yes, of course, four."

"They were police officers, Sir. Our own people."

Pickett stood, moving a hand toward Pedersen in a warning gesture. "Maybe we should wait till we have a bit more information before anything gets issued to the public," he said to Boucher.

"Of course, of course. I'll give the lab a head's up about the fingerprints on my way back. Let them know they might be looking at a couple hours overtime, but I'll clear it. How many people are we talking about?"

"About a thousand," said Nguyen.

"Uh... maybe we should hold off on fingerprinting until I run it past the budget people. Don't move on that until you get a go-ahead from me. Nice working with you, boys," he said as he left.

"Anybody think our honorable chief is going to actually mention it to the budget weasels?" said Pickett.

"Exciting times!" said Pedersen. "Kill two cops; keep Riverbend on the map!"

"Ah, well, consider the source, Jim. Where now with Maguire?"

"We'll keep Rivera and Olson going on second interviews," said Pedersen, his voice still stiff with outrage. "Lu and I will dig deeper into Maguire's background." He tapped Middleton's notebook against his palm. "He's so squeaky clean, I keep thinking nobody's that good."

"Don't forget Jerglens," said Pickett.

"No, we won't," said Pedersen. "I'm beginning to wonder if he's not a lot smarter than we think. He acts like a pig-headed moron. But what if it is just that? An act."

#   #   #   #   #   #

Chapter 13: Wednesday morning, July 14

Stangler sagged, red-eyed and half asleep, in the Police Department break room, booted feet crossed at the ankles, resting on a nearby chair. He held his sugar shot of choice, a can of Dr. Pepper.

Across from him, Pickett hunched over a styrofoam cup of coffee, elbows on the table. Middleton sat with six small bags of salted peanuts in front of him, four empty.

"Sure you got enough peanuts, there, Wiley?" asked Stangler.

"We manly men need the heat energy," smiled Middleton. "Especially on-the-go super detectives like me." He threw a handful of peanuts in his mouth and crunched them contentedly. "Now, little bitty guys who prance around on high heels with boy-toy hair; they don't need---"

"Enough!" said Pickett. "The joke's getting old. How are you coming on Goetzman?"

"We've talked to everyone who was at the dinner," said Stangler, "every hotel employee working anywhere during the relevant times, every guest. Nothing."

"No one saw anything?" asked Pickett.

"A handful of bankers and hotel people saw her leave the ballroom. A couple guests passed her when she was entering her room. No one saw her after that."

"Except the killer," said Pickett. "And Reichel?"

"Ah, man! Nothing. Hanson and Liebowitz' crew couldn't see him. No one saw him until that housekeeping guy went out on the dock for a smoke. Why the hell did he leave? Wiley, you told him not to leave, right?"

"Right."

"So, dammit, why did he leave!" He lifted his boots and kicked the chair over. "Pisses me off." He sat up, put his elbows on the table and dropped his head in one hand. "Now the kid is dead. Goddammit, why did he leave?"

"Funeral scheduled?" said Middleton

"Family's having him shipped back to Wyoming. They're bitter; don't want a police ceremony. Boucher's going to send one of the assistant chiefs out. Bakken, I think."

Three young females, computer input techs, walked in and stopped, looking surprised. They were accustomed to the detectives getting what they wanted from the machines and then leaving, rarely sitting around.

"Don't mind us," said Pickett, "we're hiding from helpful windbags."

"What?" said one.

"Never mind; shouldn't have said that."

There were three vacant chairs at the table, counting the one Stangler had kicked over.

Middleton stood up, pulling his chair back. "Please have a seat, ladies," he said. Circling the end of the table, he picked up the fallen chair, pushed Stangler's legs aside, and sat down.

"Huh? Oh! Sorry, mind's elsewhere," said Stangler.

"Well, bring it back and look alert," said Middleton. "These goddesses have the impossible job of translating your chicken scratches into coherent incident reports for the case files. Without them you'd look like the uneducated wienie you are." Pointing at each for Stangler's benefit, he said, "Jessica, Laura, Sandi. Where's Anne?"

"One of us needs to stay by the phone," said Jessica, heading for the vending machines, "and we have to get right back."

"How is your case going, Lobo?" asked Laura, looking at him sideways through her lashes.

"Oh, well, you know," he said. "Things are always slow at first...uh..."

"Laura," said Middleton.

"...Laura, but thanks for asking."

"No developments on the thing we're not supposed to mention?" she asked.

"No," said Pickett with underscored firmness.

The girls quickly bought their snacks and left. Turning at the door, Laura said, in a low husky voice, "See you around, Lobo."

"Yes, sure. See you around, Laura," he said.

When the girls were out of hearing, Middleton said to Pickett, "Do you suppose if I let my hair grow and wore high-heels, they would---"

"Quit. Enough. If you keep baiting Stangler, he's going to kill you. If you start with the girls, Amarantha will kill you. And then I'll kill you because I can't afford to be short-staffed right now."

"Okay," said Middleton, "but just because you ask so nicely."

"Where were we," said Pickett burying his head in his hands.

"If she was killed where she was found, someone got her to come back to the ballroom," said Stangler. "Maybe that ties in with the larger shoe prints in her room.

Why didn't he kill her in the privacy of the room without the risk of being seen if he simply wanted her dead?" said Pickett.

"He didn't simply want her dead;" said Stangler, "he wanted public discovery of the body and the note.

And anyone who would kill a working cop during an active crime scene is not afraid of taking risks."

"Goddammit, that's bold," said Pickett.

"We won't be able to keep the notes under wraps much longer. He's going to put it in a conspicuous place next time."

"Ah shit! You're thinking there'll be a next time before we catch him?"

"We don't have enough to go on," said Stangler. "There's no real motive. We're checking buses and planes from San Francisco. SFPD is checking Coastal Banking people who can't account for the time, but it's a big job and they have cases of their own, so we're not holding our breath. Besides, it's just elimination work. The same note as with Maguire makes it a home-grown killer."

"Someone at the rally and at the protest?"

"We'll check with Rask and Stummer when they come in. If there's a connection, they'll find it."

"Dammit, Stangler, we don't need any more lawsuits for police brutality! You didn't encourage them to get rough, did you?"

"No, Sir, I did not. All I said was that the job would be too tough for any but detectives with superior interrogation experience."

"Ah, shit!" said Pickett, getting up and throwing his empty cup in the trash container. "One of these days I'm *really* going to have to kill all four of you."

#   #   #   #   #   #

Chapter 14: Morning, Thursday, July 15

"You guys cops or bankers?" said Stangler as Rask and Stummer sauntered into the detectives' room at 10:30 in the morning.

Both detectives were in their late 50's, thickly set, with bellies that would have been paunches if they hadn't been hard-muscled. John Rask, with dark, thinning hair and a beefy face, looked like a Mafia enforcer. Now, as most of the time, he was chomping on a wad of gum. Two years ago, Rask had used Nicorette gum to quit smoking. The cigarette habit had been conquered, but the Nicorette cud remained. When chivvied about it, Rask would growl, "Don't knock it, moron. I get my nicotine without tar, carbon monoxide or carsinjens... carsonjeans... whatever. I'm laughin' my ass off at guys with lung cancer."

Bishop Stummer's gray hair was closely cut to the shape of his skull. Despite his constant smile, he looked like an evil prison guard.

Both wore their guns fully visible toward the front of their belts.

Although they'd been in the department longer, the two older detectives didn't appear to resent Stangler's elevation to senior detective. They treated him with the same disrespect and insubordination they gave everyone.

"Blow it out your bunghole, Stangler," said Rask cheerfully, pulling over a chair and sitting down.

"It isn't that it's mid-morning," said Middleton. "It isn't that you always look like a cow on uppers with that gum; it's that you're reeking of bacon."

"Yup," said Stummer. "Double orders of bacon, eggs, and pancakes at Danny's Diner."

"We was out late, workin' on the Goetzman case. Breakin' heads is hard work," said Rask. "We deserved a good breakfast."

"Pickett's going to fire me if you generated any lawsuits out there playing John McClane," said Stangler.

"Nah, we was gentle. Just sorta recreational head-bashin'; nothin' serious. We was downright cheerful till we got here and ran into the Pillsbury Doughboy."

"Who?"

"Boucher dogged us down the hall," said Stummer. "The moron wants to sit down and review the case--help us."

"Yeah. I told him I was headin' fer the can," said Rask, "and was gonna sit down and review last night's beef stew. I offered real nice to let him help."

Stangler and Middleton didn't give him the satisfaction of a laugh.

"So," said Stangler, "did you find anything?"

"Well, you know," said Rask, "beef stew is---"

"Cut it out!"

"Okay, okay, don't get pissy. We talked to 72 protesters--"

"Seventy-two!" said Stangler. "That's damn near all of them!"

"Yeah. Damn, we're good, huh?"

"I'm surprised! You two apparently aren't as stupid and ineffectual as everyone says."

"You wanna hear what we found out or do ya wanna sit there and be cute?" said Rask.

"I would like to hear what you have to report, detectives," said Stangler. "Please."

"Are we in the wrong place?" Stummer asked Rask. "That actually sounded polite."

"Talk!" said Stangler.

"Well, first off," said Rask, parking his wad of gum inside a cheek, "it wasn't nothin' organized."

"You know," said Stummer, "like there's no organization called 'People Who Lost Money In The Bank Failures.'"

"Yah," said Rask. "The way it happened was like one or two guys inna neighborhood would get to bitchin' about the bank mess 'n decide they'd all go to one of the guy's basement, drink beer, make some shitty signs, 'n show up at the hotel."

"When they got to the hotel," said Stummer, "they discovered a lot of other people had the same idea. We ran down almost all of them because, although nothing was planned, most of them recognized each other."

"You know," said Rask, "like Joe Blow rekenized the manager of his supermarket, or the guy who does his lube job. His car's lube job, not---"

"Never mind," said Stangler. "We know what you mean."

"Anyway, they're havin' a good time yellin' like morons, then somebody shows up with a big pail a' eggs n' they all have fun chukkin' eggs at the hotel, excep' one moron threw a rock 'n broke the big front window. Nobody knows who brought the eggs or who threw the rock a' course."

"You know those two little bushy trees in the cement pots on either side of the front walkway?" said Stummer. "Someone got the bright idea to collect all the disposable plastic lighters in the crowd, sprinkle their contents on the trees, and then light them."

"But here's the deal, see," said Rask, switching his gum into rapid chomp mode, "No one wanted to get inna hotel because they wanted t' protest outside where they could be seen."

"We asked everyone if they belonged to the New Guards," said Stummer, "and got nothing."

"Not a twitch," said Rask.

Stangler was satisfied with that. Even though Rask sounded like a sixth-grade dropout, both detectives had been at it a long time, and could probably tell a guy's rap sheet by looking in his eyes.

"So as far as you guys can tell, the protestors are a dead end?"

"Maybe, maybe not," said Rask, "we been savin' the best till last."

"*La pièce de résistance*," said Middleton.

Rask ignored him. "Guess who was one a' the protesters? Jerglens!"

"What!"

"Chukkin' eggs and wavin' a sign," said Rask. "We can't get the douche-bag to say where he went after the patrols broke it up, though. Most of 'em say they went home, and we got wives and roommates backin' that up. Jerglens says it's none a' our business. We leaned on him a little, but got nothin' but smart-ass talk."

"You want us to pull him in?" said Stummer.

"No, let's hold on that until we get something more definite."

"So," said Rask, "does the boy wonder have any ideas about where next?"

"Not any good ones," said Stangler. He stood and thought about it for a minute. "It's a busy hotel and she was killed out in the open. Someone has to have seen something, whether he knows it or not. Go back and buttonhole hotel people again, minute by minute, six till midnight--even the ones who weren't near the ballroom. Maybe they heard something from someone else. Get a picture of Jerglens and take it along; maybe we'll get lucky and someone saw him inside the hotel."

"It's all up to you, Batman," Middleton said to Rask. "Go find that one golden clue that will unravel this whole case."

Rask gave Middleton a withering look. "You're a real moron, you know that, Middleton?" He turned to Stummer. "Figure we need lunch before we start bashin' heads?"

Stummer looked at his watch. "Oh, hell yes."

"Do not touch anyone!" said Stangler.

"How the hell 'r we gonna get decent information if we don't touch anyone?"

Stangler gave him a long look.

"Yeah, yeah, okay," said Rask, turning to leave. "We'll be as polite as Emily Poppins."

#   #   #   #   #   #

Chapter 15, Saturday afternoon, July 17

Pedersen, Nguyen, Rivera and Olson hunched around a desk in a corner of the detectives' room.

"High point of the assignment was six Dairy Queen cones," said Rivera. *"No encontramos nada."* She handed a thick bunch of interview forms to Pedersen. "We gave Thursday's and Friday's to the computer ladies. This is today's."

Detective Carmen Rivera was 5'6", golden in color with long straight black hair she kept in a braid coiled on the back of her head. Brittany Olson was a 5'8", white-blonde with an extreme boy-cut.

Rivera's former partner was retiring to form his own security service just when Olson was promoted to detective, hence their assignment as partners. There was a five-year experience difference, Pedersen knew, but it didn't show. Both Rivera and Olson were in their early 30's with what others in the department regarded as spectacular bodies, but steely attitudes. People often heard Stummer explaining, "Just when a suspect thinks he's dealing with Little Miss Muffet, wham, he suddenly finds himself face-to-face with the spider--and it's a black widow."

Nguyen was studying Spanish, and had spent the past few minutes working out what Rivera had said. "Found... nothing," he translated.

"Close enough," said Rivera.

"*Casi--*" started Nguyen.

"C'mon guys, can we do this in English, please?" said Pedersen. "I don't know why you want a third language, Lu, you never say anything anyway."

"Okay," said Rivera. "We talked to everybody again--even that crusty night watchman. He's kind of a hoot when you get him going."

"We brought up New Guards with everyone," said Olson, "but didn't get anything. We were watching for it. If we'd seen so much as a shadow of recognition, I think we would have caught it."

"We got nothing useful," said Rivera. "Everyone says Maguire was a nice guy and they respected him. Even Jerglens' friends--who all have to consult Mr. Penis before they answer a question--told us they didn't trust him because there was something sneaky about a guy who was polite all the time."

"You ate six ice cream cones?" said Lu.

"One each day!"

"Tell us you had some luck," said Olson.

"Sorry," said Pedersen. "He was a solid family man, his finances were what you would expect, he was a regular church-goer, he volunteered for youth organizations, even his mother-in-law liked him. We couldn't find the slightest reason someone would want to kill him." He stuck the interview forms in a file folder, and stood up. "You two go home, take Sunday off. See you Monday morning."

"What are you going to do?" asked Olson as they got up to leave.

"Lobo and Wiley are checking Jerglens as perp. We get Jerglens as victim. We'll start turning over his background, see if we find any creepy-crawlies under the rocks."

#   #   #   #   #   #

Chapter 16: Late night, Sunday, July 18

The dark shiny van stood just beyond the corner of a building, its motor idling, front and back doors standing open. Two figures in dark coveralls and masks ran toward it. One of them threw something with a long wooden handle in the back, where it landed with a clatter, and slammed the rear doors. Both anonymous figures climbed into the front seats, and wasting no time, but calling no unnecessary attention to their departure, sped off into the night.

#   #   #   #   #   #

Chapter 17: Morning, Monday, July 19

The word had gone out. Meeting with the mayor. Conference room, 9:00 a.m. Be there.

The conference room was just big enough for a long highly polished table, ten padded chairs, a whiteboard at one end, and a video cart on the other.

Riverbend's nine detectives were there, grouped at one end of the long table, four sitting, five standing behind, all with a look of barely-contained animosity. When the mayor requested a meeting, it meant he intended to vent.

At the opposite end of the conference table sat Captain Harlow Pickett, looking uncomfortable; Chief of Police James Boucher, absorbed in reading his notes; Mayor Ronald Duponte, arms crossed and staring impatiently at a spot on the far wall; and a man none of the detectives recognized.

A chair left empty halfway down the table on either side made a visible division between brass and the lower ranks.

Boucher stood, giving a last look at his notes. "Gentlemen, we have a---"

"And ladies," said Rivera.

"What? Uh... oh... yes. Gentlemen and ladies, we have a serious situation." Looking up, he noticed Wishink in a dirty torn armless sweatshirt, three-day stubble, cigarette tucked behind his ear, slouched in one of the chairs. Boucher bent over and whispered to Pickett. Pickett whispered back.

"He's a Detective?" Boucher blurted out loud, looking up with a startled expression.

Wishink didn't react, glowering his opinion of morning meetings and the Chief of Police.

Pickett wiped a hand across his face, momentarily obscuring his expression. Leave it to Boucher not to know all of his staff. "Detective Wishink often works undercover," he said.

"Oh, well, of course!" said Boucher. "Didn't recognize you in that getup, Wishink. Heh, heh. Keep up the good work."

"Judas Priest!" said Rask quietly, leaning an elbow on the video equipment cart, cracking his gum.

"Gentlemen and ladies," said Boucher, switching from jovial to frowning concern, "we have a very serious situation in Riverbend." He looked around, one finger raised, to make sure everyone was hanging on his word. "We have a serial killer."

"What!" said Duponte, getting to his feet.

A low rumble of angry surprise broke from the gathered detectives. Half-finished questions beginning with, "How did he...?" rose and were quickly smothered as each detective realized it wasn't wise to let the Chief of Police know that a critical case element had been deliberately kept from him.

Boucher waited until the detectives quieted. He paused to look around the room. All eyes were on him. It was deadly quiet.

The mayor remained standing, glaring at Boucher. He hadn't forgotten two incidents in the past when the police chief had caused a storm of acrimony with his penchant for leaping to melodramatic conclusions.

Boucher's glance slid off Duponte, then turned toward Pickett, whose thin face carried no readable expression. "How is it that I wasn't informed? A serial killer! And I had to discover it by accident going through case files on the computer!"

Chagrined looks passed among the detectives. None of them had expected Boucher to actually read a case file, he having never done so in the past. Too late, they realized his recent spate of helpfulness had gone that far.

"As your Chief of Police, I am getting serious pressure from Mayor Duponte," Boucher said, carefully not looking at the mayor, who was still standing, "but that's okay. As Chief, I should be able to take a little stress, even though it's not my...." Apparently deciding not to go farther with that thought, he wiped his hand across his forehead. "As Chief," he continued, "I have a duty to protect the people of Riverbend. Ten minutes ago, I sent out a press release, quoting the New Guards' notes to the media, and warning our citizens that there is a serial killer among us."

An angry reaction broke out from the detectives so suddenly it caused the chief to flinch. Pickett rose to his feet open-mouthed.

"You did what!" shouted the mayor.

The chief raised his voice to be heard over the angry swell of reaction and switched to his usual smarmy style, "Now I know that we have the finest staff of detectives in the state. And I have the utmost confidence in each and every one of you. I cannot say how much---"

"Thank you Chief Boucher," the mayor shouted over him.

Boucher looked around in surprise and sat down, his expression struggling between polite acceptance and unwise irritation.

Pickett slowly resumed his seat, his angry expression this time easily readable.

Duponte, a darkly handsome man in a well-cut suit, waited for comments to cease, taking the time to make eye contact with each detective.

"As Chief Boucher has pointed out," Duponte began in a voice cuttingly thin and icy, "he has been receiving pressure from me. We have four murders occurring in the space of a week, and nothing is being done about it. 'Still questioning relevant people,' is the answer I get from your department head." He stabbed a vicious look at Pickett. "Detectives! My original purpose in asking for this meeting was to tell you to shorten the questioning and shorten the coffee breaks! Get some results!"

From somewhere came a quick intake of breath.

"Am I understood?" His twitching fingertips touching the table surface reflecting his pent-up anger, he looked around the silent room. No one moved. "Now!" he continued. "Now, our illustrious chief of police tells us... Tells the press! We have a serial killer!" He took a couple deep breaths, looking at the detectives. "Which of you is in charge of this mess?"

"I am," said Stangler, standing with arms crossed in front of his chest, jaw muscles clenched.

"Doesn't the department have a dress code?" Duponte snarled, eyeing Stangler's hair.

Stangler held his stance, giving Duponte an unwavering stare. No one broke the silence.

"Well, skip that for now," said Duponte. "Detective..."

"Stangler," said Boucher, pleased to remember the name.

"Detective Stangler," said Duponte, "Do we have a serial killer?"

"We don't think so."

"You don't *think* so? What the hell does that mean? Don't you know?"

"We think we have a vigilante," said Stangler, every muscle in his body tight.

"Are you being insubordinate? Can you give me a straight answer? Were these four murders committed by the same person?"

"Yes," said Stangler.

"Yes! Four separate murders by the same person mean you've got a serial killer, you half-wit!"

Standing beside, and slightly behind Stangler, Middleton shifted his weight so his elbow firmly pressed the back of his partner's arm--a clear signal that this was not a good time to go ballistic.

Seated at the table in front of Stangler, Pedersen leaned forward and said, "Sir, if you would calm yourself and let us explain, it---"

"Shut up," said Duponte. Looking back to Stangler, he said, "How many suspects do you have?"

"None."

Rask and Stummer exchanged covert glances. Stangler was apparently not going to mention Jerglens.

"None!' Duponte placed his knuckles on the table and leaned forward, looking as though he intended to vault its length. "Four murders by the same person, and you can't find someone who has a connection?"

"No," said Stangler flatly.

"'No!' Just 'No?' Duponte canted farther forward. "That's it?" he shouted. A fine spray of spittle dropped to the table.

"We're checking to see if the Maguire murder was mistaken identity," said Stangler through a clenched jaw.

"Mistaken identity!" Duponte reared back to his full height. "What sort of idiotic excuse is that?"

Pickett looked up at Duponte. "Mr. Maguire was universally respected."

"That's true" said the unidentified man near the head of the table.

"In the dark and from behind, he strongly resembled a man who was not well-liked," said Pickett.

Duponte gave him a look that could peel paint.

Turning back to Stangler, he said, "So you're nowhere near close to an arrest?"

"That's right," said Stangler, his tone carrying an ungiving finality.

Pedersen, Nguyen, Rivera and Olson were frozen. Rask, Stummer and Wishink smothered grins.

The unidentified man suddenly stood up. "I'm Pastor Clark," he said.

Duponte looked at him in furious astonishment.

"Michael and Annette Maguire are my parishioners... were... are. We are deeply concerned by the lack of progress in the case."

Reverend Clark was short, pale, and balding, but had a powerful sonorous voice.

"Who let him in here!" spat Duponte, his face flushing dark red, pointing an accusing finger at Pastor Clark.

"Uh... well..." stammered Chief Boucher, "he represents a large portion of the community and I thought---"

Clark's voice rolled over him. "The district president of our Synod has contacted the national Synod president, and he will be contacting Washington asking for help. Perhaps the FBI or the National Guard---"

Pickett buried his face in his hands, shoulders jerking, as his grim attitude dissolved into silent laughter.

"Are you fucking crazy!" thundered Duponte, abandoning all control and swearing at an important constituent.

Clark sat down suddenly with a shocked expression.

"A serial killer!" Duponte screamed. "An idiot who wants to call in the National Guard! And the Keystone Kops looking like hippies! I'm the mayor of a fucking circus!

"That's enough, Duponte," said Stangler, uncrossing his arms and lunging around the table toward the mayor as voices rose around the room.

In the same instant, Pickett stood, Middleton reached for Stangler and Emily opened the conference room door and shouted over the din.

"Lobo, you've got another dead body!"

* * * * * * * * * *

Stangler walked a wide perimeter around the body of René Storley, memorizing details. She lay on her left side at the front of classroom 303 in Eleanor Roosevelt High School, her face in a pool of dried blood, the back of her head dented and matted. A ring of keys rested a few inches from her right hand. Tucked into that hand was a note that could be read from where
he stood.

"OUR SACRED DUTY
DEATH TO ABUSERS AND USURPERS
DEATH TO THE HOUNDS
OF ABSOLUTE DESPOTS
NEW GUARDS FOR FUTURE SECURITY"

Half a sheet of plain paper, hand printed, black ink.

The custodian who found her and the uniformed officers first on the scene had seen it. But that was of little consequence now, what with Boucher's press release. And one way or the other, after this they would have been forced to admit the homicides were the work of one killer. They would still have tried to hold back the notes, though, if not for Boucher's interference. Wouldn't they?

Middleton walked in, notepad in hand. The door stood open and he was careful not to touch it.

"Custodian's in a classroom down the hall," he said. "Klindworth and Tufte are on the front door. We're waiting for the Crime Lab."

"Is Boucher right, and we're wrong?" said Stangler. "If we had released information to the public sooner, would this poor woman still be alive?"

"Move over, I'll join you on that guilt trip," said Middleton. "Duponte was right when he said all we've done is question people. I feel like a hamster in a wheel, running like the devil but not getting anywhere."

Stangler gave Middleton a long frowning look. "Nah," he said, "hamsters don't get that big."

"*Touché,*" said Middleton, moving to get a different view of the body. "Tell me how we could have prevented this. Warn all the abusers and usurpers in town not to let anyone get behind them?"

"A teacher. Did she abuse any kids?"

"Who knows?" said Middleton, with a sarcastic edge to it. "We'll have to question all the relevant people."

"It looks as though she walked into the room with her keys in hand, was struck by someone behind her, and fell forward. Why did she turn her back on someone? Was it someone she knew?"

"Maybe not. When you take someone home with you, don't you unlock the door and step in first? It's her classroom, maybe it went like that."

They looked around. The classroom was typical-- blackboard across the front, cork board to one side of the door, metal teacher's desk, wastebasket, rows of wood and metal student chairs with the one-armed writing surfaces, wide waist-high shelves full of textbooks across the back. Nothing out of the ordinary- -other than a dead body.

"Let's talk to the custodian," said Stangler.

Coming out of the room, they could see silhouettes through the obscure glass of the doors at the end of the hallway.

"I told Klindworth and Tufte we asked for them particularly because of their experience," said Stangler. "They know what to watch for. If anyone tries to pull them aside, they'll take him down."

"And get credit for catching a serial killer."

"Win-win."

As they walked down the hall, Middleton looked at his notes. "There was a meeting of teachers and parents in the big music room at 8:00 last night, conducted by Ms Storley. Purpose of the meeting was for the teachers to explain the contract situation to interested parents. From what little I could get out of the custodian, I gather it was mostly parents sounding off about the dearth of dedication in educators."

"Did he actually say 'dearth of dedication?'"

"*Au contraire*, what he actually said was they were hollering that the teachers put money before the kids. The meeting broke up about 9:45."

In classroom 308 they found the custodian seated at the teacher's desk. "Mr. Harwood, this is Senior Detective Lovar Boris Stangler," said Middleton."

Stangler shot Middleton a quick "Oh yeah?" raised eyebrow look. Laying on full name and title was Middleton's method of approaching tough nuts to crack.

Middleton slid sideways onto the seat of a too-small student chair, the writing arm digging him in a kidney. Stangler stood.

The custodian was thin with a gray brush cut, wearing dark blue work clothes. He glared at them.

"You were here last night during the meeting?" said Stangler.

The custodian flared the nostrils of his chiseled nose and jerked a nod.

"Tell us how the evening went."

The custodian folded his lips in a tight line. His rigid posture matched his tone of voice. "The meeting ended. They left. I locked up."

"Can you elaborate a little more? When the meeting ended, did you---"

"Checked the music room, locked it. Folding security grille was across the hall intersection. All other doors locked. Only way out was south doors. They all left, including some jackass yelling about his right to be in a public building without being pushed out. I locked the doors."

"You saw Ms Storley leave?"

"Yes! I've said that twice."

"We're not accusing you of any oversight, Mr. Harwood," said Stangler. "Just answer the questions as best you can. Could anyone have hidden anywhere?"

"No. I've already told you. Everything was locked."

"But teachers have keys?"

"Only to their own classrooms. I've already told you; no one could hide anywhere."

"Elsewhere in the school?" said Middleton, looking up from his notes.

"Again, in case you missed it. Everything. Was. Locked. The grille was locked. I'm the only one with a key."

"How did you leave the building?" asked Stangler, walking slowly down one side of the classroom, hands in his pockets, appearing to casually peruse the empty cork board.

"Grille. East hall. North utility door. My truck."

"What route did you take, leaving the premises?" Stangler walked the rear width of the classroom.

"West perimeter. South driveway."

"As you passed the parking area outside these south doors, did you see any cars?" Stangler came up the other side of the classroom.

"No. No cars, no trucks, no skateboards, no flying saucers, nothing."

Stangler finished his walk standing close to the teacher's desk, hands still in his pockets, appearing unruffled.

"Does assisting the police in a murder investigation irritate you, Mr. Harwood?" he asked quietly.

"I've work to do and you're holding me up with stupid questions."

Stangler turned slightly toward Middleton. "Help me out, here, Detective Middleton," he said in a mild conversational tone. "I'm not sure if this asshole should accidentally fall off his chair and break an arm, or if I should take him down to the station for the 24 hours I can hold a material witness while asking stupid questions. What do you think?"

"Hey!" said the custodian.

"Sounds like Mr. Harwood doesn't like those choices," said Middleton. "Maybe he'd rather be a little more polite and helpful."

"That's a thought." Stangler turned, braced his knuckles on the desk top, leaned into the custodian, and spoke in cold threat. "Shall we try it again? See how it goes?"

Losing a little color in his face, the custodian dropped his eyes, tightened his mouth, and held very still.

"Where were we?" said Stangler. "As you passed the parking area outside these south doors, did you see any cars?"

Harwood took a breath and held it.

"Nicely."

Harwood widened his eyes, let the breath out, and in a somewhat less acid tone, started. "A few vehicles were at the in-drive, waiting to turn into the street. No one was left in the parking lot."

"Did you recognize any of the vehicles?"

"One was René's. There was a gray Lincoln and a dark van. I don't know what the parents drive."

Stangler sauntered to a student chair, sat down, stretched out his legs. "Tell us about discovering the body, Mr. Harwood. Start with when and why you came here this morning."

"I came sometime after 7:30 to get my notes for a new boiler recommendation I wanted my wife to print up. I forgot them last night. René's car was by this south entrance. Just because it was pretty early and she was always nice to me, I decided to stop and check on her. I used my keys to come in the entrance doors. Looking down the hall, I could see her classroom door was standing open. When I got there, I saw her. I don't know CPR. I used my cell to call 911 for an ambulance."

"Her car wasn't here when you left last night?"

"No. I already said... uh... no."

Middleton gave him a small smile. "We usually ask twice, Mr. Harwood, to make sure we got it right."

"Fine."

"Did you see her purse?" asked Stangler.

Harwood tipped his head back and shut his eyes for a moment, thinking. "No."

"Was the room used exclusively by Ms Storley?"

Harwood nodded. "Pretty much so. It could happen that a class session or a meeting would be moved into a different teacher's room for the odd reason, but mostly their rooms were theirs."

"Did you notice any large objects missing from the room?"

"Large? Like what? A desk?"

"Anything that might be used as a club. A metal pipe? Piece of equipment?"

"No. There wouldn't be anything like that in there in the first place," said Harwood. "Come summer, the rooms are cleared out, desks removed, floor re-finished. We find anything, it goes back to wherever."

"You touch anything besides the entrance doors?" said Stangler.

"I don't think so."

"Light switches?"

"No, it was daylight by then. I leaned on her door frame, watching in case she moved or said something. Then I went to the hall doors when I heard sirens coming."

"Did you think she was still alive?"

"She looked dead to me. I was hoping I was wrong. Listen, I'm really not a... uh... asshole. She was a nice lady and... and there she was in a puddle of blood." He swallowed hard. "It's just...." He looked up briefly at Stangler, then down at his own hands, tightly clenched. "She was dead and I could still smell her perfume."

"Ah, man, I know what you mean," said Stangler.

Middleton looked up from his notes. "You're sure it was perfume you smelled? Not something else sweetish?"

Stangler glanced at Middleton, aware of where he was going. Some people described the odor of dissipating chloroform as being a sweet smell.

"No," said Harwood, clearing his throat. "It was perfume. She wore Paloma Picasso, same as my wife. Eighty-four dollars for a quarter ounce, and that's on eBay. Women." He lifted his face and squinted at a far corner in thought. "Hang on a minute... I take that back. I said Paloma just because that's what she always wore, but now I think on it, I don't think it was."

"It wasn't Paloma?" said Middleton.

"No. Something else nice, but not her usual. She must have changed."

"Could you tell what it was?" said Middleton.

"Oh hell, no. I can tell Paloma just because that's what the wife wears, but after that I can't tell one perfume from...." Harwood buried his face in his hands. "Oh, god."

"What?" said Stangler.

"She had this little joke she would tell. She said the best perfume to wear if you wanted a man to follow you home was Essence of Roast Beef." He pulled a handkerchief from his back pocket and wiped his eyes.

Doors at the end of the hall could be heard opening and closing, then the voice of one of the uniforms, giving directions. Middleton pulled himself out of the cramping student chair to poke his head out their door.

"Crime Lab."

"Holmes?"

"Yup."

Stangler turned back to the custodian. "Yes, okay," he said. "You can go, but we'll probably have to take you through it again once we learn a little more."

The custodian stood, wiped sweaty hands on his pants, and started for the door. Middleton politely blocked him.

"It's a good idea if you go through the grille and out the back way," he said. "I know you'll have to walk all the way around the building to your truck, but the State Crime Lab people are touchy about anyone near a crime scene."

"Fine," said Harwood, and obediently turned right out the door, heading in the opposite direction from the activity in room 303.

Middleton came back to the teacher's desk and sat in the larger chair with an exaggerated sigh of pleasure. "Everyone saw her leave; the custodian saw her car was gone."

"So she must have come back--with someone," said Stangler, "and they went to her classroom. Why? School's out; there's nothing there."

"Maguire left the rally; the watchman says he wasn't there when he made his first rounds. Several people saw Goetzman leave the ballroom and go to her room. The custodian saw our teacher leave. They all came back."

"They all came back," said Stangler. "They all came back. Why? Was it all for the same reason? Abusers and usurpers. Blackmail?" He thought for a moment. "And Simonson and Reichel left," said Stangler. "Why?"

Middleton heaved his considerable shoulders in a shrug.

Stangler pulled his legs in and stood. "Maybe Surecock has found something interesting."

Just as Middleton stood, shouting broke out down the hall.

"What the hell! Out! Out! Right now!"

An answering, "Who the hell do you think you are!"

Stangler and Middleton stepped out of room 308 and slowly walked down the hall, grinning at the sight of a furious Bradford C. Holmes gesturing angrily at a backpedaling Mayor Ronald Duponte.

"I'm the person who's going to see you in handcuffs if you don't move, right now! This is a crime scene you ignorant asshole!"

Klindworth burst through the door and ran up the hall, stopping short of the combatants, looking from one man to the other, uncertain what to do, the sounds of his shoulder radio crackling an underscore to the shouting.

"Do you know who I am!"

"I don't care if you're the fucking Easter Bunny, get out or I'll have you arrested!" Turning to Klindworth, Holmes shouted, "Who the fuck let him in here!"

"Uh...!" said the red-faced officer.

"I'm the Mayor of Riverbend!"

"Officer! Put Mayor Asshole in handcuffs!"

"Enough!" screamed Duponte. "If we have a serial killer, I damn well want all the facts and I want them now! You report to me, you fucking asswipe!"

"Bullshit! I don't report to any fucking politician!" Holmes made a sweeping gesture that ended in a point at the mayor. "Put him in cuffs if he doesn't move right now!"

Duponte's eyes fell on Stangler and Middleton. "Detectives! Don't just fucking stand there! Do something! This madman is threatening me!"

"I'm sorry, Mr. Duponte," said Stangler with patently false regret, "but at a crime scene, Dr. Holmes' jurisdiction supersedes ours. He has the authority to arrest anyone who interferes with evidence collection."

"Ridiculous!" said Duponte, backing up a step.

"Officer?" said Holmes threateningly.

Duponte drew himself up to a dignified huff, straightened his tie, and turned toward the detectives. "You will hear more from me about this!" he said chillingly, then turned and walked with exaggerated dignity toward the exit doors, followed by a relieved Klindworth.

Holmes turned back into room 303. Duponte and Klindworth went out the south doors.

"Is that true? About jurisdiction?" said Middleton.

"Hell, no, but if he keeps that up, I may begin to like Dr Holmes."

One of the south doors opened and Klindworth stuck his head back in. "Did you guys see Tufte? Did he come in here?"

"Goddammit!" said Stangler as he and Middleton began to run.

#   #   #   #   #   #

Chapter 18: Noon, Monday, July 19

(Theme Music:)
(Voiceover:)
     THIS IS KRBM-TV, NEWS AT NOON. UP TO THE MINUTE REPORTING ON WHAT'S HAPPENING IN THE RIVER LAND WITH NOON NEWS ANCHOR SALLY FELDNER.

(Anchor:)
GOOD NOON TO YOU, MONDAY, JULY 19.

IN A STARTLING PRESS RELEASE EARLY THIS MORNING, CHIEF OF POLICE JAMES BOUCHER ANNOUNCED THAT THE CURRENTLY UNSOLVED MURDERS OF LOCAL BLUE RIBBON WORKER MICHAEL MAGUIRE, COASTAL BANKING SYSTEMS' SANDRA GOETZMAN, AND POLICE OFFICERS LUKE SIMONSON AND PAUL REICHEL WERE THE WORK OF A SERIAL KILLER.

MESSAGES CLAIMING RESPONSIBILITY WERE LEFT AT BOTH DEATH SITES FROM AN ORGANIZATION CALLED NEW GUARDS. ACCORDING TO POLICE SPOKESMAN A.F. BRODHEAD, IT IS NOT CERTAIN WHETHER THE UNKNOWN NEW GUARDS IS ACTUALLY A GROUP OR ONE INDIVIDUAL.

KRBM'S SIX O'CLOCK NEWS WILL HAVE INTERVIEWS WITH PEOPLE ON THE STREET WHO, DESPITE THIS NEW INFORMATION ABOUT THE NEW GUARDS NOTES, ARE BEGINNING TO CALL THESE "ENCORE" MURDERS.
....
NO MORE THAN TWO HOURS AFTER CHIEF BOUCHER'S PRESS RELEASE, WHAT APPEAR TO BE

THE ENCORE KILLER'S FIFTH AND SIXTH VICTIMS WERE DISCOVERED.

THE BODY OF RENE STORLEY WAS FOUND IN HER CLASSROOM AT ELEANOR ROOSEVELT HIGH SCHOOL AND THAT OF POLICE OFFICER WAYNE TUFTE WAS FOUND OUTSIDE ON THE SCHOOL GROUNDS.

ACCORDING TO POLICE AT THE SCENE, CAUSE OF STORLEY'S DEATH APPEARED TO BE A BLOW TO THE HEAD, WHILE TUFTE WAS SHOT IN THE HEAD. UNCONFIRMED SOURCES SAY A SIMILAR NEW GUARDS NOTE WAS DISCOVERED WITH MS STORLEY'S BODY.

STORLEY WAS A RESPECTED TEACHER AT THE HIGH SCHOOL AND PRESIDENT OF THE RIVERBEND EDUCATION ASSOCIATION. SHE HAD RECENTLY BECOME A MAGNET FOR CRITICISM DUE TO THE ONGOING TEACHERS' STRIKE. A SUNDAY NIGHT MEETING INTENDED TO SMOOTH TROUBLED WATERS BECAME A SHOUTING MATCH, ACCORDING TO SEVERAL WHO WERE PRESENT. GREG WORMDOLF, PRESIDENT OF THE HIGH SCHOOL'S PARENT-TEACHER ASSOCIATION, STATED THAT FEELINGS WERE RUNNING HIGH AT THE MEETING, BUT NOTHING THAT WOULD LEAD TO VIOLENCE.

OFFICER WAYNE TUFTE HAD SERVED RIVERBEND'S POLICE DEPARTMENT FOR 14 YEARS. HE LEAVES A WIDOW AND TWO SONS, 19 AND 21.

IN A STATEMENT MADE OUTSIDE ELEANOR ROOSEVELT HIGH SCHOOL, CHARISMATIC MAYOR RONALD DUPONTE SAID HE WAS SHOCKED AT THE MURDERS AND HE INTENDED TO TAKE A PERSONAL INTEREST IN IMPROVING POLICE

RESULTS, INCLUDING FORMING A COMMITTEE TO INVESTIGATE STATE INTERFERENCE IN LOCAL CRIME INVESTIGATION.

WATCH KRBM NEWS AT SIX WHEN WE WILL HAVE INTERVIEWS WITH OTHER TEACHERS CLOSE TO MS STORLEY.

....

IN A RELEASE FAXED TO THE MEDIA THIS MORNING, THE STATE ARTS BOARD ANNOUNCED THE TEN MINNESOTA ARTISTS WHO WILL RECEIVE $50,000.00 GRANTS TO PURSUE THEIR WORK. AMONG THEM WERE ROCHESTER ARTIST RANDY YNGSONG WHO CREATES DICHROIC GLASS SCULPTURES AND RIVERBEND ARTIST NICHOLAS OVOLENSKI WHO CREATES LANDSCAPE PHOTOS OF NUDE BODY PARTS.

SHORTLY AFTER THE ANNOUNCEMENT, SEVERAL PEOPLE GATHERED IN FRONT OF THE RIVERBEND ARTISTS COOPERATIVE WITH SIGNS PROTESTING OBSCENITY IN OVOLENSKI'S WORKS. THE COOPERATIVE IS NOT OPEN ON MONDAYS AND ITS MANAGER COULD NOT BE REACHED FOR COMMENT.

....

THE BURNED-OUT SHELL OF THE OLD FEINGOLD MEN'S WEAR BUILDING WAS THE SITE OF THE LATEST GREEN BERET VISITATION.

WHILE ACRIMONIOUS NEGOTIATIONS BETWEEN FEINGOLD HEIRS AND THE CITY COUNCIL CONTINUE OVER THE COST OF CLEANUP, THE FIRE SITE HAS REMAINED AN EYESORE ON THE DOWNTOWN STREETS. LAST NIGHT, THE MYSTERIOUS GREEN BERET DO-GOODERS BEGAN CLEARING BURNT LUMBER AND BROKEN BRICKS ON THE SITE.

WHEN PASSERS-BY JOINED THE EFFORTS, THE
GREEN BERETS QUICKLY LEFT.   THOSE WHO
STOPPED TO HELP, SAY THE GREEN BERET GROUP
APPEARED TO INCLUDE BOTH MALE AND FEMALE
MEMBERS, BUT THEY WORE COVERALLS, GLOVES
AND CLEAR PLASTIC MASKS TO OBSCURE THEIR
FEATURES.

CLEANUP OF THE FIRE SITE CONTINUED AFTER
THEY HAD GONE.   WE WILL SHOW CLIPS OF
CLEANUP VOLUNTEERS ON KRBM NEWS AT SIX.
GOOD DEEDS ARE BECOMING CONTAGIOUS IN
RIVERBEND.
....
WE'LL BE RIGHT BACK WITH "WINDY" WINDHORST
AND THE WEATHER.   "WINDY" WILL TELL US
WHAT TO EXPECT FROM THE COLD FRONT
MOVING IN FROM CANADA.

#   #   #   #   #   #

Chapter 19: Afternoon, Sunday, June 27
ONE WEEK BEFORE
THE MAGUIRE MURDER

Muggs and Martin sat on the low stone wall surrounding the Garden of Peace Cemetery, basking in the mid-morning sunlight, listening to the church bells tolling throughout the city. They didn't talk; it was enough to simply enjoy the day. Martin marveled how having nothing could be so pleasant.

Cherry Orchard Road, a three-lane macadam, crossed in front of them. Most days it was filled with a steady stream of traffic; Sundays it was sparsely traveled. Its environs comprised almost exclusively of marginally maintained commercial locations and the dearly departed, Cherry Orchard had no sidewalks, only broad mown-grass margins.

Martin saw a man striding along the grass. He was tall, possibly as tall as 6'4", and looked like the hero of a Wagner opera, but costumed in faded jeans and scuffed motorcycle boots instead of a breastplate and winged helmet.

As the Germanic warrior came closer, Martin thought he was going to speak to them, but instead he sat on the wall on the other side of Muggs without a word.

Muggs turned to the man. "Erich, this is Martin. Martin, Big Erich."

"Hello," said Martin.

Big Erich nodded politely, without looking directly at Martin, but said nothing.

All three sat for awhile, enjoying more sun and church bells, the differing lengths of services spreading the concert out.

When all the bells had tolled, Muggs hopped off the wall and said, "Let's go hit the parks."

"Okay," said Martin, sliding off the wall, not quite sure what she meant to do, but willing to find out.

Big Erich didn't say anything, but he stood up.

Of Riverbend's 19 parks, 11 had softball diamonds. Walking in sunshine from park to park, the three of them carefully combed the grass for dropped coins under small wooden bleachers and where concession vehicles had parked the night before. Along the way, Muggs found a discarded purse in a ditch, which served to carry their pooled findings.

Although Muggs and Martin kept up a desultory conversation, with Muggs offering remarks from time to time to their companion, Martin had yet to hear Big Erich speak a word. He couldn't be deaf, Martin thought, because he appeared to hear Muggs. Mute for some reason, maybe? He would ask Muggs about it when they were alone.

Come sunset, they took advantage of a Kwik Trip special that was attempting to take the sting out of gas prices by offering three hot dogs for a dollar. Taking their food to the last park on their circuit, they filled cardboard cups with water from a spigot and sat at a picnic bench to eat and divvy the remaining coins.

The park was on a rise, with a sweeping view of the city and a southwest curve of the river. A ruby, purple and gold sunset spread across the western horizon. To the east, the same sunset was reflected like a stained glass window on the surface of the river--a stereoscopic sunset.

Big Erich spoke, almost to himself,

"'Softly the evening came.
The sun from the western horizon,
Like a magician extended his golden wand

o'er the landscape.
Trinkling vapors arose,
and sky and water and forest
Seemed all on fire at the touch,
and melted and mingled together,'"

"Who wrote that?" said Martin.
"Longfellow," said Big Erich.

#   #   #   #   #   #

Chapter 20: Evening, Monday, June 28
ONE WEEK BEFORE
THE MAGUIRE MURDER

In its small parking area, next to three lines of
railroad tracks, five cars nosed up to the side of an old
ceramic block warehouse whose windows were boarded
over. Sun-faded sheeting covered the roof, chipped
blocks marred the smoothness of its walls, but the
utilitarian structure still appeared solid and weather
proof. The front had a roll-up door and a regular door,
in front of which Wilfred Burkhalter waited for the
other four to gather. As they arrived, he handed two
keys to each.

"That one's for this lock," he said. "The controls
for the overhead are inside."

"What about this one?" asked Frahdley, holding
up what was obviously a vehicle key with a remote
locking device.

"You'll see."

He unlocked the door and pushed it open to reveal
blackness. Moving inside, he flicked a switch. Rows
of overhead fluorescents bathed the interior in bright
cool light. The other four stepped inside.

"How on earth...?" said Cantrell, looking around.

The place was immaculate. The walls gleamed,
the cement floor was clean to the point of whiteness,
the high ceiling beams held no dust, no cobwebs.

"Power sprayer," said Burkhalter.

The wall to their right held all the furnishings the
building had to offer. From front to back, a partitioned
office area, storage area, counter with deep sink, washer
and dryer, enclosed lavatory. Halfway along and out a

bit was a long folding table and chairs. Dead center in the large room was a dark gleaming van.

As the other four moved forward, taking in details, Burkhalter pulled the door closed and flipped the dead bolt.

"What color do you call this?" said Madden, tapping a finger lightly on a curve of the van's body work.

"The factory calls it 'black-blue.'"

"I like it."

"I didn't see papers on this building go through," said Turner, who kept an eye on all commercial real estate transactions in Riverbend.

"No," said Burkhalter. "I've owned it in my construction company's name for thirty or so years. We use it less now that most of our new developments are bid out."

"And the van?" asked Turner.

"Registered in the name of no one we know."

"All right!" said Frahdley, punching a fist forward in satisfaction. "The bat cave and the bat mobile!"

"How old did you say you were?" said Madden.

"Come on, lighten up, Doc. Doing good doesn't have to be deadly serious."

"Over here," said Burkhalter, moving to the storage shelves, "is what Chris is certain we need."

He picked one piece from a folded stack, shook it out, and held it up to reveal a dark navy coverall with a front zip. Handing the coverall to Frahdley, he pointed to a row of calf-length rubber boots lined up on the floor, and a pile of black leather gloves in a bin.

"Uniforms. Wellingtons. Gloves. Total concealment. All easily replaceable in any farm store."

"Perfect," said Frahdley. "Perfect. Hats?"

"I thought I'd let you take charge of getting the hats, Chris."

"Can do!"

"Don't forget the secret decoder rings," said Madden.

"Push me too far, you son-of-a-bitch, and I'll break your fingers."

"All right. All right. Let's get down to business." Burkhalter moved to the table, pulled out a chair and sat down, the others following suit.

"Audra will take us through her plan of action for our first project. She'll---"

"Falcon."

"What?"

"'Falcon' will take us through our plan of action, Owl."

"Yes. I stand corrected, Bear," said Burkhalter. "Falcon will take us through our plan of action."

Madden directed a long look at Frahdley and then Burkhalter, much like a wolf deciding which rabbit's neck to snap first.

"I don't think a reminder is necessary," said Burkhalter, "but just to say it's been said again.... Whoever is the lead on a project is the final say. We will all hash it out beforehand, looking for red flags, but come the time to put it into action, we follow the plan and the lead unquestioningly." He gestured to Cantrell to go ahead.

"Just a minute," she said, writing in a small notebook. "I've begun to see some advantage in Chris' idea of uniforms."

"Bear."

"Bear's idea."

She finished her notes and started talking. Questions and explanations continued for over an hour until everyone was satisfied with what would happen.

Later, as members of the group were leaving, Madden held back.

"That idiot Frahdley has no place in this group," he said to Burkhalter. "He's going to blow everything."

"I don't think so, Lawrence," said Burkhalter. "I checked on him more than anyone. The corporate word is that the golly-gee act is his way of amusing himself, but not to let it fool you. People say underneath he's capable of anything."

#   #   #   #   #   #

Chapter 21: Morning, Tuesday, July 20

"That's quite a crowd out front," said Pedersen as he and Nguyen walked into the detectives' room. "I think I even saw Ann Curry."

"From the Today show?," said Pickett, looking a little hollow-eyed this morning. "You think they'd send her out for something like this?"

"Maybe not, but she's one neat lady."

"Yes," said Nguyen.

"You make it in okay?" asked Pickett.

"Yes," said Pedersen. "We parked down on South Oak and came in the side door. I thought they'd be gone by now."

"So did we," said Brittany Olson. She and Rivera had been the first to arrive, carrying pressed cardboard trays holding sausage and egg biscuits, hash brown nuggets, and tall coffee containers.

Rask and Stummer sauntered in, using toothpicks. "Mayor Viper's got himself that circus he was talking about," said Stummer.

"Did you come in the side door, too?" said Pedersen.

"Hell, no, why should we do that?" said Rask. "We came in the front door, same's usual. Sure hope we didn't hurt any a' them shitheads with the cameras."

Pickett groaned and shook his head. "Were Stangler and Middleton still out there?"

"Front and center, on either side of Duponte," said Stummer. "Stangler's so pissed his lips have disappeared and his face is purple.

"And Middleton?"

"Smiling and brown."

"What's Hizzoner telling the media this morning?" said Pickett.

"Same old, same old," said Stummer. "Murder is rare in Riverbend, where everything is wonderful except the cops are stupid. But Mayor Ronald Duponte, that's Duponte with an 'e' on the end, spell it right, is going to put on his cape of invincibility and show the cops how to do it right."

"Is Boucher out there, too?"

"You have ta ask?" said Rask.

A staccato of boot heels in the hall preceded the entrance of Stangler and Middleton, Middleton catching the door to close it quietly behind them.

"I need to kill somebody!" said Stangler. "I seriously need to kill somebody!"

Middleton pulled a chair toward Stangler, then moved to the cork board, rotated it to the white board side and picked up a marker. Stangler grabbed the chair by the back, looked around as though he wanted to throw it, then threw himself in the seat, whacking his elbow on a nearby desk in the process.

Middleton smiled. "Press conferences with Mayor Duponte are a bit trying," he said.

The door opened quietly, and a well-dressed man stepped into the room, closed the door behind him, and sat at a desk.

"Wishink! What the hell?" said Rask.

"You shaved," said Rivera. "You got a haircut. That's a tie. Are you okay?"

"He's wearing socks," said Middleton.

"Will you knock it off," said Wishink. "It's career week or some such shit at the school. I gotta go in and tell my daughter's social studies class what I do."

"What are you talking about?" said Olson. "It's summer and there's a teacher's strike."

"Yeah, well, the wife's got her going to Blackthorne Academy. Kids can do classes all year round."

"I've heard of Blackthorne," said Pedersen. "They're based on the old Summerhill School experiment in England, where kids pass ahead by subject, rather than by grade, right?"

"Yeah."

"Does it look like it works?"

"It damn well better work. For what it's costing me for a private school, she's gonna have to support me by the time she's 20."

"Why'd they pick you?" said Rivera.

"They're going through everybody's old man," said Wishink.

"Gonna shock the kiddies with what you do?" said Stummer.

"Hell, no. I'm gonna tell them I'm like you wusses."

"Okay, enough," said Pickett, flapping a hand dismissively. "Duponte is right; we're nowhere. This guy is knocking off a citizen and a cop every Sunday and it looks as though he's going to keep right on. So far we don't know jack shit and we have no idea where to look next. Let's hear what we've got on this new one."

"Starting with Tufte," said Rask. "I mean, what the fuck? Tufte?"

"Ah, man," said Stangler, standing up. "We thought we were on top of it. We hand-picked Tufte and Klindworth. They had 24 years between them."

"They were bait," said Nguyen matter-of-factly.

"No, they weren't bait!" said Stangler. "They were experienced police officers we could trust not to go off on their own. They knew what could happen and were ready for it." He rubbed his eyes with two fingers of one hand. "What the hell can get someone as careful and suspicious as Tufte to leave his post?"

"So what the fuck happened?" said Rask.

"Ah jeez, we just don't know, John. Duponte bulled his way in and made a stink, Klindworth had to come in and pull him out, and during that time Tufte was killed. He was found the other side of an extension of the building, in front of a side door that leads to the boys' locker room. Lu's right. An officer at a crime scene is nothing more than bait to this guy. Ah man...." Stangler's throat roughened up and he had to swallow hard.

"Hey, hey! None a' that!" Rask's shout startled everyone. "It's Tufte's fault for being stupid, goddammit!"

"Rask's right," said Rivera.

"Are there funeral plans?" said Olson.

"Pending," said Pickett. "I'll let you know. "There's a fund being set up for his boys to finish college. Let's move along."

Stangler and Middleton went through the Storley facts and preliminary crime scene report. The description of Duponte's confrontation with Holmes caused an uproar. A needed release. The two detectives were obliged to retell the incident several times until everyone settled down to gasping and wiping eyes.

"No murder weapon was found," Middleton said. "Something rounded and pretty good-sized. Maybe a baseball bat."

"A bat?" said Rask. "Judas priest! She let someone walk up behind her with a baseball bat?"

"Her purse was locked in her car, only her keys with her. As though all she intended was a quick in-out."

"I don't get it," said Rivera. "Why would anyone come back late at night to an empty classroom in the middle of the summer?"

"We've talked to people at the meeting that night," said Stangler. "Everyone liked her. Teachers say they were thankful they had someone as even-tempered as Storley leading them. Parents are furious about the strike, admitting they had voiced some pretty harsh things, but said they had nothing personal against Storley. They all say they admired her as a teacher and as someone in a difficult position trying to keep things objective."

"Everyone liked Maguire, too," said Pedersen. "What is going on here?"

"You should have seen her," said Stangler. "Nice dark green ladies suit, blouse with a little floppy bow at the collar, high heels. Dressed up to look nice for the meeting. She wasn't halfway through her life yet."

Silence for a moment.

"Yeah, okay, it's shitty," said Rask, cracking his Nicorette. "But there ain't no way we can do anything before a homicide." He emphasized "before."

"You know why?" said Stangler. "Because all we've done so far is write reports on what he's done! We've got to start figuring out what he's going to do next. The FBI profiles serial killers to get ahead of them. We've got to start making those same judgments."

"You wanna call in the FBI?" said Rask.

"Hell, no, I don't want to call in the damned FBI."

"So what do you want?"

Stangler stopped pacing, crossed his arms on his chest and scowled. "I want to be smarter, faster, meaner."

"Sit down, Lobo," said Pickett. "You're right, but the killer is leaving us notes, for god's sake. We should be able to nail this guy before the next one."

"There has to be a pattern," said Stangler, sitting back down, "but damned if I can see it. Duponte is right; we're Keystone Kops bumbling around missing everything."

"Ah, shit," said Rask. "Lemme guess. We're lookin' at more overtime talkin' to every parent and kid inna whole damn school. I only been getting home to change shirts. My wife thinks I'm havin' a affair."

Rivera and Olson burst into laughter.

Rask pointed a beefy finger at them. "Can it! The point I'm tryin' ta make is that it's a waste a' time lookin' to find somethin' hinky about Storley, when we know it's not about her." He looked around the silent room. "Well, don't we? This is some nut case on a weird mission that ain't got nothin' to do with the victims' lives."

"I don't think so," said Olson. "He's not killing them because they're all redheads, or they all look like his mother, or they all were in McDonald's the day he was overcharged for his burger. 'Abuses and usurpations' refers to something they, themselves, are actually doing."

"Brittany's right," said Pickett. "These killings are not random. The notes refer to actions of the victims."

Pedersen rapped his pen against the edge of his desk. "Nuts! Do we have to sift through Maguire's life again?"

"You two have anything new on Maguire?" said Pickett.

"The only secret he had was a fancy set of cookware on lay-by for his wife's birthday," said Pedersen.

"That's it?" said Pickett.

"He was a nice guy," said Nguyen.

"Ladies?" said Pickett.

"Same thing," said Rivera. "Everyone had serious respect for him. It almost makes you suspicious. Everyone except Jerglens, that is."

"Jerglens!" said Stangler. "My god, we almost forgot, Wiley. You guys won't believe this. Mr. and Mrs. Lester Jerglens were at the teachers' strike meeting Sunday night."

"That means we can get a search warrant!" said Stummer.

"Hang on," said Pickett. "He had a legitimate reason for being at both the Blue Ribbon rally and the parents' meeting. No judge will give us a warrant because he coincidentally happened to be in the hotel protest. Did he say where he went after the parents' meeting?"

"Said it was none of our business," said Middleton. "His wife had nothing to say."

"We checked Jerglens pretty thoroughly," said Olson. "He was in debt, suspected of petty theft, considered foul-mouthed and a trouble-maker, but no one cared enough to kill him. Oddly enough, he was often cited at work for high production numbers, and his wife and kids actually like him. Go figure."

"Rask," said Pickett, "you and Stummer get anything going back through the hotel people?"

"Nuthin'," said Rask.

"The 55 minute window between the function guy leaving for the kitchen and the time he returned is when she was killed," said Stummer. "And can you believe it? No one saw or heard a thing. We showed Jerglens' picture around. No luck."

"This guy is ballsy," said Rask. "He's takin' some serious chances, 'specially with gettin' cops to go offsite."

"Jerglens doesn't have the brains to plan a wienie roast, let alone a murder," said Rivera.

"We're just not looking at it from the right direction," said Pickett. "Frankly, I'm at the point where I'd welcome wild leaps of intuition."

"We might have one," said Middleton.

He had everyone's interest.

"The custodian said that while he waited, he could smell the victim's perfume, and it wasn't her usual, which was Paloma Picasso. We took a sample to the pathologist and he was positive the victim was, indeed, wearing Paloma Picasso."

"What's the big deal about what perfume she was wearing?" said Stummer.

"The custodian could smell a different perfume."

Olson gasped and said, "He was smelling someone else's perfume!"

Simultaneously, Rivera said, "Another woman had been in the room!"

"And there was a high-heeled footprint in Goetzman's room that wasn't hers," said Stangler.

"That's bullshit!" said Rask. "You're saying the perp is a woman? A woman strong enough to strangle someone? And then walkin' around with a baseball bat? Pull my other leg."

"The victims, even the cops, let someone get behind them," said Stangler. "They wouldn't have done that if it was a strange man. If it is a woman, it changes motivation. Her concept of 'abuses and usurpations' could be very different than a man's."

"Ya mean like she's killin' off everyone who wore the same party dress as hers?" said Rask.

"That's okay," said Rivera, reaching over and gently patting the top of Rask's hand, "we know you're old and stupid, but we won't hold it against you."

"Hey! Laugh all ya like, but ain't no woman strong enough to strangle someone standing up," said Rask.

"How about a man dressed as a woman," said Wishink.

"Gimme a break! A man in woman's clothes ain't gonna fool nobody."

"It's a long shot," said Wishink, "but there's a group of female impersonators in town who do a cabaret every year."

"I don't know, Lobo," said Pickett, "it seems to me this is not the type of thing a woman would do. Or *could* do, for that matter. But everyone keep it in the back of your mind."

"So what now?" said Rivera.

"Let's do a little more shifting. Jim and Lu, sorry, run through Maguire one more time, see if he was doing anything that could have set someone off."

"Look for a woman," said Stangler.

"*Recherchez la femme*," said Middleton.

"Do Goetzman, too," said Pickett. Doesn't seem like she'd have any 'abuses' in Minnesota, but maybe this woman angle will turn something up. Carmen and Brittany, get on with all these parent-teacher interviews. John---"

"You think jumping people from case to case is a good idea?" said Rivera.

"Actually, I do. Different eyes might see something different."

Rivera nodded to herself and leaned back in her chair.

"John and Bishop, get with Lobo and Wiley on Storley's personal life."

"I'd like us to run with this idea of it being a woman," said Stangler.

"Seriously?" said Pickett. "You want to spend time on it? One shoe print and a sniff of perfume aren't much to hang a theory on. Even if we had more to go on, we'd have to believe that a woman would have the strength to strangle another full-grown woman who wasn't bound."

"Rantha could," said Middleton.

Pickett stopped and stared at Middleton. Amarantha was tall and a workout queen. She wouldn't, but she definitely could.

"All right," he said, "you have my permission to check Amarantha's alibis."

"Come on, Harlow," said Stangler, "what if it's a cross-dresser? At least let us check out that angle."

Pickett threw up his hands. When Stangler used his first name, the captain knew his senior detective wasn't going to let go of the idea."

"All right, all right. Just don't spend too much time on it."

"Hey!" said Rask. "You want someone like me talkin' to a bunch a them trans... transvested... whatever. Judas Priest!"

"I like it a whole lot better than turning you loose on outraged parents," said Pickett.

"They're not transvestites, they're female impersonators," said Wishink.

"What's a' difference? They both dress up in ladies' clothes, don't they?" said Rask.

"Transvestites are serious about being treated as women; female impersonators dress up more or less for fun."

"You got a name where we can start?" said Stangler.

Wishink wrote on a small notepad, tore off the page, and handed it to Stangler. "This Jason Palmquist is one of the best, and that's where he works."

Stangler passed the paper to Stummer. "You two set up an appointment when we can talk."

Rask narrowed his eyes at Wishink. "How come you know guys in ladies undies?"

"I know a lot of guys, Dickwit," said Wishink, "including your wife's boyfriend."

Rask let out a short burst of laughter. "Nice try, Wishink."

"Call this guy," said Stangler. "Don't embarrass him by walking in where he works."

"Would we do that?" said Stummer.

"Yes, you would. Don't."

"Why? You think we look like cops?"

"No. I think you look like Mafia enforcers."

"All right, let's move it along," said Pickett. "Lobo, what are we all looking for generally?"

Notepads came out, pens clicked.

"We're looking for something all three were doing. 'Abuses and usurpations' sound political to me. We should check out political affiliations."

"How about donations?" said Rask. "Maybe they all gave money big time to some crackpot outfit like the ACLU."

"You think the American Civil Liberties Union is crackpot?" Rivera's eyes were wide in astonishment.

"Oh, hell yes. Don't you?"

"Factual things to look at," said Stangler, before Rivera could jump in again. "All three were killed shortly after a gathering of people, all on a Sunday night, all were convinced to come back to the gathering place, all killed from behind, all left with the same note."

Stangler leaned forward and looked at Rivera and Olson. "I want you two to be thinking hard from a woman's standpoint. Why would a woman kill these people? Maybe talking to a bunch of mothers who are pissed off will give you something to go on. If you get any ideas, no matter how crazy, tell the rest of us right away."

He looked at his notes again. "Man or woman, why do the weapons change? Why a different method of death, different weapon, every time? But always the same for the cop. With a serial killer we should be able to see some sort of a pattern, but we do and yet we don't."

"I said before, I thought we had a vigilante," said Pedersen. "Now I'm thinking maybe terrorist."

"Judas Priest!" said Rask. "I can maybe *maybe* see some half-baked terrorist galloping his camel into Rochester and taking a pot shot at the Mayo Clinic, but Riverbend? Who would waste his time blowing up Riverbend?"

"Those of us who just got curb and gutter assessments," said Stummer.

"Right," said Rask grinning widely. "Forgot about you guys out on Palmer Road."

"I've been thinking," said Middleton.

"Judas Priest!" said Rask.

"Be more polite," said Nguyen, looking straight at Rask, and holding the look.

"Humph," said Rask, shifting in his chair, but making no further remark.

"Maybe we do have a serial killer," said Middleton. "What if his fixation is cops? And his pattern is that he has to make a high-risk kill first, in order to earn his cop kill."

"The notes were left on the civilians," said Stummer "That means they're the prime target. The cops were just... hell... an encore."

Rivera groaned.

"Don't say anything," said Stummer. "It could have been worse. They might have called him the

Piggy-Back Killer." He looked around. "You know, cops are pigs and this is one kill on top of another?"

"All right," said Pickett," enough talking. We've got maybe a vigilante, a terrorist, a psycho killer with no pattern, a serial killer targeting cops, or a killer who's a strong woman or dresses like a woman. Let's go catch someone. Lobo and Wiley, why don't we head up to Jevne's office; spare him the trip down here."

People stood and gathered their papers. The door opened and Boucher bustled in with great purpose. "Meeting over? I wanted to hear progress reports."

"Come to my office in 15 minutes and I'll fill you in," said Pickett with a noticeable lack of enthusiasm.

As the detectives filed out, Boucher stepped in front of one and held out his hand.

"I don't believe we've met. I'm Chief James Boucher. Are you a consultant?"

"Chief," said Pickett. "That's Detective Wishink."

* * * * * * * * * *

Emily walked into the detectives' room, two fingers behind her glasses, rubbing her eyes. She stopped, then staggered around a little, patting the air with exaggerated gestures. "I was heading for the ladies room; is this it?" She cupped her hands behind her ears. "Is anyone there? Sorry, I have terminal eye strain and can't see. Will anyone help a poor blind woman?"

"Very funny," said Stangler.

"You'd make a good mime," said Middleton.

"I'd make a good police secretary, too," she said, "if I weren't on the never-ending web site search. What did you want?"

"Sorry, Emily," said Stangler. "I was wondering if you'd gotten anything yet."

"All I've gotten so far is an education in useless information. Did you know there are companies who specialize in making prongs for diamond rings? The prongs have registered names--Safeguard, New Guard, Perma-Guard, Absolute Guard, Secure Future, Security Guard. Too bad I can't find a Guard against going blind."

"Sorry. It could be a big break if you find something."

"Yes, fine. I understand that and I'll keep at it, but the next time you want a progress report, you come to me."

"Yes, Ma'am."

She turned and marched out, much more briskly than she had entered. Three uniformed policemen stepped aside to let her pass, then came in--Klindworth, Harders, Kaminski.

Stangler glared at them. Middleton waited patiently.

Kaminski cleared his throat. "We gotta do something."

"Agreed." said Stangler. "What?"

"Tufte---"

"Don't you 'Tufte' me!" said Stangler leaping up from his chair. "He was an experienced cop! He carried a sidearm, a baton and a radio! He was told not to leave his post! He was told to detain anyone who approached him, regardless!" Stangler barged around his desk and up to the three cops. "What the fuck more do you want from me!"

"The man's dead! You watch your mouth, shithead!" Kaminski tossed his hat and reached for Stangler.

Middleton stepped between them and pushed Stangler back. Harders and Klindworth grabbed for Kaminski.

"Whoa! Whoa!" shouted Middleton. "No disrespect was meant!" Blocking his partner with his bigger size, he spoke to him with emphasis, "We all know you meant no disrespect, Lobo." He held on for a moment, then let go of Stangler and stepped aside.

Stangler glared at Kaminski, looking as though he would just as soon have the fistfight. "Okay." He pushed his hair off his face. "Okay. I meant no disrespect to Tufte. It's just... Man, why did he go off and get killed? Klindworth, we warned you two; we trusted your experience. Why did Tufte leave? Who did he think he could trust? I want some answers."

"That's what I was trying to say, asshole," said Kaminski. "He could have taken down anyone who looked hinky to him. If his own mother walked up talking funny, he would have cuffed her. So what the hell happened?"

"That might be it," said Middleton.

"What?" said Kaminski, shifting his attention to the large detective.

"It may be a woman or a man dressed as a woman," said Middleton.

"Get real," said Kaminski. "You're saying some babe or some fag walks up to Tufte and says, 'Please, Mr. Policeman, come over here and turn your back so I can shoot you?'"

Middleton held Kaminski's stare for a moment. "Would Tufte have been taken in by a man?"

"He sure as hell wouldn't have been taken in by a woman holding a gun!" He scooped his hat up from the floor and turned to leave. "C'mon guys, we'll figure it out. At least we don't have our heads up our asses."

* * * * * * * * * *

"Don't know why we have to come along on this," said Rask as he got into the back seat.

Middleton pulled the car out of the Law Enforcement Center parking lot and turned toward the northwest edge of Riverbend.

"Don't know why he wants us to come to his house," said Rask. "Bishop tried for a bar."

The car turned left onto the Blackwell Beltway.

"Thing's a wild fox chase anyway; no guy inna dress is gonna seriously fool anyone."

The car turned and passed between the decorative stone arrangements marking the Green Meadows addition.

"I mean, couple grapefruit in a bra, wig, lipstick. Good for fun at the lodge Christmas party, but Judas Priest, you'd have to be an idiot not to see they were guys."

The car moved along several blocks of low natural stone homes with immaculate landscaping and concealed accent lighting.

"This guy is inna photo in their brochure. He's tall and skinny. No way could this squirrel pass as a woman."

Avoiding a battery-powered kiddy ATV, the car pulled into a driveway.

"All jeez, he's got a wife and kid. Are you sure we want to do this? Here?"

Middleton turned toward the back seat. "Rask, will you just shut up? What's your problem?"

"My problem is I'm gonna be embarrassed. I don't like talkin' to fags."

"He's not a fag," said Stangler, getting out of the car.

"I don't like talkin' to squirrels, either," said Rask, heaving his bulk out of the car. "Bishop, say somethin'."

"New territory for me, too, John."

The front door was opened by a tall woman in a silver lamé dress.

"Please come in," she said, indicating they should pass her and take seats in a living room with pale gray leather furniture.

Her hair was in a dark pageboy with bangs. The dress was draped low at the neckline and was short enough to reveal long shapely legs. Silver sling-back high heels made her even taller than she was.

"Anyone ever tell you ya look a lot like Cher, Ms Palmquist?" said Rask.

"Yes, I have heard that before." She smiled and tipped her head sideways making a wing of her dark hair and a glittery chandelier earring brush her half-bare collarbone. "Please call me Mariah."

"Sure thing," said Rask.

"I'm a little overdressed, but I have to be at a reception by nine, so I thought I'd save time to talk to you by getting ready beforehand. If you'll excuse me, we've got coffee and cookies coming. I'll be right back."

As she left the room, trailing a waft of perfume behind, the detectives could see the back of her dress. Its draped folds bared the entire length of her spine. It was evident she was wearing no brassiere.

"Judas Priest!" whispered Rask. "With a babe like that at home, why would any squirrel waste his time playing dress-up?"

"Would you let her walk behind you with a baseball bat?" said Stangler.

"Hell, I'd let her walk *on* me with a baseball bat."

"She said she'd made time to talk to us," said Stummer. "I thought I made it clear to Palmquist that we wanted to talk to him."

Mariah came back. "Refreshments are on the way," she said, settling herself in a leather chair with her long legs at an angle and her skirt tugged down modestly. She jumped up almost immediately at the sound of a rattling tray. "That was quicker than I thought."

A pretty young woman carrying a large silver tray with cups, cookies and coffee pot entered the room.

"That's too heavy for you; you should have called," said Mariah, taking the tray and setting it on the coffee table.

"Gentlemen, this is my wife, Molly," said Mariah. I'm sorry, I don't know all your names."

"Don't get up," said Molly, as they all started to rise.

"Judas Priest!" Rask muttered to Stummer, "Lezzies."

After each detective had introduced himself, Molly sat on a hassock and began to distribute cups and pour coffee.

"Jason said you wanted some insight on the serial killings," she said, "and I'm consumed with curiosity about how he could help. I hope you don't mind if I sit in? He did explain that he's due at a reception later on, yes?"

"Judas Priest!" said Rask, turning purple and burying his face in his coffee cup. Stummer stared, frozen. Middleton leaned back and haw-hawed.

Stangler smiled. "That answers our first question, Mr. Palmquist. Frankly, I would have asked you for a date if you weren't already a married woman and four inches taller than me."

"Thank you," said the soft voice of Mariah. "You're short, but a cutie. I might have accepted."

Rask coughed a mouthful of coffee back into his cup and without looking up, reached over and set it back on the tray.

"I'm sorry if I embarrassed you, Detective Rask," said Palmquist, dropping into his normal baritone. "Please call me Jason."

"Hrrrmph. Yeah, well," said Rask, taking a good squint-eyed look at him.

"What was your first question?" said Molly.

"The victims of these murders," said Stangler, "all appear as though they let their killer get close behind them, which they wouldn't do with a strange man. On the other hand, some of the killings require a man's strength. That led us to wondering if we were dealing with a man who looked like a woman. Our first question was could a man possibly fool people into thinking he was a woman, up close?"

"Doesn't it seem queer to you? What he does?" Rask said to Mrs. Palmquist.

"Rask!" said Stangler.

"That's okay, I get that question all the time," said Molly Palmquist. Turning to Rask, she said, "It's a hobby. A lot like being a magician or a *trompe l'oeil* painter. The object is to fool the eye. He doesn't think he's a girl any more than a magician thinks he actually has magical powers." She smiled sweetly. "And even though it's strapped down, his equipment still works very nicely."

"Aw!" said Rask, turning a deep purple again, while everyone else laughed.

"Oddly enough," said Palmquist in his natural voice, "the hobby has gone from fun to money maker. I said I was going to a reception later? People pay us to come to their events. The titillation of having a female impersonator among the guests adds a certain cachet."

"Are there others in Riverbend as good as you?" said Stangler.

"Oh, yes. I don't know everyone, but I would say as many as 30 show up off and on for the performance cabarets."

"So, dressed as you are, you could easily get close enough to an unsuspecting stranger to kill him?"

"Yes. Before you go, would you like me to get out my calendar and see if I have an alibi?"

"Yes, please," said Stangler.

Palmquist draped his hands on his knees, made a red lip-sticked moue, and in his Mariah voice, said, "And here I thought you were cute."

Stangler grinned. "Next question. What problem would a female impersonator have with a meat packer, a banker, and a teacher that would warrant their being killed?"

"None," said Palmquist, back to a baritone. "I can see one of us taking a punch at another over stealing part of an act or a costume---"

"Told ya it'd be about dresses," muttered Rask.

"... but that's all. Remember, this is a hobby. Female impersonators are taxi drivers, students, butchers, what-have-you. One of us may be your killer, but the motivation would spring from his regular lifestyle."

"Can you give us the names of the impersonators in Riverbend?" said Stangler.

"No, but Bernie Rasmussen, who operates the Blue Moon, can. He stages all the cabarets. I've got to run. Molly can check my calendar for you, see if I was out killing anyone the last three-four weeks."

He stood up, leaned over his wife, kissed the air above her forehead, said, "Lipstick," and was out the front door in a clack of high heels.

# # # # # #

Chapter 22: Afternoon, Monday, July 5
THE DAY AFTER
THE MAGUIRE MURDER

Martin sat on a flat rock at the edge of Badger Creek. Behind him was a dirt path that followed the meanderings of the creek. Behind that was a steep incline of riprap that was part of the city's flood control project. Some springs had seen the creek rise to near the top of the concrete chunks, but it was shallow in early July.

His bare feet rested in the narrow sandy margin of the creek, toes touching the water, pants cuffed up. He held a slender branch stripped of leaves. Tied to the end was a long string ending in a bent safety pin with a worm on it. He smiled at his worm, lying on the pebbled bottom, bouncing a little in the current.

Muggs sat on a broad piece of riprap, smoking and looking at Martin over a lowered newspaper.

"You're not going to catch any fish here."

"I know."

"It's too shallow."

"I know."

"Even if you caught one, that pin wouldn't hold."

"I know."

"So what are you doing?"

"I'm watching my worm."

"You're not making sense."

He didn't answer.

She smoked quietly for a while. From where she sat, she could see the pin and the worm. "Okay. Let there be light. What am I missing?"

Martin smiled to himself and nodded his head. "When I was a little kid, just learning to read, there

were a lot of boys' adventure books. Pretty innocent
then, compared to now. Anyway, they always went
fishing with a crooked branch, a bent pin and a worm.
They hadn't a care in the world. I'm zoning into that
feeling."

He twitched his worm. "In all the illustrations,
the boy had a rag around his big toe, but I'm catching
the feeling pretty good without it."

"So it's an anti-stress technique. Why didn't you
say so?"

"You're just jealous you don't have a pin and a
worm."

"Hah!" Muggs ground out her cigarette, found a
discarded candy wrapper, folded it around her cigarette
butt and tucked it in her pocket.

"Is this your newbie?"

Martin looked up and saw a slender compact man
in maybe his late 30's, with a shaved head and a spider
web tattoo running up his neck.

"Yup. Laine, this is Martin."

"Hello," said Martin.

"Is he feeble-minded?" said Laine.

"Nah, he's getting in touch with his childhood."

"He's not going to catch anything."

"He knows."

Three quick running steps were heard at the top of
the embankment, a body somersaulted in the air over
their heads, and a small woman with a blonde ponytail
dropped to her feet on the walk beside them.

"Whoa!" Martin said, standing and turning.

"Jee-sus! Do ya have to do that?" said Laine.

"Nice you could drop in," said Muggs. "Martin,
this is Kathy."

Kathy glowered at Martin, head bent so she was
almost looking through her eyebrows. "What're you
doing? You're not going to catch any fish that way."

"He knows," said Muggs. "He's remembering his childhood."

Martin sat back down. Kathy squatted and looked at his worm. "Can I try it?"

He handed her the branch.

"Then what?"

"You watch the water bumping your worm and you remember how when you were young, there was this overhead walkway that crossed four railroad tracks and you and your buddies would lay on it terrified and feel the heat and the shaking and the noise when the trains went under."

"When I was young," she said, handing him back his twig, stepping back to sit on a piece of riprap, "I had to go to a gymnastics coach every day after school, and I couldn't have ice cream cones because I had to stay lean."

"When I was young," said Laine, "my father beat the crap outta me."

"Big Erich on the horizon," said Muggs.

They all turned to watch him come. He looked at Martin for a minute or two, then said,

> *"Blessings on thee, little man,*
> *Barefoot boy, with cheek of tan!*
> *With thy turned up pantaloons,*
> *And thy merry whistled tunes;"*

"Except he's tan all over, not just his cheeks," said Kathy.

"Don't be so sure of that, Missy," said Martin. "I might have a butt like a baboon for all you know."

Kathy staggered a few steps, pretending to be overcome with laughter, then ended the performance in a tucked tight flip that had her feet beginning and ending in almost the exact same spot.

"Who are you quoting?" said Martin, as Big Erich folded himself down to sit beside him.

"Whittier." He watched the water bumping over the rocks.

"Big thing in the paper is this guy getting killed over at Blue Ribbon," said Muggs. "Everyone says he was a nice guy, but he was leading a walkout, so someone shot him."

"Wrong move," said Martin.

"So what's that supposed ta' mean?" said Laine.

"Alive, he was leading a movement," said Martin. "Dead, he's a martyr leading a cause. If they wanted to defuse the movement, they should have bribed him and then made it public."

"Whoever shot this union guy shot a cop, too," said Muggs. "This article makes it sound like the killer waited around a while until a cop stumbled on him."

"Now that's stupid," said Laine. "They made a clean kill with this walkout guy, they should'a gotten out of there--fast." His voice got softer. "Never remain at... a kill scene. Never... lose control of... your immediate surroundings. Evacuate... silently.... Never... kill... Never... kill...."

Puzzled, Martin turned and looked at him.

Muggs shook her head in an admonition to be quiet.

"Laine!" said Kathy, quickly crossing to him. "Let's go look for agates along the river." Backing up and pulling him along, she moved them down the walkway. "Maybe we'll find something good washed up. What do you think?" She let go of his arm and suddenly did three back flips.

"Jee-sus! Do ya have to do that?" said Laine.

"He learned two trades in the Army," Muggs said. "How to program computers and how to kill."

# # # # # #

Chapter 23: Evening, Monday, July 5
THE DAY AFTER
THE MAGUIRE MURDER

Wilfred Burkhalter sat in his leather chair behind his glass-topped desk. His secretary had just left, after stopping in his door briefly to make sure he knew she was leaving. He picked up his phone and dialed a number.

"Audra? I'll say it again, we can congratulate ourselves on a job well done." ... "Thank you. We worked well together." ... "Your choice of where to start was excellent." ... "We're in the news. Not as fully as I would have liked, but our cause will grow, I'm sure of that." ... "Yes, you're right, but haste makes waste." ... "The coveralls? All clean and folded. I've added laundry to my list of skills." ... "I'm calling everyone to suggest we don't have a planning session for a few weeks. We'll see each other Sundays, and our first four goals and leaders have been discussed and approved. Later we can sit down and review what was done and what improvements should be made. Does that meet with your agreement?" ... "Good. I'll see you Sunday, then."

Hanging up, he smiled. He liked a woman who had a good mind and was quick to come to a point. His wife was like that. Used to be like that. Grandchildren had eroded her forcefulness, but never mind, she was entitled.

He picked up the phone and dialed again.

"Ch--- uh, Bear, this is Owl. Are you all set for next Sunday?" ... "Good. That's good to hear." ... "I'm calling everyone to suggest..."

# # # # # #

Chapter 24: Early afternoon, Thursday, July 22

Stangler and Middleton crowded into Emily's small office.

"Why do you have an office and the detectives have a corral?" said Middleton.

"I'm more important," said Emily, looking up at him over her big bug glasses.

"Find anything on New Guards?'" said Stangler.

"Sure. Right now I'm doing some fascinating reading on new safeguards against the H_1N_1 'flu virus. Do you know how many hits you get searching for 'New Guards?'"

"Yeah, you told us," said Stangler. Twenty-three million."

"Twenty-three *billion*."

"We're sorry," said Middleton. "We know it's a huge pain in the neck, Miss Emily, but we're desperate. Would you please try searching for 'usurpations and abuses?'"

"I'll try 'New Guards' plus 'usurpations and abuses' just as soon as I finish checking the 13,400 hits for 'New Guards' plus 'Minnesota.'"

* * * * * * * * * *

The funeral for Tufte was massively attended. Stangler knew the officer's family had grown up in Riverbend and he had a wide network of back-slapping law enforcement buddies, but the size of the turnout was still surprising.

The church filled. Overflow sat on folding chairs in the social hall and listened to the service over a speaker.

The procession held up traffic half an hour, National Guard members working the intersections. TV cameras were positioned at intervals along the route, each with a feed to its national affiliate.

Bar lights flashing, the motorcade included marked police cars from Rochester, Winona, Red Wing, and even farther. A limousine accompanied by police outriders carried the governor and his wife.

Stangler and Middleton rode in the back of a patrol car, Middleton with his uniform hat on his lap, his head inches from the roof liner. Turning slightly in the passenger seat, Pickett said, "Would you have expected something this big?"

Staring at the back of the driver's seat, taken up with his own thoughts, Stangler didn't answer.

"I'm not surprised," said Middleton. "Serial killer, third cop, national TV; people want to be part of a memorable event. They can see it again on the news and say they were there. And of course if you're thinking of making a bid for the presidency, it doesn't hurt to have your sympathetic presence on camera."

"Cynical."

"That's me all over."

After the conclusion of the graveside services, the governor and his wife, and after them, members of Riverbend's law enforcement, filed past Mrs. Tufte and her two sons, shaking hands, offering condolences. When Stangler reached her, she grabbed his hand with both of hers and thrust her face at him.

"You used him," she said in a low fierce rasp.

Stangler tried to tug his hand away, but she held on tightly.

"He would be alive today if you hadn't used him for bait, you cold son-of-a-bitch!"

Middleton suddenly enveloped her in a bear hug that made her almost disappear in the bulk of his arms. Startled, she dropped her grip on Stangler.

"He was a fine man," Middleton said, loud enough to be heard by the waiting line. "We will all miss him."

Tufte's tall grown sons balled their fists and glared red-eyed at Stangler. He looked away and moved on.

Middleton released Mrs. Tufte, steadying her briefly as she regained her balance. He shook the sons' hands. "Your dad was a good cop," he said.

* * * * * * * * * *

Later, as the news footage began to roll, Stangler watched with uneasiness. The cameras had caught the condolence line from behind. The picture showed Mrs. Tufte holding Stangler's hand, leaning forward to say something impassioned, then Middleton hugging her, and Stangler dropping his eyes and moving on, seemingly too emotionally overwhelmed to shake with the sons.

Stangler sighed with relief.

#   #   #   #   #   #

Chapter 25: Early evening, Saturday, July 24
THE PRESENT TIME

The five street friends walked into the maze of blue and white balloons, streamers and tulle filling the Riverbend Convention Center's arena for the Weber-Billings wedding reception. A palpable wall of conversations rolled over a string quartet and buffeted the entrance.

Muggs and Martin were in the lead, looking like a couple, Muggs' hand tucked cozily into Martin's bent arm. Laine had Kathy pulled close with a possessive arm across her shoulders. Big Erich brought up the rear.

"This is spooky," muttered Kathy. "There're close to 500 people in here, and they're all shouting."

Muggs raised an arm and waved excitedly at a distant table, the occupants of which were not looking her way. "There's Judy and Bill!" she said, loud enough for those around them to hear. "Let's see if we can sit by them after we get our plates."

They joined the line for the buffet table, a 35-foot array of choices. The lady in front of Muggs turned and said, "There goes my diet."

"Don't I know it," said Muggs in a chatty tone. "I used to take just a tiny dab of everything at these affairs, but even that can be too much."

Martin looked around. He worried that, even clean, their jeans and shirts would make them stick out as obvious party-crashers. Muggs assured him they would not, and he could see she was right. Reception attire was everything from sequins to cargo shorts. It was a bittersweet moment. Sara would never have let him go to a friend's wedding without a suit, and here he was at a stranger's wedding in jeans and shirt tails. He choked up, thinking of Sara and Miranda. Then he slammed the door on that thought, angry with himself for letting it open a crack.

Behind Erich, a man in a suit, going bald way too early for his apparent age, looked up. "You one of Tim's college football buddies?"

Erich smiled and nodded.

"What position?"

Erich appeared to be giving it serious thought. "Offensive tackle."

"Of course, of course. I could have guessed."

"You look a little old to have gone to college with Tim," said the lady who was with the balding suit.

"G.I. Bill," said Erich, turning to pick up a blue napkin with intertwined rings and "Tim & Sandy" in silver.

They found seats together at a round table across the arena from the wedding party. The five already seated at the table introduced themselves by first name and declared themselves friends of the bride. Doing the honors for their group, Muggs made them friends of the groom.

"You folks from Riverbend?" asked a man in a large Hawaiian shirt straining to do its job. "Real mess you've got here with that serial killer. Almost didn't come."

"How many times I have to tell you," said the equally bountiful woman next to him. "He's killing cops and union leaders, not CPA's."

"I don't think so," said the small man with lank hair on Hawaiian Shirt's other side. "The woman with the banks wasn't any part of a union. He's looking for high profile victims. If he kills whoever is in the news, it will get him in the news. Publicity, that's what all those guys want."

"What about the policemen?" asked the boney woman in hat and white gloves next to him. "Maybe it's those policemen he wants, and the first murder was a way to get the policeman to come. Maybe revenge for a speeding ticket or something."

"Now that is sincerely stupid," said Hawaiian Shirt. "Sorry, Alma. He kills a person, someone calls 911, the cops show up. How does he guarantee which cop shows up? Use your head, for Christ's sake. Sorry, Alma."

"What I want to know is how he kills everyone from behind?" said the bountiful woman. "How can he sneak up on all those people? What do you think, Chuck?" She turned to the fifth member of their party, a long lean man in a narrow leather tie with his elbow on the table holding his head up.

"Cloak uh invis'bil'ty."

"How much champagne have you had?"

"Nuh neerly enuff. Yuh gotta drink uh gallon uh the horse piss b'for yuh git a buzz."

"I need to reload," said Hawaiian Shirt, picking his plate up and pushing himself from the table.

"Good idea," said Laine, as he and Kathy rose with their plates.

"Bring me six glasses sh'mpane," said Chuck. "Hate w'ddings. N'ver did like conspic'us consum'shun."

* * * * * * * * * *

"Right out there," said the woman in worn blue jeans and a floppy shirt, pulling the screen open on a patio door, and giving Stangler a lingering look as he and Middleton stepped out onto a large plank deck with ornamental iron railings. The house was in a new subdivision east of Eleanor Roosevelt High School.

New house, new deck, new sod creating an instant back yard. A man in nothing but cut-offs and sandals was hosing off the deck. Like his property, he appeared to be in top condition.

"Oh, no. She didn't," he said, seeing the two detectives. "I told her it would be a waste of your time."

"Ninety percent of what we do is a waste of time, Mr. Fitzhugh," said Stangler. "It comes with the territory."

Noticing where Middleton was looking, the homeowner pointed to white streaks on the deck. "Grackles making bombing runs."

"Get an owl," said Middleton.

"An owl?"

"One of those big plastic ones. Stand it up on the railing."

"That'll keep the grackles away?"

"Yup."

"You saw the vehicles at the high school this past Monday morning?" said Stangler.

"Yes, but I'm sure they were all yours." He raised his voice as Mrs. Fitzhugh came out on the deck, hair combed, makeup on, wearing white short shorts and a red polka-dot halter top. "My wife has gotten you out here on a fool's errand. She watches too many police programs."

"Tell us what you saw."

He shut the hose off and dropped it. "Come over here." He moved to the other end of the wrap-around deck. "I was standing here Monday morning, checking to see if the sod wanted watering."

"We bought the place for the view," said Mrs. Fitzhugh. She took Stangler's elbow, leaned against him and pointed. "You can see the river over there to the left, and if you look straight ahead you can see clear across the city to the hills on the other side."

"The high school is at the bottom of the bluff," said her husband, "and from here you look almost straight down on top of it."

"What time Monday morning?" said Stangler, disengaging his elbow and crossing to the railing on the other side of Fitzhugh.

"I don't know... I'd finished reading the paper... maybe somewhere between 10:00 and 10:30?"

"What did you see at the high school?"

"Nothing exciting, just you guys. There were no ambulances or fire trucks, anything like that. I figured it was a break-in and vandalism. Later on we read someone was killed, and my wife got all excited, assuming I had seen something important."

She turned her back to the railing, put her elbows on the top bar, and hooked a bare foot on a lower bar, posing. "I did the right thing, don't you think, detective?" she drawled at Stangler.

"Yes." He turned to her husband. "Tell me exactly what you saw. Take your time."

Middleton had his notebook out. Fitzhugh stared at it for a moment.

"Uh, yeah. Okay. In front of the doors on the south side were two sedans, one dark maroonish, the other light-colored."

Storley's car; our car, thought Middleton.

"There was an older, rusted pickup."

Custodian.

"A blue and white patrol car."

Klindworth and Tufte.

"There was a big white van with lettering on the side too small to read from here.

Crime lab.

"Along the side a ways," he said, pointing, "was a dark van. New and shiny, black or a really dark blue or green."

Bingo.

"Did you see anyone?"

"Yes. There was a cop... uh, police officer, standing by the south door."

Tufte.

"Only one?"

"Yes, just the one."

"And then what?"

"I went inside. The wife was making brunch."

Stangler closed his eyes and looked pained. Middleton slipped his notebook back in his pocket with a sigh.

"What? Did I say something wrong?"

"No, you did just fine."

"Waste of time, huh?"

"No. It's good your wife called in." Stangler paused for a minute, wondering if he should say anything.

Fitzhugh waited. There was obviously something else.

"Had you stayed three minutes longer," said Stangler, "you would have seen who killed Officer Tufte."

#   #   #   #   #   #

Chapter 26: Afternoon, Sunday, July 25

The bowl was an ugly faded brown plastic, the spoon was cheap stainless steel with a bend in the handle, but the stew was excellent. Tearing a piece from a slice of day-old bread, Martin dipped it in the brown gravy surrounding his chunks of vegetables. Sara had been a good cook, setting the table with grilled fish, steamed vegetables and fresh fruit. The three of them would have lived long healthy lives, if two of them hadn't been killed.

Now he was eating fried foods, red meat, gravies and white bread. He felt a lurch of guilty disloyalty that he was enjoying them. "This is good," he said.

"Huh!" said Kathy. "Better be. We had to sit through a sermon to get it." She shoved her half-full bowl toward Laine.

"Share it?" said Laine, looking at Big Erich. Getting a nod, Laine scraped half of Kathy's leftover stew into his bowl and shoved the remainder toward Big Erich.

"You had something better to do?" said Muggs.

"I already know everything there is to know about God," said Kathy.

"Really."

"Yeah. He doesn't give a crap for us, so why bother?"

Martin rose, deposited his dishes in the dirty dish bin, and walked back to the serving line.

"You only get one bowl," said the lady who ladled out the stew.

"Yes, I know," said Martin. "I would like to talk to the cook."

"You have a problem with the stew?"

"Not at all. I just want to talk to the cook."

A young volunteer worker slid up beside Martin, eyes wide and wary. "Is there a problem?" he said.

"No," said Martin, "I just want to talk to the cook."

Captain Wibben appeared on the other side of Martin. "Is there a problem?"

"He says he wants to talk to the cook," said the stew ladle lady.

"Are you going to cause trouble?" said Wibben.

"No," said Martin, holding eye contact with him.

After a moment, the Captain made a gesture at the ladle lady and she hurried into the kitchen at the back of the serving area.

A lady in white appeared. Everything about her was massive. The ladle lady following close behind was obscured from sight. Looking warily at the three men on the other side of the counter, the cook asked, "Is there a problem?"

"This man asked to speak to you," said the Captain.

"You only get one bowl," she said to Martin.

"That's right," said the volunteer.

"I wanted to compliment you on the stew," Martin said. "It was delicious."

"I have to make do with whatever gets donated," she said, narrowing her eyes suspiciously.

"You do an excellent job. People should tell you that more often."

"He's right, Mrs. Robinson," said Wibben. "I eat here every Sunday myself because it's so good."

"Is that all?" she said. "Everybody had his say?"

Martin nodded.

"I gotta get back to work." She headed back to the kitchen. Halfway there she turned, and looked at Martin. "It's good, you say?"

"Better than good," said Martin.

"Humph," she said, passing into the kitchen.

* * * * * * * * * *

"Why did you do something like that?" said Kathy, sprawled in the sunlight on top of the retaining wall bordering a controlled housing patio area. "You could have gotten yourself thrown out."

"I was showing appreciation. There's nothing wrong with that."

"You're street people."

"And? I shouldn't be grateful for what good-hearted people feel moved to give me?"

"Apathetic Martin is turning into Proactive Martin right before our eyes," said Muggs.

"It's a trap," said Kathy. "Once those religious nuts get a hold, they'll try to run your life."

"I'll keep that in mind," said Martin.

"Not much new news," said Muggs, reading yesterday's newspaper on a sunlit bench. "The cops still don't have much to go on with these killings. The paper's starting to repeat the notes in a box every issue, asking anyone who knows anything about the New Guards to call a police tip line. 'Our sacred duty. Death to abusers and usurpers. Death to the hounds of absolute despots. New guards for future security.' Doesn't make sense to me."

Big Erich spoke softly.

> "'When a long train of abuses and usurpations, pursuing invariably the same Object evinces a design to reduce them under absolute Despotism, it is their right, it is their duty, to throw off such Government, and to provide new Guards for their future security.'"

Martin sat up straight and stared at Big Erich. Muggs lowered her paper and looked at him, mouth open in surprise.

"What's that?" said Laine, eyes closed, face to the sun. "One of the newest al-Qaeda manifestos justifying killing Americans?"

"The serial killer is Islamic?" said Kathy, sitting up.

"No," said Muggs distractedly, deep in her own thoughts.

"Well what is it, then?" said Kathy. "Erich, what in hell are you quoting?"

"The Declaration of Independence," said Big Erich.

"*Our* Declaration of Independence?" said Laine, straightening up and looking alarmed. "Like Thomas Jefferson and those guys?"

"Yes," said Muggs.

"They can't do that!" said Laine, on his feet now, shouting. "There's a law against that! It's like burning the American flag!" He shook his head and started to whisper. "They have to be... taken out. Keep your... heads down. Go in fast... get the job done and... get out."

Kathy bounced off the wall, landing on her feet, springing into a flip that landed her so close in front of Laine that he fell back onto the bench.

"Jee-sus! Will you cut that out? What's wrong with you?"

Bouncing on her toes, she circled behind the bench and made her fingers do little spider dances on his shaven head.

He brushed at his head. "Will you be serious for a change?" Looking at Muggs, "We've got to do something about this."

"Maybe," said Muggs.

"We do, you know," said Martin. "If the cops knew where this guy was coming from, maybe they could find him."

She looked at him with a wary expression. "And just exactly how to you propose belling the cat?"

\#   \#   \#   \#   \#   \#

Chapter 27: Sunday-Monday, July 25-26

"Say what you want, but I think three minutes longer, Mrs. Fitzhugh would have had you hog-tied and stuffed in her hope chest." Driving at walking speed, Middleton negotiated a clogged street bordering the riverside Greek Festival. Vehicles filled both sides and the tired, happily over-fed people treated the narrowness that was left in the middle as a sidewalk, moving aside casually just enough for the unmarked vehicle to pass. Many patted the fenders and cried, "Opa!"

"Just watch where you're going and shut up," said Stangler.

It was Sunday night. Detectives and officers alike were patrolling the streets, looking for a new-looking dark van. Windows would be looked into. License numbers would be taken. Everyone was alert for suspicious circumstances. Or a woman with a gun in her pocket.

So far, the Greek Festival environs had produced 15 dark SUV's, but only one dark van. This one with "Zorbas" emblazoned on its side. Mr. Fitzhugh could not have missed that name. Nevertheless, Middleton wrote down the license while Stangler got out and peered through its front windows. "Full of bakery racks," he said, getting back into the car.

"Why a new, shiny van?" said Middleton. "Wouldn't it be smarter to have an old scruffy nondescript one?"

"Amateurs who don't know better?"

"Or a sign of the times? Scruffy is suspicious; new and clean is an upright citizen?"

"Could be."

Marked patrol cars had been assigned specifically to areas where events were occurring, and they would stay in their areas throughout the night. Detectives were moving from event to event, hoping their random routes would be a complement to the patrols.

"The Rendezvous on South Island?" asked Middleton.

"Won't we be going right by that thing in Founder's Park?" said Stangler.

"Art in the Park," said Middleton. "Yeah, we will, but that ended at 6:00. There was a bit of a stink about it, I hear."

"What?"

"The people didn't pick up the area. Garbage and junk left all over. More than normal. Someone called the City Council chairman, he called the LEC, we called Art Center people, they promised to clean it all up tomorrow noon."

"Not much of a stink."

"'The rest of the story.' The Jehovah's Witnesses in town for their convention have the park reserved for outdoor sunrise services every morning this coming week. They got sight of the mess left for them and are protesting it as a hate crime."

"That should keep Duponte off our necks for a day or so."

"You wish," said Middleton. "So. The Rendezvous?"

"Fine."

As they passed Founders Park on the east side, a shiny dark van moved slowly along the west side, heading south. It flared under a street light, disappeared in dark shadow, only to flare again under the next street light. Its pace was sedate, almost as though looking for something. Half a block behind, a second shiny dark van also traveled south, flaring and disappearing in its turn.

Technically a peninsula, South Island was a land mass in the middle of the river about one-fourth of a mile wide and a mile long connected by an isthmus just wide enough to accommodate two lanes of traffic, if the cars went at a crawl and no one had his elbow out the window.

Tonight was the last of an annual four-day event occurring on the island. The Rendezvous drew people interested in re-creating the lives and skills of the French fur trappers, Voyageurs who roamed the river from the 1600's to the early 1800's. Participants wore buckskin, cooked over campfires, fished with spears, lived in hide tents, had hatchet-throwing contests, and exchanged stories of staying alive in the wilderness.

The vehicles of the Rendezvous enthusiasts, which might have destroyed the antique ambiance of the camp, were hidden behind dense growth at the north end of the island. Visitors parked on the shore and traveled to the island in a mini bus that went back and forth throughout the day.

The modern Voyageurs took in money from the sale of moccasins, raccoon hats, flint hatchets, thong amulets and fringed garments--most in child sizes. The sponsors of the event kept tight control on authenticity-- everything offered for sale had to be hand made of natural materials.

The mainland visitors' parking area had a few new dark shiny SUV's, but no vans. Middleton's hand out the window holding his badge got them across the isthmus in their car. Dousing the headlights to avoid dispelling the firelight atmosphere, Middleton carefully followed the pitted road that took them to the concealed Voyageur parking area. There they found four dark vans--dented, rusted, covered in scratches. Nothing that would qualify as new and shiny. They turned and headed back off the island, up the highway, past a sprawling Menards home center.

"I'll cruise the barn dance at the History Center," said Middleton.

* * * * * * * * * *

"I'm too old for all-nighters," said Rask, collapsed at his desk, head resting on his arms, eyes closed against the morning sunlight. "What time is it?"

"Fifteen minutes later than when you asked last time," said Stummer.

"What time was it when I asked last time?"

"Ten thirty-five."

"This is stupid," Rask said, standing up. "I need breakfast. I need sleep. I'm goin' home. You find a body; call me."

"Me too," said Stummer, standing, glancing at Stangler for a reaction.

Reading reports on his desk, Stangler didn't even look up, making a "Fine. Go." gesture with his hand.

"Probably a good idea," said Middleton. "I'd hate to admit we're sitting here disappointed because no one has found a dead body."

Stangler looked up from notes he had been making. "Twelve new-looking shiny dark vans. Two out of state, five antique dealers, one dog kennel owner, one Zorba's, two personal owners, one sociology professor."

"A sociology professor could be trying to reform the world, one abuser at a time."

"Maybe, but he was spotted over by Founder's Park, near midnight, long after everyone had gone. No Jehovah's Witness called in a dead body this morning."

Stangler looked at his notes again. "Does five antique dealers seem odd?"

"No. I think Riverbend's got more antique shops than mosquitoes."

"Do mosquitoes have antique shops?"

"I'd laugh if I weren't falling asleep."

"Six homicides occurring every Sunday night, and nothing last night. So what now?"

"Now we get some sleep," said Middleton, heading out.

#   #   #   #   #   #

Chapter 28: Afternoon, Monday, July 26

"What did you expect?" said Kathy. "'Welcome, Mr. Scruffy Street Person. We've been waiting for you to come and tell us how to run our cop shop?'"

The five of them sat in one of the reading areas of the air-conditioned public library. Martin was quieter than usual, unhappy about the summary rebuff he and Big Erich had received at the Law Enforcement Center. "I expected to be sent away without any thanks, but I thought someone would at least listen to what I had to say."

"And you took Big Erich with you, because...."

Martin smiled at her. "I thought his presence would guarantee that I wasn't sent away too forcefully."

"So what now?" said Muggs. "Forget the whole thing?"

"We can't forget it," said Laine, his voice starting to rise. "These people hate the United States of America."

"Hey," said Kathy, grabbing his ears and shoving her face against his. "Keep it down or I'll bite off your nose."

"Will you be serious," he said, shoving her off, but speaking quietly.

"This is going to sound corny," said Martin, "but we do have a civic duty to help."

"And broccoli can cure cancer," said Muggs.

"All right. I am galled by the treatment we received. It would be very satisfying to find their serial killer and gloat when we hand him over."

"Yes!" said Laine. "Let's do it."

"Hey, hey, let's have a dose of reality, here," said Muggs. "Catching a serial killer is not one of the things on my to-do list."

"We need their tactical information," said Laine. "We go in under cover, break in at night when the LEC is closed, and steal their files."

"I don't think the LEC closes, Guerilla Boy, we could just walk in," said Kathy.

"The police aren't dumb," said Martin. "They've got any kind of fingerprints, blood, DNA, that could be found, and they're working that end. I think what we could do is work on the *why*. We've got the key to the note, to the philosophy behind the killings. Using that, if we can figure out why the victims were selected, then we can use the same selection process to predict the next victim before he or she is a victim."

"And try again to tell the police?" said Muggs.

Martin shrugged.

"This guy thinks he's a patriot," said Laine.

"Why 'he?'" said Kathy. "Maybe it's she or they."

"Doesn't matter," said Martin. "We need to look at *why* he, she, or they do this."

"Okay, I'll brainstorm, but I won't go hunting," said Muggs. She thought for a moment or two and then in a thinking-out-loud voice, said, "He considers himself a patriot and he's unhappy with the present government."

"Unhappy?" said Kathy. "He's killing people!"

"He's killing civilians," said Laine. "A good soldier... does not... kill---"

Kathy reached over and pinched his nose shut. "Not in the library," she hissed.

"Willyouuucuuuutthatouuuut!" he said, jerking his head away.

"Okay, he's seriously pissed," said Muggs. "He wants to throw off this bad government, and he believes the Declaration of Independence gives him the authority to do so."

"He's keying off abuses that the present government creates or at least allows to exist," said Martin.

"But he's killing people," said Kathy. "I mean *people* people. Why isn't he attacking government agencies or politicians?"

"I'm not sure," said Martin. "Crawling before he can walk? Starting out with people who take advantage of what the government allows?"

"Okay, make a case against Maguire," said Muggs. "He was leading a walk-out for money that wasn't there that could send a company into bankruptcy."

"And the government allows unions to do this, to operate punitively, to tie up production in negotiations, to freeze out replacement workers," said Martin.

"Really?" said Kathy.

"More or less," said Martin. "I'm trying to think in black and white like the killer."

"The union didn't walk out," said Muggs.

"Which makes it a big success. Killing Maguire appears to have stopped the walk-out," said Martin.

"Why the cop each time?" said Laine.

"I know!" said Kathy. "Cops keep the law the government makes. They're the hounds of the despot."

"An abuser and a hound, every time," said Laine. "Man, he's good. Catching a cop every time has got to be tough."

"All right," said Martin, "let's put ourselves in the mind of the killer, and define the thought process that lead to Goetzman and Storley. Then we'll select our next victim."

#   #   #   #   #   #

Chapter 29: Morning, Tuesday, July 27

Middleton and Stangler watched Patricia Konburg climb into her new black shiny van, back out of her driveway, and speed away.

She had been an easy interview, despite frequent peeks at her watch. "Sorry to keep doing that. It's my work day. I have to have Someplace In Time open and ready for business by 9:30. Yes, I was at the History Center Sunday night from about 7:00 to 10:30. Do I like barn dances? Well, I don't *dislike* them. Don't dislike them, you know. I was making contacts. You know, like looking for sales? You see a woman wearing a piece of antique jewelry and you go up to her and say, 'What a lovely brooch,' or whatever. Or whatever she's wearing, you know. And she'll say, 'It was my grandmother's. She left me her jewelry and I'll never wear all of it, but I don't know what to do with it.' They never know what to do with it, you know. So I look surprised and talk about what a coincidence, I'm an antiques dealer. I hand her my card and tell her to call me; I can give her an idea of the value of her grandmother's jewelry and what she might do with it. What she might do with it, you know. And bingo, just like that the barn dance becomes a business trip. I can claim the ticket price and the mileage as a legitimate expense. It is a legitimate expense, you know. And if the lady calls me, and why shouldn't she, because I was just another person enjoying the fun, and it was dumb luck that I happened to be an antiques dealer, so she can trust me not to have an ulterior motive. Sees no ulterior motive, you know. Except, of course, I do have an ulterior motive, but in a nice way. I'm hoping to buy her grandmother's jewelry. Really hoping to buy, you know. Now if I strike up a conversation with someone who's a collector---"

"Let me get this straight," said Middleton. "Most of your social occasions fit the definition of business?"

"Absolutely. I work at it, you know. You would be surprised at how much mileage a person can claim if you're careful. Say I make a trip to the printers on 16th Street, that's business mileage, you know. If on the way I stop at the grocery store on 13th Street, that's okay. I still had to go all the way to 16th Street for business purposes and so my grocery mileage is a freebie. If I---"

"Excellent!" said Middleton. "So if I gave you some dates and times, you could look in your books and tell me where you were?"

"Hah! Not only where I was, but the ticket price, the round trip mileage, and the name of the potential customer. All in my tax records, you know."

She opened a large columnar journal and pointed to entries recording where she was at the times of their three homicide events. Looking up suddenly, she grew big-eyed. "Am I a suspect? Do you think I killed these people? Good gravy! Do I need an attorney?" She glanced at her watch. "Oh, dear, I'm going to be late."

"There goes a very clever business woman," said Middleton as they watched her drive away.

"Too gabby."

"Can't have everything." He took out their list. "Next van owner is out in South Lake Estates."

Stangler's phone vibrated. "Stangler." He shook his head slowly in disbelief. "Okay, we're on our way." Defeat was written all over his face. "10-54 at the Artists Co-op."

* * * * * * * * * *

The body of Nicholas Ovolenski lay on its stomach toward the back of the small Artists Co-op gallery. The note they hoped wouldn't be there was there, thrust between his now-stiff fingers.

"OUR SACRED DUTY
DEATH TO ABUSERS AND USURPERS
DEATH TO THE HOUNDS
OF ABSOLUTE DESPOTS
NEW GUARDS FOR FUTURE SECURITY"

Although he lay at the farthest reaches of the small gallery, most of his lower body could be seen from the front windows of the store. There was a small entrance wound in the back of his head.

"M.E. guesses he's been dead 30 to 40 hours," said Middleton. "Puts it at Sunday night."

Stangler nodded. The familiar odor of cordite and blood was fading into the familiar odor of a body dead for a while.

"Lady who found him is over there." Middleton tipped a nod at a long-haired woman sitting on a stool sipping a take-out coffee. She looked like bluish skin stretched over nothing but bones and then draped and tied with madras shawls and scarves.

Through the window behind her, uniformed officers could be seen urging a crowd of lookers to move on. Business traffic on the rest of the block moved as usual but with heads turned wondering what the crowd was about.

"Did you warn the uniforms?" said Stangler.

"Yes. Carefully, individually, in great detail. No one took me seriously. They figure Tuesday morning on a business day with the street full of people--who's crazy enough to try to shoot a cop."

"Sunday night?"

"Thought of that. I had dispatch do a voice check half an hour ago. No one's gone missing."

"Okay. What's the scarf lady's name?"

"Ruth Sandvig, but 'Rosetti' is her professional name and she prefers it."

"Ms Rosetti," said Stangler, approaching her.

"Just 'Rosetti,' if you please." She slid off the stool and swayed against him, running her hands up his chest. "I feel faint," she said.

Stangler grabbed her elbows and pushed her down on the stool again. She clamped onto his left wrist and pulled his hand into the nest of drapery between her breasts. "My heart is having palpitations."

Stangler jerked his hand free.

"Don't you feel the magnetic currents?" she asked. "There is a connection. Our auras are melding."

"You discovered Mr. Ovolenski when you opened the gallery this morning, at?"

"Look at your rich glossy hair," she said, reaching up to stroke it. "All the Rosetti's had good hair, you know. Our psyche's must have bonded 170 years ago, and we still feel the bond today."

Stangler stepped out of reach. "Ms Sandvig, what time did you open the gallery this morning?"

She tightened her lips and narrowed her eyes. "It's 'Rosetti,' and I gave all that information to one of the boys in blue."

"I would appreciate if you would give it again to me."

"I don't feel like it. You're not being simpatico."

"Fine. Detective Middleton, will you please take Ms Sandvig to the LEC and put her in a holding cell until I can question her more fully."

"Sure," said Middleton, frowning fiercely, flexing his shoulders, and pulling a pair of handcuffs from his pocket. "You want me to cuff her?"

"Oh, all right!" she said. "I'll answer your stupid questions. Again."

They went over the facts. Again. She arrived at 9:50, saw Ovolenski and called 911. She locked the door--it wasn't locked when she arrived--put up a closed sign and waited. The gallery did not open for business Sundays and Mondays, all the artists who minded the gallery had keys to the front door, and yes, again, the door was unlocked when she got there, the lights were not on.

"Did you touch the body?"

"No."

"Not even to see if he was just injured?"

"He smelled dead."

"Did you notice anything missing or disturbed in the gallery?"

"No."

"And so, for all you know, the door could have remained unlocked from the time Mr. Ovolenski came in until you arrived?"

"Yes."

"Who do you think would have a reason to kill him?"

"I don't know," she said thoughtfully, losing her attitudes. "Jealous rage maybe? He was doing some marvelous work. A breakthrough in subtext. The State Arts Board had just announced a grant to him of $50,000.00. It would have freed him up and made his life a lot easier."

"Could the killer have wanted the money?"

"Nick said the check wouldn't be issued until August 1."

"Is some of his work here?"

"The black and white photos back in that alcove where he is."

The Crime Lab van arrived. Dr. Holmes could be heard barking at the crowd of lookers and issuing orders to the officers maintaining the perimeter. He blew through the door in a wave of complaints.

"Is that how you maintain a scene? I'm afraid to look at what I'll find inside!"

"Who are you?" said Rosetti sliding off her stool again. "You have such a brilliant aura; I'd like to paint you."

"What on god's green earth is *that*?" said Holmes. "Looks like she died two months ago." He headed for the body while his team followed, carrying equipment.

"Well!"

Telling Ms Sandvig to stay put, the two detectives stepped outside while the Crime Lab people worked.

"Wiley," said Stangler. "You know I don't doubt your word...."

"But you'd feel better if you warned the uniformed guys yourself."

"Yeah."

"Go ahead, no offense taken."

"It's not you, it's me. I feel as though it's all my---"

"Lobo, I know. Go talk to them. Who knows, maybe coming from two of us they'll start watching over their shoulders."

Middleton watched his partner go from officer to officer, talking earnestly. He understood the guilt that was weighing heavily on the senior detective. Middleton frowned. No, truthfully, he didn't understand it at all. The police victims had disobeyed an order and left their posts. He deeply mourned their loss, but they were grown men and they, not him, not Stangler, were responsible for their actions. Although he didn't understand Stangler's feelings of guilt, nevertheless he grieved for the way they were tearing his partner apart.

Shortly after they went back inside to check the progress of the Crime Lab, an officer rapped his knuckles on the glass door. Middleton went, and came back with a young woman. "This is Randi Willett. She works at the cafe next door 11:00 to 7:00, Saturday through Wednesday. She passes the gallery coming and going and usually takes a minute to see what's on display."

She was maybe 19 and wearing a yellow and white waitress uniform. Stangler smiled at her. She dropped her eyes and blushed, but didn't say anything.

"You passed here on Saturday, a little before 11:00. What did you see?"

"Just the two guys who usually work on Saturday. I think their names are Dan and Bruce."

"Any customers?"

"Not that I could see."

"And when you went home a little after 7:00?"

"The gallery was closed and the lights were out."

"Did you try the door?"

"No. Why would I do that?"

"Just checking. How about Sunday?"

"It was closed and the lights were out both times when I passed. I didn't try the door."

"And Monday," said Stangler, letting her describe it her way.

"Monday morning, I could see the... feet... and legs back there. Like... like... a figure on its stomach."

"You didn't call 911?"

"Nooo." Tears started to run down her cheeks. "I thought... I thought it was... art! They do really crazy things here, you know, and it's art! Like they make a pile of sand with beer cans sticking out of it, and call it an art work. And once they had a person seated in a lawn chair, and he looked just like a person, but he was some sort of cement-like stuff, and I saw the legs and feet and figured it was art!" She grabbed a napkin from a table with a big coffee pot and blew her nose loudly.

"Did you try the door?"

"No, I never touch their door when they're closed. Why would I do that? Why do you keep asking?"

"The door wasn't locked when the store opened this morning. We wondered how long it had been that way."

"Oh. I never thought to check the door." She hunched her shoulders, looking guilty.

"That's okay. Most people wouldn't. Tell Detective Middleton here how you can be reached and then you can go back to work."

Stangler moved closer to the Crime Lab activity.

"Keep out of the damn way! Don't touch anything!" Dr. Holmes in fine form.

Middleton collected Rosetti's keys, a contact list of the gallery's dealers, and her alibi. "Meditating and painting in solitude till far into the night." After taping a sign in the window, "Closed until August 3," she left.

Stangler came back up front and they watched the bagged body leave on a gurney, Crime Lab following shortly after.

"Anything of interest, Dr. Holmes?" said Middleton.

"He probably thought being shot was pretty interesting," said Holmes, without stopping.

Middleton shook his head. "Sometimes I feel like a big dog on a six-foot chain, with a cat at seven feet."

They moved back to the corner of the gallery that held Ovolenski's work.

"Photographs," said Middleton, leaning forward to examine two round smooth hillocks with a narrow cleft between and a lone bare wind-swept tree growing right at the apex of the cleft. The photo was taken with a lens that produced a dream-like quality--almost as if shot on a foggy day.

Another larger photo showed two dome-like huts with round tops and bundles of grass surrounding them.

"To quote our little waitress," said Stangler, "they do some really crazy things here. What is that?"

Middleton moved over to see. "There are some pieces of what, bark?, lying here on the surface, so this must be a tree branch stripped smooth and lying sort of across another, and in the cleft where they cross there's moss? Hard to tell with this hazy photo effect."

"Here's one I recognize," said Stangler. It's a lighthouse rising out of sea grass on a rocky shore."

"The sides of the lighthouse look odd," said Middleton. Then, "That's not a lighthouse." He reached and pointed to the first photo. "Look. This is someone's buttocks with a twig stuck in." Tapping the second, he said, "Not huts; breasts."

Stangler stared at the next two. "Well, I'll be damned. Someone actually gave him $50,000.00 to do more of these? Do people seriously consider this art?"

"Don't know about others. I think they're sophomoric potty jokes."

They turned out the lights and locked the door behind them. "'A breakthrough in subtext!' Now I've heard everything," said Middleton. "I'm surprised someone didn't kill him for having such bad taste."

With the body and the Crime Lab gone, there was nothing interesting to see. The onlookers had not lingered and the street was back to normal weekday traffic.

"We're through here, Harders; you can wrap it up," Middleton said. Harders thumbed his radio and said, "We're outta here guys. Dispatch, Units 13 and 8 leaving 106 Fourth Avenue West. We'll be at the LEC in five minutes."

Two uniforms climbed into one of the marked cars in front and tipped two-fingered air salutes to Harders and the detectives. One leaned out the window as they were pulling away. "Don't let anyone get behind you, Harders!" he shouted. and laughed.

Harders looked to see if the detectives were okay with a little ribbing about all their warnings. Satisfied all was okay, he adjusted his equipment belt more comfortably, looked toward an alley entrance halfway down the block and waited.

"Who're you with?" said Stangler.

"Kaminski."

"Is there a problem?"

"Nah. Someone was doing a helluva lot of banging down the alley. Probably a garbage truck. Kaminski went to tell 'em to keep it down. He'll be back in a minute."

Harders touched his radio. "How ya coming Kaminski? We're clear to go." He waited for a response. "Kaminski?"

"Goddammit!" said Stangler. He and Middleton sprinted across the street, reaching for their guns.

"Ohhhhh shit!" shouted Harders, right behind, unsnapping his own gun.

#   #   #   #   #   #

Chapter 30: Noon, Tuesday, July 27

(Theme Music:)
(Voiceover:)
THIS IS KRBM-TV, NEWS AT NOON. UP TO THE MINUTE REPORTING ON WHAT'S HAPPENING IN THE RIVER LAND WITH NOON NEWS ANCHOR SALLY FELDNER.

(Anchor:)
GOOD NOON TO YOU, TUESDAY, JULY 27.

THE ENCORE KILLER HAS STRUCK FOR A FOURTH TIME. HOURS AGO, THE BODY OF NICHOLAS OVOLENSKI WAS DISCOVERED AT THE ARTISTS COOPERATIVE GALLERY IN THE DOWNTOWN CENTRAL SHOPPING MALL. THE WELL-KNOWN ARTIST WAS REPORTEDLY SHOT IN THE BACK OF THE HEAD AND LEFT WITH THE NOW-FAMILIAR NOTE CLAIMING RESPONSIBILITY BY THE UNKNOWN, AND POSSIBLY FICTITIOUS, NEW GUARDS.

APPROACHED AT THE SCENE, STATE CRIME LAB SPECIALIST, DR. BRADFORD C. HOLMES, OFFERED NO COMMENTS GERMANE TO THE INVESTIGATION.

OVOLENSKI, 36, WAS UNMARRIED AND IS REPORTED TO HAVE NO IMMEDIATE FAMILY IN THE RIVERBEND AREA. JUST LAST WEEK HE WAS AWARDED A $50,000.00 GRANT FROM THE MINNESOTA STATE ARTS BOARD TO PURSUE HIS WORK IN INTERPRETIVE PHOTOGRAPHY.

POLICE SPOKESMAN A. F. BRODHEAD CONFIRMED THAT THE INVESTIGATION WILL INCLUDE

QUESTIONING PROTESTORS OF OVOLENSKI'S WORK AS OBSCENITY ALONG WITH ANY AND ALL PERSONS WITH CONNECTIONS TO THE ARTISTS COOP GALLERY AND THE ARTIST. KRBM WILL HAVE MORE DETAILS ON NEWS AT SIX.

....

"Excuse me, I am being handed a late bulletin."

THE BODY OF POLICE OFFICER TADEUS "TED" KAMINSKI WAS FOUND IN AN ALLEY NEAR THE ARTISTS COOPERATIVE. UNCOMFIRMED SOURCES SAY HE WAS SHOT IN THE HEAD. THAT IS ALL THE INFORMATION WE HAVE AT THIS TIME. WATCH KRBM NEWS AT SIX WHEN WE WILL HAVE MORE DETAILS.

....

THE OFFICE OF MAYOR RONALD DUPONTE HAS ANNOUNCED A PRESS CONFERENCE AT 4:00 TODAY. SOURCES AT CITY HALL WHO DO NOT WISH TO BE IDENTIFIED SAY HE WILL BE ANNOUNCING A SPECIAL TASK FORCE TO HEAD UP THE ENCORE KILLER INVESTIGATION. IT IS ASSUMED THE SPECIAL TASK FORCE IS IN REACTION TO THE ALARMING INCREASE IN HANDGUN SALES OVER THE PAST TWO WEEKS. HUNTERS PARADISE ON NORTH MAIN REPORTS THEIR HANDGUN SALES ARE UP 300% OVER JULY OF LAST YEAR. KRBM NEWS AT SIX WILL HAVE ON-THE-STREET INTERVIEWS WITH CONCERNED CITIZENS.

....

RIVERBEND'S GOOD WORKS GREEN BERETS HELPED AVERT AN ALLEGED HATE CRIME ISSUE LATE SUNDAY NIGHT. AN UNUSUAL AMOUNT OF TRASH AND DETRITUS LEFT AFTER THE ART IN THE PARK EVENT SUNDAY AFTERNOON THREATENED TO PUT A BLIGHT ON THE JEHOVAH'S WITNESSES SUNRISE PRAYER MEETING IN FOUNDER'S PARK MONDAY MORNING. WHILE

THE TWO ORGANIZATIONS WRANGLED, THE GREEN BERETS MADE A LATE-NIGHT VISIT TO THE PARK, LEAVING ITS LAWNS AND PATHWAYS PRISTINE AND A GREEN BERET WITH THEIR SIGNATURE MESSAGE--"HELPING MAKE OUR WORLD BETTER."

....

THE FARMERS' TRACTOR CAVALCADE IS SCHEDULED TO START ITS LONG JOURNEY SOMETIME THIS WEEK. RESPONDING TO MINNESOTA FARMER ARVID HAUGEN'S PLEA FOR A SHOW OF STRENGTH FOR GREATER FARM SUBSIDIES, OVER 50 FARMERS AND THEIR TRACTORS ARE SCHEDULED TO LEAVE HASTINGS, TRAVELING DOWN TO HANNIBAL, MISSOURI AND THEN EAST TO WASHINGTON, DC.

IN AN INTERVIEW, HAUGEN SAID THEY ARE WAITING FOR TRACTORS EN ROUTE TO REACH THE RALLYING POINT. HE IS CERTAIN MORE TRACTORS WILL JOIN THEM AS THE CAVALCADE PROGRESSES. THE FARMERS' GROUP WILL TRAVEL SECONDARY ROADS WITH DRIVERS SLEEPING IN FIELDS AT NIGHT.

HAUGEN CONCEIVED OF THE CAVALCADE AS A MESSAGE TO THE GOVERNMENT, CALLING ATTENTION TO THE PLIGHT OF SMALL FARMERS WHO NEED LARGER GOVERNMENT SUBSIDIES IN ORDER TO SURVIVE.

....

WE'LL BE RIGHT BACK WITH "WINDY" WINDHORST AND THE WEATHER. "WINDY" WILL TELL US HOW LONG WE CAN EXPECT THE HIGH TEMPERATURES TO REMAIN BEFORE THE PREDICTED COLD FRONT MOVES IN.

#   #   #   #   #

Chapter 31: Afternoon, Tuesday, July 27

"So now you're in charge of a Special Task Force investigating New Guards," said Rask as the Captain pulled the door closed. "What the hell else is new? Dirt bag just wanted to get his face in the news again."

"I hate these damn press conferences," said Stangler. "That asshole is using these homicides as opportunities. He doesn't give a fuck for any of the victims. Ah, man, why did Kaminski.... You'd think by now.... Everyone was warned.... You warned them, didn't you, Wiley."

"Yes, Lobo, I did."

"And I warned them. We both warned them."

"Get off it, Lobo," said Pickett. "It's not your fault."

"Yeah. Sorry. It's just... Cops. Why cops?"

"Why anybody?" said Pickett. "Don't lose focus." He stared at Stangler, ready to use rank if the discussion went any farther. Stangler frowned but kept silent. "All right," said Pickett, "we all hate that cops are being killed and we all hate Duponte's news conferences. Let's move on."

"All those damn jackals followin' so close 'n tryin' to stick their microphones up yer ass," said Rask. "Can't be blamed if I accidentally break a few fingers brushin' em away."

"Goddammit, John, will you be careful," said Pickett. "We've got national media out there. If there's any stink about police brutality, Duponte will see that we're all unemployable. Everybody sit down. Let me shift a few assignments and then Wiley you can fill us in on this goddamned cop killer."

"And the artist," said Rivera.

"Oh, god, yes, the artist. I sound as though I don't care enough about the civilian victims. This whole case.... Ah, well, never mind. Go on, Wiley."

Half an hour later, the meeting was starting to break up.

"Has Emily turned up anything on New Guards yet?" said Pedersen, standing.

"No," said Middleton. "Too many possibilities. But she's keeping at it, even the seemingly dumb stuff."

"The only progress we've made," said Stangler, is Rivera and Olson finally got Mrs. Jerglens to rat on Lester. He's been going to AA meetings late Sunday nights." He tipped a one-finger salute. "Good work, ladies." He started gathering up papers. "The moron would rather be suspected of murder than let us know his alibi was an AA group. Dumb jerk."

"Huh," said Rask, shifting his Nicorette cud, "I got the winner in dumb stuff. Two homeless idiots wandered in yesterday, claimin' they knew who the New Guards was. Squirrels will use any excuse ta get a night in a cell anna free meal."

"What?" said Stangler.

"I said---"

"I know what you said. Who did they say the New Guards were?"

"How the hell should I know? I was tired n' goin' home; I wasn't gonna humor no crazy homeless guys. Besides, they didn't say they knew who New Guards was, they said they knew what the notes meant."

"Who did talk to them?"

"No one. I told 'em to get out and not come back."

"Ah man! Go find them. Bring them in. Now."

"Yeah, yeah, don't get yer water hot. I see 'em around. We'll pick 'em up. Won't do any good. They're just squirrels trying to get somethin' free."

"Maybe," said Stangler. "Probably. But they're also the only people who have claimed to actually know anything."

* * * * * * * * * *

Kathy ran along the bike path, vaulted the iron railing, took the rocky slope in hopping leaps, and scuttled under the bridge. "They're looking for you!" she said.

"What?" said Muggs..

"The cops are looking for Martin and Big Erich! Two fat detectives asked me where you were and they knew I hung around with you and they tried to grab me, but I ran."

"You're sure it was us they were looking for?" said Martin.

Kathy gave him an exasperated glare. "No, I suppose it could have been some other big white guy and short black guy."

"If they know you, they know Laine," Muggs said to Kathy, alarm edging her voice. "If they try to grab him, he'll stand and fight."

"Against two of them?" said Martin.

"He was special ops, Martin. If they try to grab him and he goes off, he'll kill them. Kathy, can you find Laine?"

"I think so."

"Go! Get him back here just as soon as you can."

The three waited silently for what seemed like hours until they heard rocks being dislodged on the steep slope. "Jee-sus! Quit shoving! You're going to kill me!" Catching his balance at the bottom, Laine said, "Next time send a pack of Rottweilers, it would hurt less."

"Shut up and move," said Kathy, punching him on the shoulder.

"We've got to get off the streets," said Muggs.

"Why?" said Martin. "We wanted to talk to them."

"They had a chance and weren't interested. Now they want you badly enough to be out looking. Why? If it's who I think they are, they're really mean, Martin. They beat and handcuff people *before* they ask questions."

"Still, though, does it matter what changed their minds? If they're looking for me, it means they'll listen this time."

Muggs pushed him away from the others and lowered her voice. "This is serious, Martin. Maybe you feel like taking risks, but what if Kathy and Laine get drawn into it? We have to get off the streets. After that you can decide if you're going to risk your neck talking to the cops."

Martin studied her face for a moment, then turned and walked away a few paces. Muggs waited. After several minutes, Martin turned back. "All right," he said. "I know a place where we can hide."

"Where?" said Muggs.

"A place you don't know."

She looked at him indecisively.

"It's a building on private property and we won't be trespassing."

She still wavered.

"It's okay. It's safe. It's down where Stewart crosses 18th Avenue."

"All right," said Muggs. "Drivers, start your engines. Kathy, you stay close to Martin. Erich, Laine, string out; keep a distance between you. I'll bring up the rear. If anyone whistles, we all get down fast."

* * * * * * * * * *

Martin punched a key pad. There was a thunk of
the lock disengaging. He opened the heavy steel door
of the warehouse, and motioned them inside. He closed
the door and turned on the lights.

It was a small windowless two-story building that
appeared to be a three-stall garage with an open
stairway to the second level. A two-year old Lincoln
Town Car sat in front of one of the doors.

"Whose place is this?" whispered Muggs.

"Mine," said Martin.

No one said anything. Mistrust and suspicion
radiated at him in waves. The uncomfortable silence
lengthened.

"All right," he said softly. "Come on upstairs and
I'll tell you."

The second level was bare and unfinished. There
was a small sink and counter, a small gas stove, a
refrigerator-freezer, a small wooden table with two
chairs, a single bed, an open rack with a few clothes,
and a walled-off area with a door. Along one wall was
a stack of taped cardboard boxes, a radio lying on top.

"You've got a shower in here!" said Kathy from
inside the walled area. It was an accusation.

Muggs lowered herself to sit cross-legged in an
open area. "Okay let's have it."

The others joined her.

Martin got down with them. He started softly,
head down, looking at his clenched hands. "One year
ago, my wife and young daughter were killed in a car
accident." He cleared his throat. "Others can deal with
something like that and get on with their lives. I...
couldn't." He cleared his throat again. "I sold off
everything I owned, except what you see here." His
voice gained a little strength. "I went out on the streets

because I was lost and didn't care what happened to me."

The silence lengthened. Finally, Big Erich said softly:

"'Ever has it been
that love knows not its own depth
until the hour of separation.'"

"Shakespeare," said Muggs.

"Kahlil Gibran," said Big Erich.

"So what did you used to be?" said Kathy

"I was the owner of Driver Business Reengineering."

"Well that's as clear as mud," said Muggs.

"Business reengineering is a technique to help organizations rethink how they do their work."

"Efficiency experts."

"No. On a larger scale than that. It's the development of sophisticated information systems to support innovative business processes."

"Computer programmers?"

"No. It's hard to explain."

"Are you rich?" said Kathy.

"Very rich. I've found peace and friends."

"Are you money rich?"

"I suppose I am, but what I'm left with doesn't compare to what I've... lost."

"What's in those boxes?"

"Mostly sentimental things. Some cash and certificates."

"Can I take a shower?"

"Be my guest."

"Sold your ideals for a measly shower?" said Muggs.

"Yup," said Kathy as she headed for the bathroom.

Martin looked at the remaining three. "I wasn't pretending. Everything I was with you was real. I just didn't want to talk about... everything."

Muggs laid back, stretched her legs out, and put her hands behind her head. "I guess we all have past lives that we don't want to talk about. Can I be next in the shower?"

"Is Martin Driver your real name?" said Laine.

"Yes."

"You good with computers?"

"I'm good at hacker level, but I don't have enough brain cells to be a serious programmer."

"I'm good with computers."

"So I've heard."

* * * * * * * * * *

"... asking these two individuals to return to the Law Enforcement Center. Anyone seeing these two men is asked to call the Law Enforcement Tip Line, 800-534---"

Muggs turned the radio off and looked at Martin.

He sighed and scrubbed his hand on his head. "I have to go back in."

"We," said Big Erich.

"No, you don't!" said Kathy. "It's not safe. They'll lock you up."

"We were right about that artist. We have to go in. If we're decent people, we simply don't have any other choice."

"We're Americans," said Laine. "We know our duty."

"But we were just *guessing* Ovolenski," said Kathy. "We don't *know* anything. It could be just a coincidence. The police know lots more than we do. Let them guess."

"The police are doing what they do--looking for the murderer," said Martin. "They don't waste their time guessing who the next victim will be. If they find the killer, there won't be a next victim."

"Good! There won't be a next victim, so we can relax. And not go in."

"We have to go in."

"Muggs, say something! Tell him he's wrong."

"He has to go in," Muggs said, her voice heavy with resignation. "And he could end up in a lot of trouble. What's behind Door #2?"

#   #   #   #   #   #

Chapter 32: Morning, Wednesday, July 28

"Why do we get all the squirrels?" said Rask as he cruised a residential neighborhood at the bottom of a bluff.

"We only got four," said Stummer. "Stangler and Middleton are covering most of them."

"Yeah, well, Stangler should'a had the girls take all of 'em. Females are better at talkin' to nutso artists." He turned a corner and started looking for house numbers. "Let's liven things up a little, put this last one in cuffs."

"We'd have to have a good reason," said Stummer, "or Stangler will chew our asses."

"How about if he bad-mouths the dead guy?"

"Nothing illegal there. How about if he refuses to talk about the dead guy?"

"Bingo!" said Rask, hitting the steering wheel. "Clear case of obstruction of justice." He slowed as they got closer to the house number they were looking for. "What's this next squirrel's name?"

Stummer consulted a list. "Howard Livingthorpe-Saunders."

"I hate 'im already," said Rask, pulling over to the curb. The street was typical middle class residential-- weed-free green lawns, brick-edged flower beds, trimmed hedges, concrete rabbits. In the middle of the block their destination stood out. What would in any other instance have been a grassy front lawn, bristled with a haphazard tangle of day lilies, raspberry bushes, ornamental grass, sunflowers, corn stalks, golden rod, tiger lilies and unidentifiables.

Stummer was attempting to disengage a raspberry cane from his pants leg when the door opened, revealing a gaunt man wearing a faded bathing suit and paint splotches.

Inside, the floor of the living room was entirely covered in old canvas drop cloths. An easel and a small table holding paints, brushes and cans were the only furniture. The easel held a large canvas with diagonal slashes of color. Propped against the walls were other canvases with the same diagonal slashes in different colors.

"Lotta paint here," said Rask.

"I'm doing a series for the Kane Bank atrium," said the artist. "'The 12 Emotions.'"

"Gonna do 12 like that, huh?"

"Take a minute to study them. Deceptively similar, yes? But on contemplation, very profound."

"Yeah? Like, ya look at 'em long enough, they make sense?" said Rask, the sarcasm dripping.

"Precisely. Look at this." He picked one up. "This is 'Frustration.' The energy flow is aubergine and brooding ochre, but notice up here the corner is filled with overlapping palette knife applications in tenebrous blue? That says it all! I feel particularly successful with this one. Doesn't it totally speak to you with a sub-text of frustration?"

Rask frowned furiously. "Yeah, it speaks to me all right. It says you're a moron."

The artist jerked his head in surprise and took a step back.

"This one on the easel," said Stummer. "Love?"

"Ah!" he said, happy to avoid Rask and talk to an art lover. "You see that? Marvelous! Yes, indeed, tender, fragile love, growing from the jaded sophistication of today's anomie."

"Yeah, well, we're here about Nicholas Ovo-what-ski. You probably don't want to talk about him," said

Rask, reaching around to his back pocket for his handcuffs.

"No, that's fine," said the mostly naked artist, steeling himself to be polite. "I didn't know him all that well, but I'll tell you anything I know about him."

Rask threw Stummer a look of frustration as his hand came back front without the cuffs. "So what do you know about the squirrel?"

"What? Oh, Ovolenski. Not much. We ran into each other in the gallery on occasion. He affected a Russian accent, can you believe it?"

"Did you think he was a good artist?" said Stummer. "Deserving of the $50,000.00 grant?"

"What's good? What isn't? He was clever."

"You think stickin' sticks 'n grass on nekkid people n' then takin' pitchers is clever?" said Rask.

"I think finding a concept that titillates the buying public is damn clever, never mind if it's art or not."

"You jealous?"

"Maybe a little envious, but true art is never about the money."

"Not even $50,000.00?" said Stummer.

"Yes, well, that's quite a prize."

"Do you think he could have been killed for it?" said Stummer.

"How could he? With him dead, the grant dies, uh, no pun intended. No one else gets it."

"Let me rephrase that," said Stummer. "Do you think he could have been killed to prevent him from receiving the grant?"

"No, too much effort for no result. It would have been smarter to let him get the money and then steal it."

"Where were you Sunday night?"

"Right where you see me now."

"Can anyone corroborate that?"

"Fraid not."

"Do you belong to New Guards?"

"I don't belong to anything."

"Know who they are?"

"Not a clue."

Avoiding the raspberry canes on the way out, Rask said, "How about we pick up lunch before we drop off reports?"

"Sound's good."

"How the hell did ya know that one was 'Love?'"

"Wild guess," said Stummer. "It was pink and red."

* * * * * * * * * *

"Where are you guys at?" said Stangler as Rask and Stummer sauntered into the detectives' room.

"Finished our artists," said Stummer. "Just turned in our reports."

"Anything interesting?"

"No alibis, but they all looked pretty tame," said Stummer.

"They're all squirrels," said Rask. "Should a' put 'em all in cuffs and hosed 'em down."

"You found that homeless pair yet?" said Stangler.

"Judas Priest, whadda ya want us to do?" said Rask. "Talk ta squirrels or look for crazies?"

"We've got patrols looking for them," said Stummer.

"Okay, here," said Stangler, handing Stummer a list. "We need that last guy checked out. Professor with a new black van."

"Ah crap," said Rask. "I been itchin' to put someone in cuffs all day, and you give us a perfesser."

"Rask!"

"Yeah, yeah."

* * * * * * * * * *

"I get lost every time I come here," said Stummer in commiseration as Rask did a three-point turn at yet another dead end "That building used to be a parking lot, and this road wasn't here six months ago."

"What's the place called now?" said Rask.

"Minnesota State University, Riverbend."

Receiving directions from a perky brunette named Sheila at the main administration office, they walked a long corridor, took another one to the right, rode an elevator up one flight, passed through an enclosed walkway to another building, circled a commons area, rode another elevator up two flights, and headed down another long corridor.

"Maybe we should a' had Sheila show us the way," said Rask. "She could a' held my hand so I didn't get lost."

"Probably ruined her whole day when you didn't ask."

The one black van reported almost as an afterthought because it wasn't in what anyone thought had been the right place at the right time, turned out to be the one van that was closest to the fourth murder site--Founder's Park was only three blocks from the Artists Cooperative. But a college professor? Rask and Stummer knew they headed for another dead end.

The door to office 327B stood open. Stummer knocked on the frame and they walked in.

"Come in, come in," said the slender wispy-haired man behind the desk. "Hmmm," he said, smiling and leaning back. "Not students. Not photocopy service people. Not fund-raisers."

Stummer flipped a badge.

"Ah. Police," said the professor.

"Mr. Bengston," said Stummer, "do you own a black or dark blue van with the license number. TLP---"

"Discovered. I knew it would happen sooner or later. Yes, gentlemen, I'm your culprit."

Rask and Stummer exploded left and right, pulling their guns as they moved.

"Good heavens!" said Bengston, lifting both hands, palms out. "Don't shoot me!"

"Stand up!" said Rask.

"Yes, yes, of course. Just be careful with those guns. I didn't think you would take a little matter of trespassing so seriously."

"Step away from the desk! Put your hands behind your back!"

"I'm doing it. I'm doing it."

Rask snapped cuffs on the professor and shoved him around front of his desk and into a visitor chair while Stummer kept a gun on him.

"Wait! Wait! Why are you so angry? Let me explain!"

"Lyle Bengston, I'm arresting you for the murder--

"Murder!" Bengston shrieked. "This has gone entirely too far! You *will* explain yourselves or you will have the biggest lawsuit of your lives!"

"You just admitted you were guilty," said Rask.

"Not guilty of murder, you morons!"

Stummer pushed the door shut, and sat in a second visitor's chair, still keeping his Glock in hand.

Rask moved to sit in the chair behind the desk. "All right, let's have it. Yer not technickly under arrest at this time, but understand, you have the right to remain silent. Anythin' you say can and will be used against you inna court of law. You have the right to consult with a attorney and to have that attorney present during questionin'. If you cannot afford a attorney, one will be provided for you. Do you understand them rights?"

"My god," said Bengston, "do people still talk like you?" Rask glared. "Yes, yes, I understand my rights."

"Knowin' them rights, do you consent to answer questions for us at this time?"

"Yes, surely. This whole scene is ridiculous."

"What were ya doin' at Eleanor Roosevelt High School Monday mornin', July 19?"

"Nothing. I wasn't there."

"Yer van was seen there."

"No, it wasn't! Maybe someone saw *a* van, but it wasn't *my* van. Depending on what time of the morning, my van was either in my garage or the faculty parking lot."

"Yer van was seen near Founder's Park around midnight Sunday, July 25."

"That's not a question, but yes, it was."

"What were ya doin' there?"

"Cleaning up Founder's Park."

Rask wasn't expecting that. "Cleanin' up the park?"

"Yes. And the week before that, Feingold Men's Wear." Bengston tipped his head sideways and widened his eyes in an expression that clearly said, "How stupid are you?" Blank stares. "Badger Creek?"

'What the hell are ya talkin' about?" said Rask.

"You idiots, we're the Green Berets. If you've seen my van around on Sunday nights, it's because we're cleaning up eyesores."

"Who's this 'we?'" said Rask.

"Myself and eight senior students."

Stummer holstered his gun.

Rask stared at the professor a few moments. He thought they had caught the Encore Killer and he didn't want to lose that hope. "Let's have the whole story, an' it better be good."

"Humph! Not with these handcuffs on." Bengston slid forward in the chair and twisted so his hands cleared the arm rests. "Take them off or I start screaming for a lawyer."

Stummer got up. "Stand up." He patted Bengston down and then uncuffed him.

The professor sat back down, jaw dropped. "You thought I might have a firearm? You thought I was The Encore Killer! This is truly bizarre."

"All right," Stummer said as the professor slid back in the chair. "The Encore Killer drives a new black van. It was seen at the high school where Ms Storley and Officer Tufte were killed. A new black van was seen near Founder's Park, three blocks away, on the night Nicholas Ovolensky was killed. When we asked about your van, you said you were the culprit and you knew you would be caught eventually. That's what we know."

"Again, that's not a question, but never mind, I'll explain. At the beginning of summer session, some of my sociology students and I decided to try an experiment to see if we could change behavior and attitudes by conspicuous example. As super heroes with secret identities are very popular right now, we decided to act in the dark of night wearing identical concealing coveralls and masks. To make sure we got in the news, we always left a green beret and a note." He glared accusingly at Rask. "All we do is clean up unsightly environmental messes. The worst we could be accused of is trespassing. Or maybe stealing worthless trash. That's what I'm guilty of. That's what I thought you were here about."

"You got a list a' your student crew?"

"Certainly," Bengston said, standing up. "If I could get behind my desk?"

Rask didn't move. "I need to look in the drawers first."

"Whatever for?" said the professor.

Rask didn't answer. "Gun," said Stummer.

"Oh, really? Are police that suspicious?"

"Suspicious as hell," said Rask, sourly seeing what they thought was The Encore Killer now morphing into Mr. Clean.

"Yes, surely, you have my permission to snoop in the drawers."

Rask opened the drawers one by one. "Uh-huh," he said as he looked in the last one, "there's a gun in here."

"There is not!" the professor shouted.

Stummer put a precautionary hand on the butt of his gun.

Rask slowly reached in and pulled out a yellow plastic squirt gun.

"Dammit, you almost gave me a heart attack," the professor said, sitting down again. "I have a Sociology 101 section this summer. Some of our students are slow to mature."

Rask got up and changed places with the professor who consulted a thin ledger and started making a list.

"We need to look at your van," said Stummer.

"Yes, it's in the faculty lot, I'll take you there. Our uniforms, masks and clean-up tools are in it. I have to call and cancel my next class first." Checking his ledger, he punched a number on the phone, turned his back to the detectives and spoke softly into the handset. Finished with the call, he stood and handed Rask the list. "I would like to keep the experiment going as long as possible. Do you suppose you could keep this quiet?"

Rask smiled at him. A smile on Rask looked like a shark opening wide for a fat tuna. "I dunno, we gotta consider charges a' trespassin' and petty theft. I don't think you're off the hook yet." He looked at his partner. "You think he's off the hook yet, Bishop?"

"Oh, hell no."

* * * * * * * * * *

Four long corridors and two elevators later, they were still walking.

"Judas Priest! Do ya know where you're goin'?" said Rask.

"Confusing, isn't it?" said Bengston. "It's because the college rises with the bluffs. The layout is reasonably logical once you get used to it. Here we go," he said, pushing through a glass door onto a green area with benches. "The faculty parking lot is around the end of this building."

"Wait a minute," said Stummer, stopping. He pointed at a three-story building bounding the green area. "Isn't your office up there?"

"Yes."

"So why didn't we just come down and out that end?"

"Ah... well... to be truthful, I was killing time."

Both detectives looked at him with deep suspicion.

"You said you wanted to talk to the students involved in our project. Our class was about to start, so I called and had them dismiss the others and meet us at the van. I was giving them time to get there."

"Judas Priest!" said Rask.

"Why didn't we kill time sitting in your office?" said Stummer.

"If I had asked you to wait for ten minutes, would you?"

"No!" said Rask.

"That's why."

"Okay, let's get on with it," said Stummer.

"My achin' feet," said Rask.

They crossed the green area, rounded the corner of the three-story building, and faced a parking lot. At the close end was a dark van and in a precise rank behind it stood eight figures with their arms crossed across their chests--all in concealing navy coveralls, black boots, black gloves, green berets and clear plastic masks.

"Judas Priest!" said Rask, reaching for his gun.

"Rask!" said Stummer, grabbing his arm. "These are just kids, right Bengston?"

"Yeah, well, they look like a goddamned special ops team," said Rask.

"Yes, they're students, and you don't swear in front of them," said Bengston. As they walked closer, he said, "Unmask, please."

The row of figures pulled off their berets and masks and became a group of grinning students, delighted at having looked mysterious enough to cause a reaction. Five of them were young women. One slender male stepped forward confidently. "My name's Philip Antonis, I'm pre-law, and you can't question us without our parents and an attorney present."

"Your over 18, we don't need your parents," said Rask.

"You're not under arrest, you don't need an attorney," said Stummer. The two detectives exchanged delighted looks. "But you can have one if you want."

"What? What's so amusing about that?" said Antonis.

"Go ahead," said Rask, "ask for a lawyer, you pre-law moron. We'll be happy ta haul ya down to the station in handcuffs and let ya wait for one."

"You can't put us in handcuffs. That would be improper procedure."

"We know," said Rask. "N' after you'd sat in cuffs for hours before we cleared enough paperwork to find the time to let you make a phone call, your attorney would be screamin' and so would your arm sockets, and we would get our patties slapped for improper percedure."

"Seems a shame to go through all that instead of answering a few simple questions," said Stummer.

"Yah, well, morons is morons," said Rask, reaching around for his cuffs.

"What simple questions?" said Antonis.

"They thought we were The Encore Killer," said Bengston.

All five women shrieked in delight and crowded around the detectives, excitedly asking questions.

"Do we look that menacing?"

"Is The Encore Killer a bunch of people?"

"A woman?"

"Can we tell people we were suspects?"

"Hey!" said Antonis. "Will you get real? These guys are accusing us of murder."

"C'mon, Phil, lighten up," said a cutie in pigtails and freckles. "We aren't murderers."

"Think of it as a sociological experience," said another coed.

To a continuing chorus of questions, and underfoot curiosity, Rask and Stummer searched the van and each pair of coveralls. Eyeing the very brief summer attire the women wore under their coveralls, they wished they could pat their suspects down, but held off, it being worth more than a patty slap to do so. Names and addresses were taken; alibis for relevant murder times were taken. They all alibied each other, which is exactly what a group of killers would do, but the detectives didn't think it was much of an issue.

Eventually the students were obliged to leave for another class, still chattering excitedly about the experience. Rask and Stummer headed back for their vehicle, got lost several times in the college's corridors first, and then irately headed back downtown.

* * * * * * * * * *

Feeling better after a mid-afternoon snack of french fries and chocolate shakes, Rask and Stummer stepped out the front doors of the LEC. "Damn, for a while I thought we had something big there," said Stummer.

"Them get-ups are dangerous," said Rask. "If I looked out my window in the middle of the night and seen them, I'da taken a pot shot at 'em. No shit, it gave me the willies seein' 'em all lined up like that."

"Yeah. Startled me, too."

"Hey!" said Rask, "look what's comin' up the steps at us."

Standing in the shadow of a building across the street, Muggs, Laine and Kathy watched Martin and Big Erich start up the broad steps of the Law Enforcement Center. As the two men neared the top, two beefy detectives came through the doors and started shouting. They pulled their guns and shouted for Martin and Big Erich to get down. Uniformed officers arrived, the two street people were handcuffed, stood up and shoved into the building.

"C'mon," said Muggs, heading for the warehouse at a run. "We've got to get them out of there."

"How?" said Kathy, matching her speed.

"Beat 'em at their own game."

* * * * * * * * * *

"Okay, we're here," Stangler called to Rask as he and Middleton passed the detectives' room. "Bring 'em into Three." Interview Room Three was the largest, frequently used for depositions.

Stangler and Middleton stood waiting in Three until Rask and Stummer shoved the two homeless men in, their hands behind their backs.

"They're in cuffs?" said Middleton.

"Hey," said Rask, "until we figure out if they're half-wit loonies or goddamn psychos, I'm gonna keep 'em in cuffs."

Middleton started to laugh. "I don't believe it!"

"What the hell?" said Rask.

"What's so funny?" said Stangler.

Laughing, Middleton said, "Look at us! A big black guy and a short white guy facing a big white guy and a short black guy. We're a negative!"

Martin and Big Erich grinned broadly. Middleton brought himself down to diminishing snorts. The other three looked unamused.

"You told these gentlemen you know who the serial killer is," said Stangler.

"No, we didn't say that," said Martin.

"Close enough," said Rask. "Say what you said to me or I'll whack it outta ya."

"Rask!" said Stangler.

"Yeah, well, ya don't want to mess around with these loonies. Gotta let 'em know who's top dog."

"Do you know who New Guards is?" Stangler asked Martin.

"No, but we think we know what his motivation might be."

"And what is that?" asked Stangler.

"Considering where the words in the note came from---"

"And where is that?" said Stangler.

"The Declaration of Independence."

"We was right in the first place!" said Rask. "Total loonies. We'll get 'em outta here."

"Hang on," said Middleton. To the two men in cuffs, "Can you explain that?"

Martin turned and nodded at Big Erich, who said,

> *"'When a long train of abuses and usurpations, pursuing invariably the same Object evinces a design to reduce them under absolute Despotism, it is their right, it is their duty, to throw off such Government, and to provide new Guards for their future security.'"*

"That bullshit ain't in the Declaration a' Independence!" said Rask.

"Yes," said Middleton, "it is. And we never.... I feel stupid."

"When we realized the source of the killer's note," said Martin, "we used his motivation to guess who might be next. We had two guesses for victims and an intuitive guess at the next police target. It was just guesswork, and maybe we shouldn't have come in. But now, since Tuesday...."

"Oh, let me guess!" Rask said jeeringly. "Ovolenski was one a' your guesses!"

"Yes."

In the stillness that followed, an argument could be heard in the hallway, voices coming closer. The door was jerked open and Muggs stalked in on high heels. She wore a tailored suit, makeup, jewelry, tamed hair, and carried a leather briefcase.

"These gentlemen are my clients," she said angrily, handing Stangler a card. "Are they under arrest?"

"Uh, no," said Stangler. His thoughts were still locked on the implication of what Rask's homeless man had just said. Now suddenly the homeless man had a high-gloss lawyer?

Martin and Big Erich goggled at Muggs. The easy-going street person they knew had been transformed into a stylish professional--sophisticated and commanding.

"Then why the hell are they in handcuffs?" she said in a voice that carried outrage and the threat of dire consequences.

Stangler gestured for the cuffs to be removed.

Martin had all he could do not to laugh out loud. The carefree woman he had rifled trash containers with was now pushing these cops around like sheep.

Rask moved behind Martin and uncuffed him. Big Erich held his hands out in front of him, chain dangling from one of the cuffs. "Sorry. It was an accident."

"Judas Priest!" said Rask, looking up at Big Erich with squint-eyed assessment. He unlocked each cuff carefully, giving the impression that he was ready to leap back instantly.

"'Margaret V. Collins, Attorney at Law,'" said Stangler, reading the card she had handed to him. "Doesn't say that much."

"That's all it needs to say, Buddy! Gives you the name of the person who will be filing a false arrest and police brutality suit."

"Police brutality! We never touched 'em!" said Rask.

"Really," said Muggs in a deadly tone. "How many hours have they been in handcuffs?"

"That's different," said Rask, flustered.

"Uh-huh, we'll let a judge decide that," said Muggs. "My clients aren't saying another word. They're leaving with me, unless you're prepared to formally charge them. With *what* I don't know. Trying to do their duty as citizens?"

"What firm are you with?"

"I'm not with any firm. I have a few select private clients. Mr. Driver, Mr. Van Vorst, you're free to go now. Come with me."

"Wait a minute," said Stangler. "I need to talk to your clients."

"Huh! In handcuffs?"

"No. Any way they like. How can I contact you?"

"You can't. I'll call you. Maybe. Gentlemen, we're out of here." She motioned them to precede her, and then took the lead in the hall, her high heels clicking smartly on the tile floor, her attitude that of someone who could buy the place and tear it down if any part of it displeased her.

"Muggs---" said Martin.

"Save it!"

They moved quickly down one flight of stairs and out the doors of the LEC. A black stretch limousine sat at the foot of the marble steps, surrounded by people with microphones and cameras. Vans with satellite links stood in the parking lot, carefully not blocking access to the Law Enforcement Center. Laine in a chauffeur's uniform leaped out of the driver's seat, pushed his way forcefully through the bodies surrounding the car and opened a door.

Eager news people swarmed toward Muggs and her companions like iron filings to a magnet. "What's your name, Ma'am?" "Are you an attorney?" "Are these The Encore Killers?" "Are your clients under arrest?" "Isn't there enough evidence to hold them?"

Muggs and Martin dived into the car. A short, big-nosed reporter with bushy hair pushed himself forward to block the door opening, thrusting a microphone at Big Erich. "What's your name? Were you formally charged or just questioned?"

Big Erich reached forward, grasped him under the armpits, lifted, rotated, set him down out of the way and climbed into the car. Laine slammed the door.

* * * * * * * * * *

Looking out the window of Three, Rask said, "Sonofabitch! I don't understand any of this! Look at that. High-powered attorney. Limo. What the hell is going on? Honest to god, Lobo, they're homeless people!" He was red-faced and on the defensive.

"He's right, Lobo," said Stummer. "We've seen them on the streets picking up cans."

"Lobo!" shouted Emily from down the hall. "Lobo!" She rushed into the room. "I've found it! At last! 'New Guards' comes from the Declaration of Independence!"

"Yeah. Thanks, Emily," he said without turning.

"'Thanks, Emily?' 'Thanks Emily!' I've spent weeks reading thousands of web sites! I'm almost blind with eye strain, and for that I get 'Thanks Emily!'"

Stangler turned to her. "You're right, Em---"

"'Thanks, Emily!' Shoving all my regular work on the back burner for 'Thanks, Emily!'"

"I'm sorry I was insensi---"

"'Thanks, Emily!' Everyone else is on my case because I've been putting you first! For what? For 'Thanks, Emily!'"

"I'm a jerk, Emily. It was just that somebody already told---"

"Don't bother to explain! You're a jerk! That's all the explanation needed!" She turned and marched out the door with heels clacking on the tile floor, her attitude that of someone who wouldn't even bother to buy the place first before she blew it to smithereens.

"'Thanks, Emily!'" echoed back.

"I think I'm looking at weeks of flowers," said Stangler.

"Don't forget groveling," said Middleton.

* * * * * * * * * *

In the back of the smoothly moving limo, Martin and Big Erich faced Muggs.

"Are you really an attorney?" said Martin.

"Why do sharks never bite lawyers?" said Muggs.

"Professional courtesy. But Muggs...."

"Hey, didn't I say we all have pasts we don't like to talk about?"

Martin studied her thoughtfully.

"Oh, okay! I used to be an assistant DA in Minneapolis, but got sick of working my ass off only to see scumbags slide out on a technicality. I may have dropped out of the action, but I'm still a shark in good standing with the State Bar."

"You look beautiful," said Big Erich.

"Thanks. I do clean up okay, don't I? Silk purse from a sow's ear?"

"But the clothes, the car? How did you do it?" said Martin.

She turned red. "Kathy and I looked for your carton with the cash in. I hope that's okay. I can pay you back in installments if---"

Martin let himself have the first big noisy laugh he'd had in over a year. "I don't mind at all. The show was worth it! They're probably still standing there with their mouths open."

"The limo may have been overkill, but I didn't want to leave any doubts about messing with us," she said.

"Wanna go hit a couple dumpsters to celebrate?" said Laine.

"I'm afraid I'm not dressed for it, Bucko. I've got a little of Martin's cash yet; let's blow it on take-out pizza."

"Yee-hah!" said Laine, making a sudden left turn. "Life in the fast lane."

"We'll have to go back and talk to them, you know," said Martin.

"I figured," said Muggs. "But at least we'll do it on our terms, and they're going to be a helluva lot politer."

# # # # # #

Chapter 33: Afternoon, Thursday, July 29

Stangler sat on the stone rim of a band shell in a small town 12 miles south of Riverbend. At the edge of the park Middleton pulled over in an unmarked car and sauntered across the grass.

"No problems shaking the news gnats?" said Stangler.

"Nah. In one door and out the other. What's the difference between a crowd of reporters and a batch of yapping puppies?"

"I don't know. What?"

"Nothing."

"What did you find out?"

"Martin Driver was a wealthy big shot, sole owner of a consulting company. His wife and daughter were killed in a car crash about a year ago, after which he sold everything out and fell off the map. No record, not even a traffic ticket. Margaret Collins was a former assistant DA in Hennepin County. Quit five years ago, no record of public practice since then, no criminal record. Erich Van Vorst was a professional motorcycle racer, but hasn't been active in the past seven years. Couple charges of assault way back but dismissed as self-defense."

"So what does it look like happened?" said Stangler. "Maybe Driver met Collins five years ago when he had the consulting firm. And if the consulting firm needed a lot of legal work, maybe he hired her away from the DA's office with a private retainer deal. Then when his family was killed he switched into something else. Do we have any idea what else?"

"Couldn't find anything," said Middleton.

"But whatever it is, he kept Collins on retainer?"

"That's what it looks like," said Middleton, "but John and Bishop say they've seen them living on the streets. I don't think they'd be wrong about that."

A black limo pulled to the curb at the edge of the park.

Laine jumped out and opened doors. Muggs stepped out once again in suit and heels. Kathy, who had been petulant about being left out of the fun, now appeared in heels, hose, slim skirt, crisp white blouse, and carrying a steno pad. Martin and Big Erich wore their cleanest street clothes. The ladies led the way to a paved walkway, not wanting to sink their heels into the turf. Laine watched them go with grouchy resignation. He didn't disagree with the others' opinion that he might zone out in front of the cops, but he still wished he could hear what was going on.

"Riverbend cops at the bottom of their budget?" said Muggs critically as she brushed the dust off the low cement edge of the band shell and sat down. "Out-sourcing their meeting rooms?

The others followed suit, Kathy pulling a pen from the spiral of her steno book and flipping the cover.

"Damn reporters everywhere," said Stangler.

"This is Miss Nelson," said Muggs. "She'll take notes for me."

Middleton leaned in Kathy's direction and looked closely at her face. "You look familiar. Should I know you from somewhere?"

Kathy gave him a sideways look of disdain and didn't respond.

Stangler studied Martin curiously. "While we've been trying to identify the killer, you decided to identify the victim. Is that correct?"

"Yes," said Martin.

"Why? Why do any thinking about it at all? Are you involved in any way? A witness to something?"

Martin looked at Muggs. She thought briefly, then gave a short nod. Martin was planning to talk freely, but he and Muggs had devised this little interchange to reinforce the idea that he had legal protection.

"No reason," said Martin. "Erich recognized the quote and we simply got to tossing ideas around, as if it was a puzzle. We first came in to tell you where the quote was from, but when we got brushed off, we assumed you probably knew it already anyway."

"You came back," said Stangler.

"As I said, playing at the puzzle, not really at all seriously, we had predicted the next two victims," said Martin. "You have to realize we didn't want there to be another victim. Our greatest hope, along with everyone else in Riverbend, I expect, was that the police would catch the killer first. We were just thinking casually. You know, the way folks do when they watch the pageant and predict who they think will be the next Miss America."

"And?"

"When one of our choices turned out to be the next victim, we were afraid. Afraid not to come in would be obstruction of justice. Afraid coming in we would be taken for the killers."

"Are you the killers?"

"No!" said all four.

"Do you have alibi's for the times of the killings?

"Yes," said Muggs. "I, and these people, including our driver, were all together on each date and time in question."

"Doing what?" said Middleton.

"None of your business," said Muggs. "All you need to know is that we all alibi each other."

For a minute or two the detectives appeared to be considering where to go next. Kathy appeared to be adding to her notes.

"Now that we know the Declaration is the source," said Stangler, "we see what you were thinking. This guy, or woman, is wiping out people who take money from the government. Right?"

"I think there's more to it than that. Your killer isn't protesting the victim so much as the fact that the government *allows* the victim to take money he or she doesn't deserve *from the people*. There's also an element of being in the public eye. The victims were well-known."

Middleton said, "Maguire because he was the publicly visible head of a union that could legally wipe out a company and leave thousands of people without jobs. Goetzman because she had helped banks trash thousands of people's finances and could not be touched by law. Storley's union robbing the kids. Ovolenski because of the arts grant for crap."

Martin nodded.

"And cops are the hounds of the despotic government which allows this to happen," said Middleton.

"Yes," said Martin.

"You said Ovolenski was one of two choices," said Stangler.

Again the look from Martin to Muggs, and the nod. "Yes. We weren't exactly sure which, because both were a little outside of the parameters."

"You think your other guess is next?" said Stangler.

"Yes. We think---"

"Hang on," said Stangler. "Now that we know the source of the quote--for which we appreciate your help--we've been doing our own thinking along that line, and have come up with some 'possibles.' Let's see if our thinking lines up."

Martin nodded.

"We've come up with Chuck Bettendorf, the guy on the City Council who's voting development projects to his own company," Stangler said. "Or Marvin Ulland, with all the lawsuits for the highway construction mess or George Rampels, the go-for-the-jugular divorce lawyer. Is one of them your guy?"

"We thought of them," said Martin, "but we decided Arvid Haugen was more likely."

"Haugen? The tractor guy?" said Stangler. "They're just a bunch of farmers."

"Farm subsidies, crop price stabilization, and federal money for leaving fields fallow all keep prices high in the supermarket. And Haugen's leading a movement to get even more money from the government."

"Stick a fork in it; we're done," said Muggs, standing and brushing off her skirt. "Mr. Driver has done his civic duty and we're leaving."

"We might be more helpful if I could see your case files?" said Martin.

"Sorry, but that won't happen," said Stangler. "Don't think I'm not appreciative. You made a good guess, an intelligent guess, and I'm talking to you because you might make another good guess. But I don't dare even mention you to the higher-ups in the department."

"Let's go," said Muggs, heading for the steps.

"How can I reach you?" said Stangler.

"I'll call you," said Muggs.

"Not good enough. Give me a phone number."

"Maybe. I'll call you."

"You are an obstinate pushy woman."

"And you are a stiff-necked suspicious man."

"Suspicious is what makes me good at my work."

"Pushy is one of my charms." She headed down the walk, the others following.

"You like her," said Middleton, watching the homeless group get into the limousine.

"She's pushy," said Stangler. "Let's get back."

# # # # # #

Chapter 34: Afternoon, Friday, July 30

Boucher took the three steps up to the chancel, bent to flip down a small step behind the podium, and stepped up to slowly survey the mourners. Below him, Kaminski's coffin stood surrounded by flowers.

"The family of our beloved colleague, Ted Kaminski, has asked me, as his Chief, to say a few words about a man who was an outstanding police officer, yes, but much more than that," Boucher began.

"Letting him talk was their first mistake," Middleton muttered.

Media people duck-walked across the front of the nave, making a show of being inconspicuous, while holding a forest of microphones aloft toward the podium. Silent rubber-tired dollies with cameras trailing heavy cords rolled slowly up the center aisle.

Watching them out of the corner of his eye, Middleton said, "Letting them in was their second mistake."

"Our brother Ted was struck down by a vicious killer...."

"Is he going to mention the Declaration?" Middleton whispered.

"No. I drilled it into him. He says he won't."

"...protecting and serving his city, while evil minds used the tenets held sacred by our forefathers to..."

A buzz of whispered exclamations rose from the crouching reporters.

"...cannot mention while the investigation continues, but we all stand here to say that no individual citizen has the right to enforce historic documents..."

The forest of microphones thrust higher. Mrs. Kaminski leaned forward and spoke in low tones, waving they should move back to the side aisle. No one moved. "What historic documents?" rose in a loud whisper. Ushers moved to the front and tried to quietly urge reporters back. They held their ground. One bold woman stood up from her crouch and said at full volume, "What historic documents?"

Boucher stopped talking in open-mouthed surprise. The ushers changed tactics and tried to take microphones away. Remarks unsuitable for a church were heard. Losing patience, the ushers started grabbing and dragging reporters. Scuffles broke out, and then open fist fights. Bodies careened into the front pews, women screamed. Boucher shouted, "Please! Please! Show some respect!" A struggling pair thumped into the coffin, making it wobble on its bier. Uniformed police left their pews and started efficiently clearing the church of combatants and electronics.

"When the service is done," said Stangler, "grab Boucher and let's get him out a back door. He'll cause a riot if he goes to the interment."

"He kept his word," said Middleton. "He never actually *said* 'Declaration of Independence.'"

\#   \#   \#   \#   \#   \#

Chapter 35: Evening, Saturday, July 31

"I cannot adequately express how pleased I am with our success so far." Wilfred Burkhalter allowed himself a genuine smile. "Audra's... uh... Falcon's plan to always have a woman as part of the elimination pair was a stroke of genius. So far every event has gone smoother than we might have expected because the presence of a woman does not arouse suspicion in the target."

"Bravo, Falcon!" said Chris Frahdley, clapping his hands loudly.

"'*Brava*,' you idiot," Lawrence Madden snarled under his breath.

"Nor are we forgetting that you are single-handedly removing the police officers."

"Hounds," said Frahdley. "They are the hounds of the despot and we should call them hounds."

"Of course," said Burkhalter. "Hounds."

"That turned out to be the easiest part," said Cantrell.

"Credit where credit is due," said Burkhalter. "Getting that... uh... hound to come two blocks away from the Blue Ribbon yard was impressive."

"Perhaps," said Cantrell, maintaining a cool exterior. "Snagging one off the street in front of the artists store in broad daylight wasn't too shabby, either." She dropped the cool attitude and gave a little pleased laugh.

Burkhalter turned to Frahdley. "While I'm handing out kudos, Bear---"

"Yes!" said Frahdley, doing a fist jerk. He adopted a dramatic tone. "And the rest of us following along in the anonymous van... in our anonymous coveralls... ready to swoop in and pick up our point men.... Great, right? 'Mission Impossible.' Tump, tump, te tah tah; tump, tump, te tah tah!"

"Yes, an excellent backup plan."

"Are we sure we don't want lapel pins? Maybe with locators in them?"

"Oh, for Christ's sake," said Madden.

"No, Bear," said Burkhalter. He addressed the group. "Operations have been going like clockwork, without the necessity of meetings, but that brings up a question. Our plans being so well laid, Bear, why did you depart from them? The plan was to get Goetzman in her room."

Yeah," said Frahdley, "but I decided to improvise. The microphone cord was symbolic. You know, shutting off the lies of the despot by using their own device. I think it was deeply significant."

Burkhalter looked at Cantrell. She shrugged, rolled her eyes, and said, "We asked her to come down and approve of a different room arrangement if we had her back."

"Nevertheless, it was a departure from the plan," said Turner, staring at Frahdley.

"Jealous that you didn't think of it?" said Frahdley.

Madden leaned toward Burkhalter to say something, anger written on his face.

"And Storley?" said Burkhalter quickly, to forestall a scene.

"Nothing to it," said Frahdley. "Batter up. Pow! High and inside."

There was a sudden silence. The other faces around the table looked shocked.

"My God!" said Gregory Turner.

"Jesus Christ!" whispered Madden, leaning forward and glaring fiercely at Burkhalter.

"What? What?" said Frahdley.

Burkhalter looked pained. "We'll talk," he said to Madden. "Let it be for now. We'll talk." To Cantrell, "How did you get her into the classroom with Chris carrying a baseball bat?"

"Bear!"

"Bear."

"Our scenario was too contrived," said Cantrell. "She almost didn't buy it. We said our neighbor's kid was at camp. He had borrowed our cell phone and forgot it locked in his locker at the "Y." It was a new padlock, he hadn't memorized the combination yet, but he had written it on the underside of his homeroom desk. We'd know which desk was his because he had scratched the logo of his favorite baseball bat on the top of the desk. Hence the bat to match the logo."

"Not only would I not believe that story, I would be royally pissed to have to come back," said Gregory Turner.

"She was," said Cantrell.

"Snake," said Burkhalter. "You and Falcon have any trouble with Ovolenski?"

"No. Distasteful as hell, but no."

"You find shooting people 'distasteful?'" said Frahdley with a sneering tone.

"I find pretentious no-talent artists, disgusting photographs passing as art, and childish public relations people all distasteful," said Turner softly.

"Fine!" said Frahdley. "You can do the next one with a baseball bat."

"That's enough," said Burkhalter. "The choice of weapons was yours, Chris."

"Bear!"

"Moving along. We'll want to publish our manifesto soon. Naturally, we want to maintain that it is our right and duty to throw off the works of the government, but like our forefathers, we should enumerate the abuses we fight against. Let's come up with some issues that we might want to cover, then work individually on rough drafts."

Suggestions were thrown out.

"Bush getting us into a goddamn war."

"Handout programs for the stupid and lazy."

"Fewer laws. We have no real freedom."

"The slippery slope into Socialism."

"Socialism hell, Communism!"

"Eliminate the unintelligent, dependent and prejudiced."

"And homosexuals, polygamists, atheists, cults."

"Stop government support of the arts.

"Stop government support of anything!"

"All right," said Burkhalter. "Take those ideas and put your thinking caps on." He turned a page on a small memo pad. "Tomorrow is taken care of. You two are all set?" he said, looking at Cantrell and Madden and getting nods. "You located masks and hats like the Green Berets? he said, looking at Frahdley.

"Done for days," said Frahdley, patting his hands in a gesture of self-approval.

"Let's look at the next two weeks," said Burkhalter. "It's time to broaden our ideological scope and send a sharper message to the government. Now that we've tested ourselves and know we have a perfect strike team, I think we're ready to take out some high profile government employees."

"Tump, tump, te tah tah; tump, tump, te tah tah!" hummed Frahdley.

The others stared at him in silence.

#   #   #   #   #   #

Chapter 36: Evening, Sunday, August 1

John Rask sauntered along the line of tractors pulled over to the shoulder of the county road. "Riverbend, check in," he said. His ear bud came alive with voices. "Lavorski. Eleven. All okay." "Harders. Two. Nothing." "Spurgeon. Nine. Nothing." "Wilson. Twelve, close to Haugen. Looks okay." "Stummer. Way out on nine. Not a damn thing." "Okay," said Rask, "I'm out on three, headin' for center. Don't none a' you assholes get sloppy. Stangler, you hearin' us okay?"

"Loud and clear," said Stangler. Middleton had backed their unmarked into a small copse of trees at the end of an in-drive about one-fourth mile away. Both would have preferred to be on site, but doubted they could blend in as farmers.

"Sheriff's outposts, you gettin' all a' this?" said Rask.

"North can hear you," came back at him. Then, "South is good."

The tractor cavalcade led by Arvid Haugen had pulled over for the night with the drivers camped in a crop-less field that was part of the Federal Land Bank Program. Family members had come along for this first night in the fields and would return home in the morning, leaving the tractor drivers to continue their determined drive toward Missouri and then across the country to Washington. This first night, however, was like a big party. A large bonfire lit the faces of those gathered around it, some holding food on sticks or skewers, some hugging and slapping shoulders as though it was a reunion. Somebody's grandmother was moving around with a tray of coffee mugs. Men and women began to fan out from the fire, carrying sleeping bags and tent packs, looking for a place to settle for the night. Kids still ran in and out of everything, shrieking delightedly when they got too far from the bonfire and bumped into each other in the dark.

Riverbend police in lace-up boots, jeans, cotton shirts, denim vests and billed caps wandered through the site. Using the field's in-drive as a clock's center, they had a system for identifying their positions.

Rask passed a Featherlite trailer, satisfied he could hear no movement inside, where four uniformed officers and their motorcycles quietly waited. Passing center, he looked up the drive to see Haugen carrying an empty plate and holding forth to men with deeply-tanned and weather-roughened faces.

"America rides on the shoulders of the small farmer!" Haugen projected. There was a chorus of "Yeahs" and "You tell 'em!" Haugen was in his fifties, slender in the waist with broad shoulders. His looks were unremarkable, but his light-colored hair gleamed in the firelight like a halo, and his voice carried earnest conviction. "Your big conglomerates," he continued, "produce only 20% of what goes on the tables of the nation. Without small farmers, America would starve to death in two years!" Cheering, whistling and clapping erupted.

Suddenly in the dark beyond the fire's reach, a series of explosions erupted. Rask started to run toward the fire, reaching behind his vest for the concealed gun, when one of the fireside men shouted, "Dammit, Jason! I told you to leave them home!" "It's not me, Dad," said a nearby boy. Rask stopped and re-settled his gun. "Ah, crap, that means it's my two," said another farmer. "I'll get 'em to cut it out." He turned and walked into the darkness as a new series of explosions broke out. Rask turned away from the bonfire, facing the empty road. "Firecrackers," he said. "Kids with firecrackers. If you see any, take 'em away. But sound like parents, not cops, okay?" Brief acknowledgements sounded in his ear.

Middleton hit the brakes and quickly backed into the trees again. "Fooled me."

A car passed in front of Rask. The cavalcade was on a secondary road and although the traffic was light, the Sheriff's Department had established a presence at both ends of the parked tractors, stopping vehicles, vetting ordinary travelers who were allowed to continue through slowly, but turning back irate media. It was a precaution that would have been taken normally, and wouldn't appear suspicious.

Rask turned back to watch the crowd around the fire. On the other side he could see Wilson. Another man turned to Wilson and said something. He answered, but kept his eye on Haugen. "Yeah," Rask and everyone with an ear bud heard Wilson say, "my Dad still owns a 1948 John Deere A, and uses it, too. You just can't wear 'em out. Starts with only one spin of the crank."

"We've got a genuine farm boy passing as a farmer," Stangler whispered.

"Dang, we're good," said Middleton softly.

"Kill the conversation, Wilson," said Rask. He saw Wilson squat down to shift a branch in the bonfire, and the other man move off. Rask had avoided mixing in. He knew corn was supposed to be knee-high by the Fourth of July, and it was good to have deep snow cover to melt in the spring, but after that, he didn't know any farmer talk. He saw Wilson stand up and take a mug from the tray of the old lady, keeping it to a murmured "Thanks." She offered a cup to a tall thin farmer, who exchanged a few words with her, but declined coffee. She moved off toward the back of the crowd. Another burst of firecrackers went off somewhere in the dark.

Still holding an empty plate, Haugen was pulled aside by two farmers. Wilson threaded a little closer and Rask came halfway up the in-drive. The two farmers bent their heads toward Haugen and talked earnestly. Haugen nodded his head in vigorous agreement from time to time. Soon, one of the men gestured to the crowd around the bonfire and left as another came up to talk. Haugen was explaining something, making gestures with his right hand, left still holding his plate.

Rask relaxed a little, turning his attention to the crowd nearby, memorizing faces, looking for potential weapons. He could see Wilson was scanning around too. A dark shiny van passed, heading north. Rask looked closely, saw the plastic masks, green berets, and tipped a finger in an inconspicuous salute. The word had been passed to the Sheriff's deputies about the sociologists, and they had let the masked do-gooders through the checkpoint. He frowned thoughtfully. That could be confusing. They should get these college kids off the streets until they caught the other van. One lone firecracker went off. The two men left Haugen, and the tall thin farmer with hat pulled low against the brightness of the fire, approached Haugen, carrying a skewer loaded with chunks of meat and potatoes. Haugen smiled and held out his plate. The man came close, put a paper napkin on the plate, and slid the contents of the skewer on top of it. He put his hand on Haugen's shoulder and bent close to say something. Haugen let out a bark of a laugh. The tall farmer moved off. A moment later, Haugen bent his head, appearing to look closer at his plate. He bent farther over, watched his plate slowly tip until the food dropped off and the napkin fluttered down, bent farther

still as if to look at the food on the ground, folded his
knees, and dropped.

"What the hell!" said Rask as he ran toward the
fallen man. "Haugen's fainted!" said Wilson's voice in
his ear bud. The crowd was beginning to notice what
had happened. There were exclamations, but no one
moved for a moment. "Police," shouted Rask, holding
up his badge. "Don't anyone leave the area! Close off
the road! Cycles!"

Middleton shot out of the in-drive and down the
highway. At the sight of Stangler's badge held out the
window, the Sheriff's car, already blocking the road,
backed enough to let them get by.

The back gate of the Featherlite dropped and four
motorcycles roared out, took the ditch flying, and
headed for the back of the crowd.

Middleton jerked to a halt at the bonfire's in-drive
and the two detectives leaped out, leaving doors open.
Rask and Wilson were bending over Haugen, feeling
for a pulse. "CPR!" said Wilson, rolling Haugen on his
back, checking for a clear airway, pulling his jacket
aside, and feeling for a two-finger width above the
xiphoid process. "What's that!" he said as his fingers
hit something hard. A round chrome ring about the size
of a quarter stood firmly upright on Haugen's chest. He
reached for it. "Don't," said Middleton. "Don't pull it
out; you'll do more damage. Do breathing, but no chest
compressions." Wilson tipped Haugen's head back,
pinched his nostrils, and started puffing breath into his
lungs.

"What the hell is it?" said Rask.

"It looks like the handle end of a skewer," said
Middleton.

"A skewer? You mean like one a' them long
things they do shish-key-bob on?" said Rask. Then he
clapped his hand to his forehead. "Godammit to hell,

we saw it happen! That tall skinny asshole carried it
over full a' meat n' potatoes! N' then as cool as you
please, he slides the food on Haugen's plate and shoves
the thing inta his chest."

"Looks like straight into his heart," said
Middleton.

"Means medical knowledge?" said Stangler.

"At least some," said Middleton.

* * * * * * * * * *

Hours later the process was still in full swing.
Wilson and Stummer were at the south barricade, Rask
and Lavorski north. Stangler and Middleton were in the
field. Ear buds removed, everyone was working with
radios. Lights had been brought in and the spread of
sleeping bags, blankets, small tents, coolers, hibachis
and jerry-rigged latrines stood out in stark light and
shadow looking almost like a battlefield the day after.

People were questioned, their identities noted,
their movements recorded, and anything they witnessed
written down before they were allowed to move to their
vehicles. They were angered by having to leave all
their camping possessions in the field. They were
further incensed when they were held aside while their
vehicles were searched. Officers working the site had
sympathetic thoughts for the people working the
barricades. When people were finally allowed to drive
away from the field, they were going to go ballistic at
being stopped and made to go through the whole
process again. It was a precaution that had to be taken,
and there would be serious trouble for anyone whose
family members and answers were not identical at both
sites. At the barricades, any tall slender male would be
closely scrutinized by Wilson or Rask, and for good

measure he would be asked to remove his cap and hold for a digital photo.

When they first got to the north barricade, Rask and Lavorski found the roadway on the other side of the Sheriff's car clogged with news vehicles and a crowd of people shouting demands to pass, questions about what happened, and making attempts to sneak through the ditches.

"Hang on, I'm gonna break a few heads," said Rask, starting toward the crowd.

"Uh, Detective, why don't you let me handle this?" said Lavorski, quickly catching up. Rask shrugged, put his hands on his hips, and waited to see what would happen. Lavorski walked around the county car and stepped into the crowd. They shouted questions. He waited silently. Eventually they all fell silent.

"Ladies and gentlemen," Lavorski said. A thicket of microphones was thrust toward him. "We appreciate you trying to do your jobs, but it is against the law for you to obstruct traffic, create a disturbance that interferes with the progress of an investigation, or violate a crime scene. Now if you will all pull your vehicles and yourselves out of the roadway and keep the shouting down so we can hear, we will be happy to let you stay and observe. If anyone stands or parks in the roadway, shouts so we can't hear, or tries to go across the field, you will be arrested. Okay? Okay, let's clear the road."

While the news vehicles were being moved onto the shoulders of the road, Rask asked the two Deputies, "You see a dark van go through here, just before all hell broke loose?"

"Yeah," said Deputy Couts, a 30-ish man in good physical shape who kept his hair marine short, "they came in earlier and went out again. It was that bunch of green berets that have been in the news for awhile. We asked them if they were scoping out how big the clean-up job would be tomorrow, and they said yes, but sometimes they'd get a surprise and people would clean up after themselves so you never knew. They were the last to get through before we blocked the road."

The first car rolled up from the campsite, a woman driver with two kids in the back who hung out the window, shouting. "That's my Cub Scout tent! They can't keep it! I want my tent! I want my tent!" "I want my Barbie doll! I'm not leaving without my Barbie doll!"

"Would you and your children please step out of the car, Ma'am?" said Deputy Couts, shining a flashlight inside. "And open your trunk, please?"

"Not again!" she shrilled. "They've already done this down there! I absolutely refuse! This is police harassment; I'm going to call our lawyer! They just looked us over and the car! Why do we have to do it again!"

"Ma'am, you can be on your way much sooner if we can make short work of this."

"Oh, for cri-eye!" she said, thrusting the car into park and popping the trunk. "Out, kids," she said, opening the back door for the kids to get out. The Cub Scout lit running, across the road, and down the ditch. "I'm gonna get my tent!"

"Get my Barbie," shouted the little girl.

"Jeremy, you get back here, right this minute! You're going to get lost in the dark!"

"Are they harassing you, Ma'am?" came a shout from the other side of the county car where a redhead with a microphone was leaning across the top, thrusting it forward. "What's your name? Can you give us a quote?"

"I figured there'd be someone to test things," said Lavorski, looking at Couts. "Can you give me a hand?"

They circled the county car, took the microphone away from the redhead, who reached up and scratched Couts across the face. Grabbing her arms, they cuffed her, and put her in the back of the county car.

"You can't do this!" she screamed. "I have First Amendment protection! You dick heads will have the biggest lawsuit you've ever seen!"

"Yes, Ma'am," said Deputy Couts. "You be sure and tell your attorneys to add assaulting an officer to their list of problems."

Lavorski looked at the microphone he was holding, which had a colorful plaque reading, "KLAC." In the light from the stopped vehicle's headlights, Lavorski walked down the roadway looking at the vans pulled over on the shoulder. When he got to one emblazoned "KLAC," he pointed at it. If this van is not out of here in three minutes, we'll call a tow and impound it."

Muffled shrieks of protest came from the back of the county car. Two men carrying cameras separated themselves from the sidelines and walked disgustedly toward the van. Lavorski handed them the microphone as they passed.

"You got your cuffs?" Lavorski asked Couts. Holding the cuffs high, Lavorski said, "Now where's that kid that was going to violate a crime scene?"

"Maaaaa!" cried Jeremy as he tore his way back up the side of the ditch and flung himself against his mother. Rask saw her put her hand over her mouth to hide a smile.

The identification and search process went quickly after that. The county car was pulled back to let her pass. Once through, she shouted out her window, "I'll pull over down the road a ways."

The entire media crowd ran after her. Silently.
On the shoulder.

With all the people sitting in their cars or on their
tractors, waiting to be checked and sent on their way,
officers on the periphery began to play their flashlights
over the camp site.

"Crime Lab's going to be here forever," said
Middleton. "Think I should call in and tell them they
need more people?"

"Huh," said Stangler, "and have Surecock Holmes
have a hernia for us presuming to do his job? He'll be
rabid as it is that we slid the note out of the napkin."

Time passed while the farm vehicles diminished
and flashlights probed the site. Every now and then an
officer would shout, "Hey, what's that?" Flashlights
would zero in on his, and someone would shout, "Just a
big cooler."

Middleton's phone vibrated. "Middleton. Hang
on, I'll ask." To Stangler, "Dispatch. Mayor Duponte is
summoning you to an 8:00 a.m. meeting."

"Gimme that phone," snarled Stangler.

"Uh, uh, uh," said Middleton, lifting it away.
"There's a reason they call me, you know." Into the
phone he said, "Extend our apologies to the Mayor, but
we will still be held up at the crime scene at that time."

"Coward."

"No, nice. No need to take it out on Dispatch."

More time passed.

"Hey, what're those?" asked one of the officers.
Multiple flashlights homed in on the spot. "It's a tray,
and a bunch of ceramic mugs. Someone must have
dropped them when things happened. Maybe tripped
over that big pile of blankets?"

"That's odd," said Middleton.

"Maybe," said Stangler, pulling his radio. "Hey
Rask?"

"Yeah?"

"Did you see anything like a tray and a bunch of mugs before?"

"Yeah. Somebody's gramma was walkin' around passin' out coffee."

"Has she passed you guys yet?"

"Not yet," radioed Rask. "We only got three vehicles left. Hang on, I'll take a look. Nope. She musta gone south."

Middleton's phone vibrated. "Middleton. Yes, sir. ... Yes sir. ... We understand that, sir. ... We have a large crime scene and a large crowd of witnesses, sir, and Crime Lab hasn't arrived yet. We can't suspend the investigation for meetings right now. Please give our apologies to the Mayor. We can probably make a 1:00 meeting." He clicked off. "Boucher."

Stangler held his radio up again. "Wilson, are you there?"

"Yessir."

"What do you know about a tray full of ceramic mugs?"

"An old lady was passing coffee in mugs on a tray."

"Has she passed you yet?"

"No, and we're on our last car. She must have gone north."

"What did she look like?" said Stangler.

"Well... short, white hair, humped over, couldn't see her face, dress, apron, couple layers of sweaters, moved arthritically."

Stangler looked at Middleton. "Ah, man, you don't suppose when the crowd started to panic...?" He thumbed his radio. "Everyone focus on that big pile of blankets near the mugs. We've got a missing old lady."

Flashlights moved over the spot. Positions were changed. Flashlights from a different direction. "Hey! That could be a body under the blanket!"

"All right," radioed Stangler. "Everyone hold your positions. We're coming around."

A voice on the radio said, "There are tarps in the Featherlite."

"Good man!" said Stangler.

"Woman," said the radio.

Moving at a trot and carrying folded tarps, Stangler and Middleton made a wide circle of the camp site toward where most of the flashlights were being held.

Stangler stopped when his phone vibrated. "Stangler. No! Now get off the goddamn phone and let us do our job!" He smiled at Middleton. "See? Nothing to it."

"Duponte?"

"In full shriek."

Approaching a dark figure with a flashlight, Stangler said, "Okay, what are we looking at?"

"Right there," said the dark figure, moving his flashlight beam back and forth on a long pile of blankets that could possibly be covering a body.

"Bishop. Didn't recognize you in the dark," said Stangler. "Let's get in there quick. Maybe she's just hurt."

Determining the shortest clear way in, stepping on tarps, Stangler, Middleton and Stummer moved toward the old woman as fast as they could. Stangler squatted and with a latex glove on his right hand reached for a corner of the blanket,. "We're the police, Ma'am. We're here to help." He pulled the blanket aside.

"That's not a woman!" said Stummer. "Is it a farmer?"

"Officer Spurgeon," said Middleton.

"Ah, goddammit!" Stangler said, lurching up and away a few steps. "Goddammit to hell!" he shouted at the night sky.

#   #   #   #   #   #

Chapter 37: Noon, Monday, August 2

(Theme Music:)
(Voiceover:)
THIS IS KRBM-TV, NEWS AT NOON. UP
TO THE MINUTE REPORTING ON WHAT'S
HAPPENING IN THE RIVER LAND WITH NOON
NEWS ANCHOR SALLY FELDNER.

(Anchor:)
GOOD NOON TO YOU, MONDAY, AUGUST 2.

THE ENCORE KILLER HAS STRUCK FOR A
FIFTH TIME. LATE LAST NIGHT, CHARISMATIC
ARVID HAUGEN, SPEARHEAD OF THE
TRACTOR CAVALCADE TO WASHINGTON, WAS
FATALLY STABBED AT THE GROUP'S FIRST
STOP. RIVERBEND POLICE INVESTIGATORS
ARE NOT RELEASING ANY INFORMATION AT
THIS TIME, BUT OTHERS AT THE CAMP SITE
SAY HE WAS STABBED WITH A COMMON
BARBECUE SKEWER IN FRONT OF OVER 30
WITNESSES, INCLUDING POLICE OFFICERS
POSING AS FARMERS. MEMBERS OF THE
CAVALCADE HAVE RETURNED TO THEIR
FARMS, AND THERE IS NO TALK AT THIS TIME
OF CONTINUING THE DEMONSTRATION.
....
AT THE SAME SITE, THE BODY OF POLICE
OFFICER ROY SPURGEON WAS FOUND,
ALLEGEDLY SHOT IN THE BACK OF THE HEAD.
A POLICE OFFICER HAS BEEN TRAGICALLY
SLAIN AT THE SITE OF EVERY ENCORE
ATROCITY. RIVERBEND CITIZENS, NOW

CARRYING ARMS IN THEIR NEIGHBORHOOD
WATCH PATROLS, ARE ASSUMING POLICEMEN
REPRESENT THE "HOUNDS OF THE DESPOT"
MENTIONED IN EACH NOTE CLAIMING
RESPONSIBILITY. OFFICER SPURGEON WAS
UNMARRIED. LATER THIS WEEK HIS BODY
WILL BE ESCORTED BY A POLICE HONOR
GUARD TO FAIRMONT, WHERE HE WILL BE
INTERRED IN THE FAMILY PLOT.

....

IN ANOTHER UNRELATED DEATH, THE BODY
OF CHRISTOPHER T. FRAHDLEY, WELL-KNOWN
PUBLIC RELATIONS CHAIRMAN FOR OUR
LADY OF HOPE HOSPITAL, WAS FOUND IN HIS
MANGLED CAR NEAR THE BOTTOM OF
DAKOTA BLUFF. ACCORDING TO SHERIFF
NOLAN, FRAHDLEY'S BLOOD ALCOHOL LEVEL
WAS .12, WHICH IS ABOVE THE PERCENTAGE
FOR LEGAL INTOXICATION. EVIDENCE AT THE
SITE INDICATES THAT FRAHDLEY MAY HAVE
MISCALCULATED THE CURVE AND BROKE
THROUGH THE GUARDRAILS. WE HAVE NO
FURTHER INFORMATION AT THIS TIME.

....

MAYOR RONALD DUPONTE'S PRESS
CONFERENCE, SCHEDULED FOR 10:00 O'CLOCK
THIS MORNING HAS BEEN POSTPONED UNTIL
3:00 O'CLOCK. AT THAT TIME, KRBM WILL
HAVE MORE INFORMATION ON THE
INVESTIGATION INTO THE ENCORE KILLER.

....

RIVERBEND'S GOOD WORKS GREEN BERETS
APPEARED AGAIN SUNDAY NIGHT, AT THE
INLET ON THE SOUTH END OF LOGAN DRIVE,
WHERE RESIDENTS HAVE BEEN COMPLAINING
ABOUT A MASSIVE ACCUMULATION OF

DETRITUS THROWN OFF HOUSEBOATS. THE
SELFLESS ACTIONS OF THIS GROUP ARE
STARTING TO SEND A MESSAGE TO
RIVERBENDERS--PITCHING IN AND CLEANING
UP GETS FAR BETTER RESULTS THAN
COMPLAINING.

....

WE'LL BE RIGHT BACK WITH "WINDY"
WINDHORST AND THE WEATHER. "WINDY"
WILL TELL US WHAT TEMPERATURES WE CAN
EXPECT FOR THE COUNTY FAIR.

#   #   #   #   #

Chapter 38: Early afternoon, Monday, August 2

Stangler unlocked the front door to his house. He didn't have much time; Wiley had dropped him off long enough for the two of them to change the clothes they'd been in all night and morning. Even though he was in a rush, he quickly went to the kitchen and gave the old cabinets a smile. After they caught the New Guards he was going to talk to Lucy Lundquist about kitchens.

Heading for the stairs, his glance picked up on the door to the large room at the back of the hall. The previous owners had used it as a bedroom. He was thinking it would make a good home office. If he ever married, he was sure she would be a professional woman--one with her own career who wouldn't hang around home complaining about the long hours cops worked.

He took the stairs two at a time, hurrying to be changed by the time Wiley came back. They had reports they had to get on top of, and no doubt they would have to deal with Duponte.

* * * * * * * * * *

"How dare you! How dare you!" shouted Ronald Duponte rushing into the detectives' room shortly after Stangler and Middleton returned. "Do you realize who I am! Do you have any idea how close you are to being fired!"

Caught standing, the two detectives turned to face the onslaught of temper. The other detectives, having just come in for an after-lunch message check, were a surprised audience.

"When I say 'come,' you come! Do you understand that!"

"Mayor Duponte," said Pickett's voice behind him, "if you have problems with the investigation, proper procedure would be to go through me."

"To hell with that noise!" said Duponte, not turning. "I want obedience! And I want information *now*, or I'm going to string this hippie up by his gonads!"

"Ronnie, are you sure you want to be doing this?" said another voice.

Duponte turned to see Captain Pickett, Chief Boucher, and City Council Chairman Vernon Jacoby. "Vern!" said Duponte. Smiling broadly and slipping into a genial tone, he moved over to shake Jacoby's hand. He ignored Boucher.

"What's the problem, Mayor Duponte?" said Pickett.

"I sent three messages to this... this... detective," he spat the word, "telling him to report to me at 8:00 this morning, and he refused!"

"Is that true, Stangler?" said Pickett.

"Yes, Sir."

"And why did you refuse?"

"We had two dead bodies, over 200 witnesses who were also potential suspects, not enough lights, and Crime Lab hadn't arrived yet. We needed every hand we had. I couldn't leave the crime scene."

"What did you need him for, Ronnie?" asked Jacoby.

"I had a press conference scheduled for 10:00 o'clock, and I needed information," said Duponte in a surly voice.

Somewhere in the room a smothered squeak cut off a laugh.

"Well! Well!" said Boucher brightly. "He's here now, and I'm sure he'll be happy to give you the information you need. Won't you, Detective Stangler?"

"No."

A quiet snort was heard. A cough covered something.

"Why do you say that, Detective?" said Jacoby.

Looking around, Duponte said, "Vern, perhaps we should take this elsewhere. Someplace more private."

"I agree this is not a good place to air a problem, Ronnie, but you chose it," said Jacoby. Turning to Stangler, he said, "Why will you not give information to Mayor Duponte."

"What the public knows, the killer knows," said Stangler. "To catch him we need to keep some things back. Mayor Duponte has been accessing our files and releasing all information to the media."

"Ronnie?" said Jacoby.

"I most certainly.... The public has a right to.... It is in the best interests.... The people look to me to...."

"What were you planning to say at your 3:00 o'clock press conference?" said Pickett.

"Well... I... ah...."

"These folks have a spokesperson, Ronnie," said Jacoby, clapping the mayor on the shoulder. "Why don't we cancel any administrative press conferences and let them do it their way. I haven't had lunch yet, how about you?"

"Lunch! Fine. Good."

As they turned to leave, Jacoby stopped and patted Boucher on the shoulder. "Unauthorized access of police files is a serious issue, Jimmy. Why don't you check and make sure we don't have any more problems in that area?"

The laughter held until elevator doors had closed on Duponte and Jacoby, and Boucher had hurried back to his office.

"Way to go, Hippie," said Pedersen.

"My life is complete, I can now retire," Stummer laughed.

"I didn't see you saying anything," Stangler growled at Middleton.

"I was afraid he was going to bite," said Middleton, laughing.

"Okay, I know you're all busy; quick, down and dirty, Lobo, what have we got?" said Pickett.

"Haugen had a skewer thrust directly into his heart, which suggests medical knowledge, by a tall thin male. Spurgeon was shot in the back of the head by a little old lady."

A surprised reaction broke out.

"Hey!" said Rask. "Wilson and I saw her up pretty close. It was a little old lady, I kid you not."

"The getaway van was rolling before Haugen hit the ground---"

"Went right past my damn nose," said Rask.

"... and the Deputy at the road block thought it was this Green Beret bunch and let them through, seconds before Rask called for a blockade. Can someone get to this Professor Bengston and ask him to suspend operations until we catch these guys?"

"We'll do it," said Rivera.

"Wait a minute. Bunch?" said Pedersen.

"The deputy says there were four of them. We don't have a serial killer; we have serial *killers*. Damn! What we have is a serial vigilante group."

# # # # # #

Chapter 39: Morning, Tuesday, August 3

"These air mattresses are making us soft," grumbled Kathy.

"You can go back to your nice cozy hard ground if you don't mind being picked up by those two Gestapa-Tubbies," said Muggs, hunched over a chess board with Martin. "These pieces are in cruddy shape; they'll hardly stand."

"Miranda would chew on them when she was first learning."

"Your daughter?"

"Yes."

"When did she first learn?"

"She was five."

The deep throb of the theme music from "Jaws" sounded.

"That's the new phone I used for Sober Stangler," said Muggs not moving to get it.

"Sober Stangler?" said Martin.

"Even sharks smile sometimes, Kiddo," she said, standing up, "but not him. I'll take a little run and call him back from somewhere along the river."

"You think they got the technology to track your phone?" said Laine.

"Don't know, but I'm not taking any chances. A chicken only crosses the road when there's nothing coming."

Big Erich silently rose to follow her.

They heard the lower door close and the lock thump. Laine slipped into Muggs' chair. "So. This is pretty much like checkers, yeah?"

"Martin?" said Kathy.

"Yes?"

"What did you do with all your money?"

"Set up some scholarships, some long-term investments, threw the loose ends in the box."

"My parents have all mine."

"Did you have money?" said Martin.

"I guess. All those endorsements and stuff."

"Do you think it's gone, or put away for you somewhere?"

"I don't know," said Kathy. "I don't care. I just wanted to get away."

"We'll have to form a club," said Martin.

"So this horse can go one, two, this way, and then one this way, right?" said Laine.

* * * * * * * * * *

"They'll be along in about two hours," said Stangler.

"I can't get that secretary out of my mind," said Middleton. "I'm certain I've seen her before. Nelson.... Nelson...."

"Mark this date on the calendar," said Stangler. "The great brain known as William Edward 'Wiley' Middleton is having trouble with a name."

* * * * * * * * * *

"Hooray! I get to be Miss Nelson again!"

"Hooray," said Muggs flatly, "I get to wear these damn high heels again."

"In a covert operation, a soldier does what he has to do," said Laine, pulling his chauffeur's uniform off the hanger.

Kathy looked at him sharply.

"Oh, knock it off. I was just making a joke," said Laine.

* * * * * * * * * *

The limo moved its way slowly through the media crowd that immediately surrounded it in front of the LEC.

"Can I run over a few toes?" said Laine.

"No!" said Muggs. "And once we're out, keep the doors locked, the windows up, and do not answer any questions."

"Can I give them the finger?"

"No!"

With Big Erich in the vanguard, the homeless group made its way to the doors of the Law Enforcement Center, Muggs snapping, "No comment" repeatedly.

Coming off the elevator on the second floor, they spotted Rask and Stummer standing in the hall outside the conference room, gesturing them in that direction.

"Gestapa-Tubbies on the horizon," muttered Muggs.

The group was in the conference room, which was a definite step up from Interrogation Three, but after 20 minutes, that was the only good news. Stangler needed definite information, which Martin was unable, or unwilling, to give. Their interchange was punctuated by hostile remarks from Rask, and acid responses by Muggs.

Furious at getting nowhere, Stangler thumped the table with his fist, shot out of his chair, and stood with his hands clenched in front of him as though looking for something to hit.

Muggs jumped up. Big Erich rose to his feet. Kathy pushed away from the table, clutching her steno pad to her chest. Rask and Stummer came slowly out of their chairs, eyeing Big Erich, poised to move. Martin hung his head.

"You were right about Ovolenski," growled Stangler. "You were right about Haugen. Why can't you tell me who's next!"

Muggs dropped into her chair. In an unusually soft voice, full of understanding for his frustration, she said, "Because he doesn't *know* who's next. Those were just lucky guesses."

Stangler stared at her in surprise.

"Well let him lucky guess again!" said Rask, still on his feet.

"Give me a break!" snarled Muggs, back in shark mode, "Why don't you ask for the next winning lottery number!"

"You know, you might be attractive if you didn't have that smart mouth," said Stangler.

"Yeah? And you won't be such a pretty boy if I knock a few teeth down your throat!"

They glared at each other.

Middleton cleared his throat. "Why don't Mr. Driver and I talk?"

"Don't stop them now," said Stummer. "It was just getting good." He and his partner eased to their seats when they saw Big Erich return to his chair.

"Mr. Driver," said Middleton, "can you tell us how you arrived at your other guesses?"

"Well," said Martin, flicking a glance at Muggs, who nodded, "in my former... employment, we believed that to stay on top of the competition, you had to imagine what that competition might do to steal your customer base. I just imagined I was the killer, and what I would do to... stay on top of the game." He cleared his throat. "I had to factor in recklessness and no concern for human life, of course."

"And you don't think you can do that now?" said Middleton. "What you are actually doing is profiling, and like only a few specially-trained FBI agents, you're very good at it."

"I don't know a particular victim, but if I were the killer, after five successful... demonstrations... I would be thinking of ramping it up."

"Ramping it up?"

"Maybe targeting social issues, something the moral majority would approve of. Maybe selecting a law enforcement person with more status. Maybe going public with my beliefs."

"You think there are some homicides the moral majority would approve of?" said Middleton.

"Not openly, no. But certainly with less public outrage."

"So who are you thinking?" said Stangler.

"Sorry. I have no idea."

"What'd I tell ya?" said Rask. "Bunch a' bullshit. These guys don't know anythin'."

"If I could see your files---" said Martin.

"Sorry," said Stangler.

"We would be out of a job if we did something like that," said Middleton.

"Okay, that's it," said Muggs, standing. "Needless to say, we haven't enjoyed this."

"Thank you for coming in, Ms Collins," Middleton said, as everyone else in the room stood.

"Is it 'Miss' or 'Mrs.?'" said Stangler.

"None of your damn business," snapped Muggs, leading the exit of her street people.

* * * * * * * * * *

"I'd like to take that long-haired jerk and... and... do something that would wipe that smirk off his face!" said Muggs as the limo pulled out into the street.

"He doesn't smirk, he scowls," said Kathy.

"Behind that scowl he's smirking."

"Where to?" said Laine.

"Let's go to a computer store," said Martin.

"All right!" said Laine.

Muggs frowned at Martin. "Are you planning to look at files that cocky bastard said you couldn't?"

"Yes."

"Good! But let's change cars first."

"I wish we could have helped him," said Martin. "If I was a cold killer and wanted to get rid of some sort of socially unacceptable element in Riverbend, what would it be?"

"Little kids in restaurants," said Muggs carelessly.

"Drunks?" said Kathy.

Big Erich shrugged.

"Faggots," said Laine.

Martin and Muggs exchanged shocked looks. "Uh... Laine?" she said.

"Yeah, yeah," came from the driver's seat. "Gay persons."

"Still, though..." Muggs raised her eyebrows at Martin.

"Call him," said Martin.

"I'd rather cross the Mojave without a canteen," she said, handing the phone to Martin.

* * * * * * * * * *

"They're thinking homosexuals," said Stangler, hanging up the phone.

"Holy cow, I've got it!" said Middleton, smacking his forehead. " She's Kathy Nelson! She won an

Olympic gold medal in gymnastics when she was
fourteen."

#   #   #   #   #   #

Chapter 40: Afternoon, Wednesday, August 4

The table had been moved closer to a wall and was almost hidden in wires and computer equipment. Two screen modules sat at either end, back-to-back. Laine had climbed a nearby telephone pole and spliced them into a cable system.

"Dueling hackers," said Laine happily as he and Martin began working their keyboards.

"Will you look at this!" said Martin, reading his screen.

"Wait a minute, this isn't going to work," said Laine. "We're gonna be hopping up and down all the time."

They moved equipment around until they were sitting side-by-side.

"Much better," said Laine. "You into the police files? What have we got?"

"It isn't one killer; it's a group of people! Four at least. One is a tall thin male, and one is a little old lady?"

"You sure you're reading that right?" said Laine.

"Maybe not. Let's start from the beginning and read everything."

Hours later, Martin stretched and looked around. "Where is everybody?"

They heard the downstairs door close and Muggs came up the steps.

"Where've you been?" said Martin.

"Out having a smoke."

"Where's Kathy?" said Laine.

"She had cabin fever and went to find a playground with monkey bars. Big Erich went with her."

"Okay," said Laine, and turned back to his keyboard.

"Let's start thinking of everything we know they're not, and start narrowing the possibilities," said Martin.

"For instance?"

"They always hit on the weekend, so they probably have regular jobs. That eliminates the unemployed, the self-employed, homemakers, and anyone getting Social Security."

"What about that little old lady?" said Laine.

"That's got to be wrong, don't you think?"

"Yeah, I do."

They hunched over their keyboards and began working.

"You guys hungry? I can make sandwiches," said Muggs.

"That's fine," said Martin, fingers busy, not looking up.

"Or I could set the place on fire."

"That's fine."

"I'm going outside for another smoke."

"That's fine."

* * * * * * * * * *

"John, you and Bishop get those two who own the candy store out at the mall," said Stangler.

"Dammit, here we go with squirrels again," said Rask, stretching his arms across his desk in a pleading gesture. "These guys are real homos, right? I'm not gonna get a big embarrassin' surprise again, am I?"

"They're gay and make no bones about it," said Stangler. "Quit bellyaching, you get to spend Sunday in a candy store."

"Carmen and Brittany, you get the lesbian lady preacher and her significant other."

"Jim and Lu, the decorator and his partner."

"How do we know one of these is the target?" said Rivera.

"We don't," said Stangler. "The homeless guy is just profiling and could be wrong. These three couples have been in the papers off and on for both their professions and their lifestyles, so they're conspicuously gay. Again, we could be missing someone. I know it's a crap shoot, but it's the best we've got right now."

"The plan is that between now and Sunday you make these people aware of our suspicions, and then come Sunday you stick to them like burrs," said Middleton. "Questions?"

"What if they don't want us around?" said Pedersen.

"Talk them into it," said Stangler. "Be as charming as hell." He looked at Rask and Stummer with resignation. "Make a big effort."

* * * * * * * * * *

"Would you like some more tea?" said Jessie Bowalter, rising from her chair. She was a plump, 50-ish lady in a floral print dress, with a soft voice.

"I'm fine," said Rivera as Olson shook her head "no."

"We need more cookies," Ms Bowalter said, grabbing up a plate still half-full and disappearing into the kitchen.

Her partner, a stocky woman with short black hair, wearing men's black oxfords, men's dress pants, and a lemon yellow dress shirt, rose from her chair and paced as she talked. When she was sitting, it wasn't noticeable, but standing revealed a very round broad bottom that was not flattered by the cut of men's pants.

"I understand what you've explained," she said, addressing the two detectives sitting side-by-side on a love seat, "I'm just summarizing. You have a profiler who guesses--guesses!--that the next victim of The Encore Killer will be a homosexual person. Jessie and I are one of a few high-profile gay couples in town, and so one of us may be a target. Come Sunday, the day he always kills on, you two are planning to act as bodyguards to the two of us. That, in brief, is the situation, am I right?"

"Yes," said Rivera.

"I don't think so," said Reverend Edwina Gossley of the New Hope Christian Church.

"You don't think what?" said Rivera.

"Here we are," said Ms Bowalter, bustling in, "cookies so fresh they're still warm." She put the plate on the coffee table and sat down.

"I don't think we need, or even want, bodyguards. No one is going to consider killing a preacher, even a lesbian preacher. We're two dowdy old ladies. There would be no fun in it." She turned to her companion. "Jessie, I'm declining their protection. Are you okay with that?"

"Whatever you say, Ned."

"There! All settled. Thank you for the kind offer, but we think it would be a waste of your time."

"Reverend Gossley," said Rivera, "don't you owe it to your parishioners to keep safe for them?"

"No, I owe it to God to do Her bidding. If She wants me dead, I will be dead."

"But God gave us intelligence and free will. Surely God doesn't expect us to willfully risk... God's most precious gift, our lives." Rivera was avoiding the pronoun issue.

"Of course not. It would be a sin for me to step in front of a speeding train or walk too close to the edge of a cliff. But to hide from what plans She may have for me, to use bodyguards, is willful negation of Her grand plan. I'm sorry, we're having none of it."

"Take a couple cookies with you," said Jessie.

#   #   #   #   #   #

Chapter 41: Evening, Saturday, August 7

A wolf whistle greeted Amarantha as she sailed into the detectives' room early Saturday evening. She smiled and acknowledged the compliment with twiddled fingers at Jim Pedersen. Tall and shapely, she wore a short white deep-necked dress that set off her chocolate skin. Its little bugle bead dangles shimmied and danced as she moved and seemed to be telegraphing, "Hey, look me over!"

"If some asshole shoots Wiley," said Stangler, "will you marry me?"

"I certainly would, Sugar, except my mama told me I should never take up with any man who couldn't look me straight in the eyes, and you can only look me straight in the elsewhere."

"You have a very nice elsewhere."

"Better stop there or you're going to get hurt," said Middleton.

"You going to rough me up, Wiley?"

"Me, violent? Heaven's no. But Amarantha will fold you like a pretzel if you get too smart."

"Story of my life," said Stangler. "Are we off?"

"Let's go out the front door," said Amarantha, "I want to see myself on TV."

* * * * * * * * * *

The Blue Moon nightclub was packed, thick with people sitting and those willing to stand for its annual variety show with female impersonators. Folding chairs filled the dance floor, facing a stage big enough for five-piece bands, but not much more. The bar had people three deep waiting to give their orders. Servers garbed in harem attire, the men with bare chests and earrings, the women with bare bellies and veils across their faces, wedged their way carefully through the press, delivering drinks.

Stangler, Middleton, and Amarantha eased their way through the crowd, heading for the chairs, looking for Molly Palmquist. Jason had sent them tickets and said his wife would save them seats.

"Mrs. Middleton, you look stunning!" said a voice.

They turned to see Chief Boucher and his wife, a short, round-faced, chubby woman in a floral print dress with a lace collar.

"Detectives Stangler, Middleton, and Mrs. Middleton," said Boucher to his wife, pointing to each as he named them. "This is the little woman," he said to the detectives. She smiled happily, obviously excited by the occasion.

Amarantha looked down with half-lidded eyes very much like a snake about to strike. "Does the Little Woman have a name of her own?"

"Sure, sure," said Boucher genially, missing the thin ice he was on, "Harriet."

"I'm pleased to meet you, Harriet," she said, extending a hand. "I'm Amarantha."

"A gauzily-veiled server squeezed up next to them. "Drink order?"

"Very fetching costume, my dear," said Boucher, eyeing how her breasts billowed from the top of her skimpy bodice.

She pulled her face veil aside to be heard better. "Drink order?"

"Well, heh, heh, heh, we're not on duty, hey boys?" said Boucher. To the server he said, "The little woman and I will have strawberry daiquiris."

She looked at the detectives. All three shook their heads.

"Those waitresses are awfully daring," said Mrs. Boucher, watching theirs head back to the bar. "But pretty."

"Maybe," said Boucher, "but I'm with the prettiest girl in the room."

"Oh, you!" said Mrs. Boucher, blushing happily and poking him in the ribs.

Amarantha leaned close to Middleton. "I thought you said I was the prettiest girl in the room."

"That was before I saw Mrs. Boucher," he whispered. Then, "I didn't expect to see you at something like this, Chief."

"I read your reports. You boys seemed pretty impressed with a man dressed as a woman. I thought I'd better come see for myself. I'm not so easily fooled, you know. Besides, I thought it would do Harriet some good to take a walk on the wild side. Shake the Little Woman up some, hey?"

"Oh, you!" said Mrs. Boucher, giving him a laughing nudge.

"I see somebody waving at us," said Middleton. "Excuse us, folks."

Molly Palmquist stood by three empty chairs on the center aisle, waving them in. "I saved these for you," she said. "Jason wanted me to make sure you had good seats."

The lights began to dim. They quickly introduced the ladies and sat down.

An MC walked onto the stage, a follow spot matching his progression. "Ladies and gentlemen, ladies who are gents, welcome to Riverbend's fifth annual Gilded Lily Cabaret! We hope you enjoy tonight's performances, and remember, your ticket price, half your drinks price, and any money you care to throw at the stage will be donated to the Helen Keller Children's Wing of Our Lady of Hope Hospital. And now, to start us off with a bang, that red-headed short stack of sass, Miss Bette Midler!"

Act after act was met with applause, cheers and whistles. The last act before intermission was Sophie Tucker--just as round and packed and raunchy as she ever was said to be. "Before I sing you a little song... about temptation... and how *not* to avoid it... what do you think of my dress? Magnificent, yes?" Wild applause and cat calls answered the question "Red velvet is always showy, but the magnificent part is all me. How about a back view? Does velvet make my... tush look big? Big enough to bounce on, you naughty boys?" Loud appreciative reaction rolled in. She turned front and bent over, revealing deep cleavage. "For all you unbelievers, is this real enough for you?" She bent her head to look at her bosom. "Hello, my lovelies, how ya doing?" She looked up. "They love to watch TV. I used to call them after their favorite shows, 'Big Valley' and 'Bonanza.'" She held for laughs. "But nowadays I just call them 'white' and 'chocolate.'" The reaction was uproarious. "Maybe I'll let them out later---"

"You go, girl!" came from the audience.

"...if enough money gets tossed up on this stage. The sick little kiddies need the best medical equipment, you know."

A shower of coins pelted her.

"C'mon, have I got nothing but little boys with little pickles out there? Take out a twenty, wrap it around a half dollar, and loft it this way. Or throw Benjamin Franklin and we can talk later about your lightning rod."

Laughs, catcalls, whistles and applause.

When her act was over and the lights came up for intermission, stage hands came out to sweep up the money.

The detectives and the ladies decided to stay where they were, rather than push through the crowds.

Rask eased through the throng. "Hey, Mrs. Palmquist, I ain't seen your hubby out there yet."

"Jason opens the second act."

"I'll be watchin' for him." He turned to Stangler. "Say, hotshot, if we're watchin' out for you-know-who to take out a you-know-what, how come we ain't got guys all over this place?"

"This isn't Sunday and as far as I know, most of these guys aren't you-know-whatses," said Stangler.

"You think Sunday for sure, huh?"

"I don't know any goddamn thing for sure, John-- excuse me, ladies--but it's been Sunday five times now, so it's the best we've got to go on."

"Yeah, you're probly right."

"You're all set for tomorrow?"

"Yeah. We made a switch, though. Carmen's preacher said no dice, so the two girls are gonna swap recipes with the candy squirrels, n' Bishop n' me are gonna sit surveillance outside the preacher's house."

"Here we are," said Boucher, pushing through the bodies that filled the aisle, wife in tow. "We're a little confused. We thought Sophie Tucker died a long time ago."

Rask gave him a puzzled look. "Yeah. That's just a guy impersonatin' her."

"That was a man!" Boucher looked dumbfounded.

"Judas Priest, Chief! They're all guys!"

"Oh. Well." Boucher blinked rapidly while his mind caught up. "Oh. Well, they're very good at it, aren't they?"

"Damn straight. They can really fool ya if ya don't know what to look for."

Stangler put his head down to hide a smile. John Rask, the new expert on female impersonators. Or, as Rask might have put it, squirrels in ladies undies.

"Are those little harem girls men, too?" said Boucher, a note of disillusionment creeping in.

"Nah," said Rask, "Them're all babes."

"Oh. That's nice," beamed Boucher.

"Oh, you!" said Mrs. Boucher, giggling and grabbing his elbow.

The lights began to dim and the aisle cleared.

"Ladies and gentlemen," said the MC, "a woman who needs no introduction--Cher!"

A painted drop of a battleship deck slid into place upstage. The musical introduction to "If I Could Turn Back Time," began playing, and Cher strutted out on impossibly high heels--huge masses of black curls, an open leather jacket under which was a V of black fabric covering her breasts and pubic area, a black garter belt holding black nylons mid-thigh--and began to sing. People leaped to their feet, wildly cheering, clapping, whistling, and throwing money. Stangler, Middleton, Amarantha and Molly had to stand to see.

When the number was over and Cher had bounced off stage with a flash of bare buns, the audience would not let go. "More! More! More!" people chanted.

Amarantha leaned to see Molly, who was beaming with pride. "If he doesn't do an encore, I'm going to start shouting myself."

The MC came out.

"Not you! Not you! We want Cher!"

"I don't know...." said the MC, toeing the coins and bills on the stage. "Doesn't look like much. The Helen Keller Children's Wing does a lot of good for thousands of children...."

Money started flying through the air. Stangler
and Middleton wrapped bills around coins and threw
them.

The battleship flew out and a rendering of the
backside of a carnival wagon dropped in. The music
started "Gypsies, Tramps And Thieves." Cher walked
quietly out in a one-shoulder dress made entirely of
long yellow fringe and did a soulful rendering of an
unforgettable old favorite--again to a hail of money and
thunderous applause.

Other acts followed to enthusiastic, but not as
frenzied, applause.

"Jason is a tough act to follow," Middleton
whispered to Molly.

"They tried putting him last one year, but didn't
get nearly as much money," she said. "Now a
committee selects the opening and closing performer
for each act, and everyone else draws for position."

When the show was over, much of the audience
stood around talking, ordering drinks from the harem
servers, and waiting for performers to get out of
costume and put in an appearance. Mrs. Boucher
joined the detectives.

"Where's the Chief?" said Middleton.

"He went off with one of those girls for a few
minutes. I think she wanted advice on their security
system."

Stangler and Middleton exchanged bland looks.
What Boucher knew about security systems was easily
as much as he knew about raising silk worms.

"Did you enjoy the show?" said Molly.

"Yes, very much. Cher was particularly good."

"Here she is now," said Molly as Jason walked up
and gave her a hug from behind.

Mrs. Boucher looked him up and down, and then again. He looked completely like an ordinary man. "I'm not sure I understand," she said.

"This is Cher," said Molly, holding on to Jason's arm.

"I'm not...."

"Jason performed the Cher numbers."

"That was... that was you? Her face was wavering between admiration and disbelief.

"Guilty as charged," said Jason.

"Oh, well... ah... you sing very well."

"Wish I could take credit, but it's all lip synching."

"Ah...?"

"He just looks like he's singing, Mrs. Boucher; it's actually a recording you're listening to," said Molly.

"Well, my goodness, I wish Jim would hurry back. He would want to hear all of this." Mrs. Boucher looked around the room.

A bare-chested man with smears of cold cream on his face ran onto the empty stage. "Is there a doctor out there? Are any of you a doctor? We have a sick man backstage!"

An East Indian lady looking more like a model than a doctor, hurried up from the back of the audience area. "How do I get back there?" The bare-chested man pointed to a short set of steps off to one side of the stage. They disappeared around the backdrop.

"I wonder what that's about?" said Jason. "Maybe I should...."

"No, stay here," said Molly. "You'd probably just be in the way."

"We'll check it out," said Middleton, and he and Stangler headed for the stage.

The bare-chested man came back. "Does anyone out there have a cell phone? We need someone to call the police."

"Hold on," said Stangler. "We're police."

The bare-chested man led them down a hallway behind the stage. Open doors on either side showed storage rooms temporarily transformed into dressing rooms for the evening. Their guide indicated the last door on the left.

Sophie Tucker, without her wig, but still in costume, lay on the floor. Although the heavy skirt covered any external signs, it was obvious that his bowels had emptied. There was no immediate sign of injury.

Stangler showed his badge to the doctor standing guard over the body. "What do we have here?" he said.

"He's dead," she said. "Somebody killed him."

"What makes you think that?"

She squatted, no mean feat in a tight dress and three inch heels, and pointed to a pair of small circular dots on the body's shoulder. "Taser burn," she said. Then she pointed to a very small drop of blood on the neck. "Injection site. Looks like something very lethal and very quick."

Squatting beside her, Stangler muttered, "Not a natural death."

"Not bloody likely," she said, rising.

Middleton turned and hurried back down the hallway.

"Do you see a note anywhere?" said Stangler.

"What sort of note," said the doctor, looking curious.

"Half page, big printing."

She shrugged and shook her head.

Stangler looked around the room, then lifted the hem of the red velvet skirt slightly, but didn't see a note.

Middleton hastened back out onto the stage. "Jason," he called, "Can you go to the front door and tell anyone trying to leave that there is a police order

for them to remain in the building? Amarantha, can
you do the same at the back entrance? If you see
Boucher, tell him to take over." Middleton pulled his
phone and began making quick calls.

"Oh, dear," said Mrs. Boucher, "I'd better go
looking for Jim. He's been gone a long time."

"No, don't," said Molly, taking her arm.

"But I don't know where he is."

"That's okay. If there's trouble, he'll be on duty.
It's best if we sit right here in plain sight where he can
see us when he comes back."

"Wiley!" rang out Amarantha's voice from
somewhere behind the bar area.

"What!"

"Get back here, now!"

Leaping off the stage and shouting, "Police!
Move aside!" Middleton got to the open back door in
seconds, where he found Amarantha outside in the
alley, standing over the prostrate body of James
Boucher. One gunshot wound in the back of the head.
A note with large printing tucked under his fingers.
"Go tell Lobo," he said. "Don't let anyone else hear.
Tell him I'm making the calls and I'll stay here till
uniforms come. Then go help Jason at the front door."

She started back in.

"Amarantha!"

"What?"

"Don't tell Mrs. Boucher anything until I get more
of our people back here."

Doing her best to look calm, Amarantha made it
back stage in time to hear Stangler say to the doctor,
"Would this take medical knowledge?"

"No, not really."

"Lobo," said Amarantha, "I've got a message from
Wiley."

"Okay," he said looking at her.

"I need to tell you privately."

With a hand on her elbow, Stangler steered her from the doorway down the hall a ways. She leaned toward him and spoke quietly.

He didn't say anything. He just slumped against the wall looking totally defeated.

Half an hour later, six uniformed policemen were going about the necessary business, the Blue Moon was an official crime scene, people were complaining about not being able to go home, and Mrs. Boucher was having hysterics.

* * * * * * * * * *

"One of those... those gitchy-goo girls... came and... and asked Jim if he would... would come and... and look at their... security system!" Mrs. Boucher's sobs ended in a wail. "He was just going to... to a back room. How did he get in the alley!" She started to rise from her chair. "I want to see him."

Middleton patted her hand and urged her to sit again. "No one can go back there until the Crime Lab comes and goes, Mrs. Boucher," he said, squatting to bring himself to her eye level. "It will be hours. You can see him after he's taken to the... to a much more well-lit place than the alley."

"Ha... Harriet."

"Beg pardon?"

"My name's Harriet."

"Would you recognize the server who asked him to come away, Harriet?"

She took a deep breath and wiped her eyes with a soggy tissue. "No. With those veils across their faces, and rows of dangling things across their foreheads, they all looked alike."

"Was it a very old woman?" said Stangler.

"An old woman!" she squeaked. "Her breasts were pooching up and her pants were eight inches below her belly button! It wasn't an old woman! Why are you asking me all this!" She began to sob hysterically. "I want my Jimmy! I want my Jimmy!"

Stangler stepped back to where Amarantha and the Palmquists stood. "Her sister's on the way and can take her home," said Amarantha.

"Thanks for calling," said Stangler. "Jason, would you mind following us around? Speak up if anything strikes you as odd."

"No problem."

"Molly, would you give Amarantha a lift home? We'll send Jason in a car. Might be several hours."

"That's fine," she said.

"Gotta go, Babe," said Middleton, giving Amarantha a quick kiss and following Stangler and Jason onto the stage.

The performers were crowded into one storeroom-cum-dressing room with a uniformed officer standing in the doorway. The makeup boxes and spangled dresses laying about made an unlikely background for what appeared to be a group of unexceptional men sitting around glancing at their watches impatiently. When the detectives entered, Jason followed unobtrusively and quietly sat down on a carton.

Working off an information sheet given to him by the Blue Moon manager, Stangler learned Sophie Tucker's name was Joe Dixon, and he identified all the others by name and by act, with the exception of two who had left while Sophie Tucker as still seen to be alive. Questioning brought out that they all knew each other more or less by sight and act, but weren't friends and didn't know all that much about each other, particularly the deceased.

"Did anyone notice anything unusual tonight?" said Stangler. "Anything catch at your attention? Something even slightly different?"

"Seemed like the same old, same old, to me," said one of the men.

"Yeah," said a second. "Except who was that gawdawful Baby Jane?"

"What a loser," acknowledged another. Several others chimed in that they had seen her.

"What are you talking about?" Stangler referred to his list and looked at the second man. "Mason?"

"There was a short old guy here tonight in a crappy dress and wig with makeup that looked like he put it on when he was drunk. Reminded me of Baby Jane from that old Bette Davis fright movie. Any of you guys see his act?"

"There was no such act," said Stangler. "You were looking at the killer."

# # # # # #

Chapter 42: Morning, Monday, August 9

"What's that noise downstairs?" said Martin, looking up from his computer screen.

Muggs rolled her eyes in exasperation. "They told you. Big Erich is making exercise bars for Kathy. If she can't go out on the streets, she needs to find some way to keep her muscles loose. Besides, she was getting jumpy from the inactivity."

"Ah. How about you?"

"I don't do exercise."

"Are you getting jumpy?"

"Is Jiminy Cricket jumpy? Never mind, I found some books in one of your cartons; I'm okay."

"Will you guys shut up?" said Laine. "I'm trying to concentrate. You got your employed list done?"

"Yes, but employed between the ages of 16 and 67, still leaves 80,000 people. I think we can look at income levels."

"What are you thinking?"

"We have a new van, so that suggests a certain level of income and maybe a big enough garage. The victims so far have seemed unsuspecting so I'm assuming there's nothing alarming about the killers. They must look and sound like upright citizens. Good clothes, good language arts skills usually means upper educational-economic level. So I think we can remove lower income levels."

"You think poor people talk and dress funny?" said Muggs.

"Thank you, Miss Social Conscience," said Laine.

"I might have been thinking in that direction," said Martin, "but the truth of the matter is people with lower incomes are too busy, and maybe too smart, to waste time running around dressed up killing people."

"Okay," said Laine, "kick out total household income below what?"

"I'm going down to watch Kathy and Big Erich," said Muggs.

"What's the national poverty level figure?" said Martin. "Is it a realistic figure for our purposes?"

"Hang on, I'll check," said Laine.

"I hope you won't miss me too much," said Muggs as she headed for the stairway.

* * * * * * * * * *

"Four people for sure," Stangler said to the group in the detectives' room. "One tall thin guy with medical knowledge; one short older man; maybe two women, one old, one young; or one young woman good with disguises and a fourth unknown."

"Fourth unknown," said Rivera. "Someone with the muscle to strangle Goetzman.

"But why did they do this one on a Saturday and why female impersonators?" said Pedersen.

"Ah, man, what a screw-up," said Stangler. "John, you were right on, and I'm a dick head."

Rask cracked his Nicorette and made no comment.

"But those guys aren't gay," said Olson. "As far as we know."

"Remember, we thought they were before we knew better," said Stangler, carefully not looking at Rask. "Our killers made the same mistake."

"Why Sophie Tucker?" said Rask. "I thought she, he, was pretty funny."

"We're thinking it was like a fox in a henhouse," said Middleton. "If our killer thought he was in a nest of homosexuals, then anyone he could catch alone for a few minutes was fair game."

"But Saturday?" said Pedersen.

"At a guess, success is making them bolder," said Middleton. "Maybe the security of their timing was most important at first, but now the emphasis has shifted to the importance of the victim. Like a Chief of Police."

A hush fell over the group. Having spent several years wishing Boucher would transfer to Outer Mongolia, they nevertheless were sorry he was dead. On the other hand, no one was prepared to hypocritically mourn his demise.

"Mr. Driver guessed the next victim would be homosexual and he thought the killers might move up to more prominent law enforcement people," said Stangler. "I hate like hell having to use civilians, but he's making all the right guesses."

"Who are these people?" said Pedersen.

"I'm not sure. From what we can find out, they're all prominent citizens who fell off the radar in the last few years," said Stangler. "No criminal history, high-profile lawyer, but John swears they're homeless."

"I'm tellin' ya, they're livin' on the streets," said Rask.

"I'm not doubting you, John. But it's just another piece of the puzzle that doesn't fit."

"Ownership of the limo?" said Rivera.

"Rented by the day," said Middleton, "but rental is pretty steep."

"Who rented it?"

"Attorney Margaret Collins."

"Duh!" said Rivera, and smacked herself on the head.

"So what are you going to do?" said Stummer.

"Dammit," said Stangler. "I guess I'd be a fool not to call them. This feels about as stupid as working with a goddamn psychic."

* * * * * * * * * *

"I wish that long-haired idiot would quit calling; I'm starting to get muscles in my calves," said Muggs topping the stairs in the warehouse. "I ran clear out to Riverside Park to call back."

"What's up?" said Martin, turning away from his keyboard.

"He wants you to come in and talk again. I asked him what he wanted; said it was too much trouble for us to come in." She put her back to a counter and slid to the floor. "Smart jerk suggested it would be less trouble if we didn't rent the limo every time."

"Checking on us," said Laine.

"What does he want us for?" said Martin.

"He wants you to tell him who's next."

"I don't know who's next. Laine, who's the biggest flouter of social conventions after homosexuals?"

"Lawyers."

"Excuse me!" said Muggs.

"Gotcha! I'd vote for televangelists."

"If we had some in Riverbend, that would be a good one," said Martin. "Tell Stangler we don't even have a guess," he said to Muggs.

"I told him that. He wasn't happy. What a nasty attitude."

"Anything else?"

"He didn't deserve any hope, but I told him we were working at it from the other direction and would call when we knew something."

"Anything else?

"That poor excuse for a detective said he guessed I wasn't married because no man would have a smart mouth like me. I told him I wasn't married because I hadn't found a man good enough yet, and that included any law enforcement types!"

* * * * * * * * * *

Stangler slammed the phone down and sat back with a scowl.

"No luck?" said Middleton.

"None. Miss Razor Tongue said they've switched to using computers to look for the killers and would let us know when they found them. When *they* found them!"

"What can they do that Emily can't?"

"I got the impression that I was such a dolt I wouldn't understand."

* * * * * * * * * *

"Okay, removing low income adults brings our 80,000 down to 65,600." said Laine. "Then what? I can find almost anything, but I have to know what I'm looking for."

"If we access airplane reservations here and in Minneapolis, we can weed out anyone definitely out of town on the dates of any of the murders," said Martin.

"Okay, that might get rid of a hundred," said Laine with a touch of frustration.

Martin scratched his head. "This would be easier if we were looking for only one person, but I think our only hope is to build a large database of possibilities, and hope that something matches up."

"Field number one," said Laine, "our sixty-five thousand. Field number two?"

"Everyone who has purchased a .25 caliber handgun in Minnesota in the past 10 years."

"Just Minnesota?"

"You're right. Minnesota, Wisconsin and Iowa."

"People hang on to guns a long time," said Laine. "They stash 'em away and forget about it until they need them. One of these guys looked like an older guy."

"Last 40 years then. As long as we're looking for a specific caliber, it shouldn't be that many. You set up the database. Allow for what, maybe ten fields?"

"Fifteen to be sure."

"Fifteen. Then you start on the gun and I'll look for anyone with a criminal record."

* * * * * * * * * *

"Wait a minute," said Middleton. "Did she say 'killers?' Did you tell any of them we were looking for more than one killer?"

Stangler sat bolt upright in astonishment. "No, I did not! They've hacked into our files! I'm going to throw the whole lot of them in a cell!"

"No, wait. You don't know for a fact that they have."

"Of course I know! If she said 'killers' plural, that means---"

"No, Lobo, hey! You don't know *for a fact* that they're hacking," said Middleton with heavy emphasis. "But if they are, it's the one thing they can do that Emily can't. Maybe we shouldn't be too curious about their activities."

Stangler shifted in his chair and glared at Middleton. "Okay, you're right. Catching these guys is more important than anything. But why does she have to be so damn smug about it!"

\#   \#   \#   \#   \#   \#

Chapter 43:Morning, Wednesday, August 11

"That is scary," said Laine. "I would rather be hauling a 60-lb pack through an alligator swamp than doing that."

He and Martin sat on the warehouse stairs, watching Kathy fling herself in gravity-defying arcs over the high horizontal bar Big Erich had made for her.

"He did a good job," said Martin. "It's even got that soft "give" to the bar, the way you see on professional equipment."

Kathy swung upright, released, did a flip mid air, and caught the bar again coming down.

"Jeez, that scares me! How can she do that? What if she falls and bashes her brains out?" said Laine.

Massive eye strain had forced the two of them to take a break. Muggs was upstairs napping on an air mattress, but they were too pumped to sleep. Watching Kathy for a bit and then maybe a stroll around the building several times should give them another 3-4 hours at the computers before they were forced to sleep. They had fallen into a workable procedure. Laine would hack into useful sites, copy the information they needed, transfer it to a flash drive and erase his tracks. They had changed Martin's computer to a stand-alone with no Internet connection. As new information was dumped into Martin's database, he looked for connections and ideas for additional searches.

Kathy made a final swing in the air, tucked herself into a double roll, and landed gracefully on the mats. Her tank top and shorts were wet with sweat. "Wheeo," she said, "shower!"

Martin and Laine came the rest of the way down the stairs to let her pass, Big Erich following. As the two hackers opened the outside door, Muggs ran down.

Squinting into the sunlight as she accompanied them around the building, she said, "So where are you at?"

"We've got everyone now living in Riverbend who bought a .25 caliber handgun in the three-state area in the past 40 years," said Laine.

"Wouldn't some of them have died or moved?" she said.

"Yeah. When that happens, the database creates sequence identity numbers to store the information."

"See anything interesting?"

"Not yet," said Martin. "Nothing has popped out yet, but we're still working."

"We've got everyone who bought a dark-colored van in the past five years," said Laine. Then we added in the date of every purchase of more than three dark coveralls from all retail stores, or more than three plastic masks from party stores. If any were bought with credit card, we have a name; if not, all we have is a date of purchase, and sometimes a zip code, but we hang on to that."

"How about people who had access to the Declaration of Independence?" said Muggs.

"We considered that," said Martin, "but it's impossible to narrow down--libraries, text books, home libraries, documentaries, the Internet, framed facsimile copies... some people even have it memorized from school."

"Radical Republicans?" said Muggs.

"Difficulty separating them out from the herd," said Martin, grinning.

"So where next?"

"Next, we're going to start making leaps of faith," said Martin, as he held the door open for the other two.

Back upstairs, Muggs curled up with a book while the two men again faced their computers.

"We know the group has one tall slender man probably with medical training, one person with great strength, one shorter older man, and likely one woman good at disguises," Martin said. "So let's do three separate sorts of what we have--men 5'10" and under who are over 60, male doctors 5'11" and over, and women between 20 and 45 who have any theatre background or cosmetics connection."

Hours later they studied the results. "This looks better," said Laine. "Three short old guys who once bought a .25 handgun, 159 women with theatre or cosmetics background, 189 taller doctors. None of them bought a van or charged coveralls that we know of. What next?"

"The most accurate times of death the police have are for Sandra Goetzman, Arvid Haugen and Joe Dixon," said Martin. "Lets plug those times in and see if we can pinpoint any of our 351 who were not using their phones for say, half an hour before any of the three times of death."

"Why?"

"I'm thinking they had to be traveling to, or getting in position for, the... strike, and would not be making any calls."

"Gotcha. This shouldn't take too long."

Forty minutes later, they stared at a screen, stunned by their results.

"Muggs," said Martin. "Put the book down. We've got to go see your favorite detective. Now."

* * * * * * * * * *

Middleton leaned sideways in the seat and tugged at the belt of his uniform pants.

"Putting on a little weight, are we?" said Stangler.

"I weigh exactly what I weighed when I first put on this uniform, but I think my incredible abs have extended."

"Sure."

They were in the back seat of a marked car about seven or eight vehicles behind the hearse, part of the cortege heading for the country cemetery. Media vans passed in the left lane at breakneck speed, rarely encountering vehicles from the other direction, but causing the few to lay on their horns and take to the shoulder to avoid a collision. Their driver cursed, easing right to make a few more inches room for the near-miss encounters. "Where's a county mountie when you need one," he muttered, gripping the wheel tightly. "Good thing for them this whole parade is only going 40."

Harders, one of the two uniforms in front, turned partway around in the passenger seat. "You think Pickett's gonna end up being Chief?"

"Not a chance," said Middleton. "It'll be Bakken or Jevne or maybe someone from the outside."

"I don't get it," said Harders. "Bakken and Jevne are Assistant Chiefs; Pickett's only a Captain, so why didn't they pick one of them for Acting Chief?"

"Because Bakken and Jevne will be candidates. People would read things into it if they made one of them Acting Chief. This way, everyone knows Pickett can handle the job until a decision is made, but no one's going to have a hernia when it isn't Pickett."

"Pickett will probably be promoted to Assistant Chief," said Stangler.

"How long's it gonna take? said Harders.

"Hard to tell," said Middleton. "Maybe three-four months. The Civil Service Commission posts the opening, interviews and tests candidates, and then recommends a short list to the city. The mayor makes the final decision."

"Mayor Viper?"

"The one and only."

"What a godawful first duty for Pickett," said Stangler.

"Shit, yeah," said Harders, turning back front.

The church service had been an embarrassment. Mrs. Boucher insisted that Boucher's successor sit in the front pew with her. She clung to Pickett throughout, sobbing hysterically, crying "I want my Jimmy." She had selected crushingly maudlin hymns, including "Beyond The Sunset," sung by a full choir and a professional soloist. Those in attendance were urged to file by the open casket and say a silent prayer, a ceremony that took a long time with nothing to relieve the silent shuffle of feet except Mrs. Boucher's uncontrolled sobs. It was rumored that the pastor had gumption enough to insist on a limit of only two personal eulogists, otherwise they'd all still be there beyond sunset.

The Bouchers' married son and daughter and their spouses sat rigid on either side of their mother and Pickett, their faces pinched, enduring the proceedings with closed expressions.

Leaning heavily on Pickett's arm as she was escorted through the church doors, Mrs. Boucher saw the crowd of shouting media gathered outside, and crumpled in a half faint that left Pickett and the son holding her up by the armpits. The crowd surged against the line of Sheriff's Deputies keeping the walkway clear, camera lights and flashes making novas of a moment that would surely make the front pages.

"Is this a heart attack?"

"Will she be a collateral victim?"

"Can she make a last statement?"

The journey of the cortege was beginning to be familiar--the uniforms, the cars, the long ribbon of flashing bar lights, the motorcycles, the participating area law enforcement, the media, the governor, the crowds with cameras.

At the cemetery it took forever for each car to pull up, disgorge its occupants, and for them to move to the grave and get lined up. The governor held up progress when he paused for comments to the crowding media. Pickett had sense enough to hold Mrs. Boucher in their limo until everyone else was positioned. Hoping for another dramatic shot, media people with microphones and cameras came close to toppling deputies in their efforts to get closer. Pickett and the son supported her limp figure as they began the walk to get Mrs. Boucher to a graveside chair, the daughter and two in-laws following behind, heads down.

"Give us a statement, Mrs. Boucher!"

"How does it feel to have your husband the twelfth victim of the Encore Killer?"

"Chief Pickett, how much longer will the killings go on?"

"When will you catch the Encore Killer?"

Out of reach of the deputies, five media people started climbing the cemetery's ornamental iron fencing, and a section of it fell under their weight. There was a surge over the fallen section. Deputies quickly surrounded Mrs. Boucher and her family, warding off thrusting microphones. Other eager news gatherers dodged tombstones and ran up the slope toward the grave site. Tested beyond patience, Riverbend police broke ranks and started corralling the interlopers, not caring if they caused a few tumbles or if a camera accidentally flew through the air to land with a crash against a marble memorial.

Order finally restored, the graveside service began. Mrs. Boucher lay into Pickett's shoulder, her muffled sobs punctuating the pastor's words. Pickett carefully eased a hand between their two bodies to adjust his sidearm more comfortably. Son, daughter and spouses sat on chairs on either side, their posture rigid and faces blank, not wanting their grief to become part of the conspicuous excess.

There was the usual 21-gun salute. There was the often-seen bagpiper with "Amazing Grace." Then, "I don't believe it," muttered Middleton. "She's hired a 'missing man' flyby."

Everyone looked to the sky as three jets in a V formation flew over, the two wing positions continuing in their level flight while the point plane turned straight upwards and disappeared into the brilliant clouds.

As the minister began the concluding, "Ashes to ashes," recitation, the governor, his wife and attending men in suits turned and quietly began to walk away. Mrs. Boucher staggered up from her chair and tried to throw herself across the coffin. She managed to place a foot exactly in the small gap between the ornamental edging holding the coffin straps and the excavation for the grave. One leg slipped down into the grave and the other doubled under her. Pickett and the son leaped to haul her to her feet, whereupon she truly fainted dead away.

Standing in the row of dignitaries behind the chairs for the family, Mayor Duponte was heard to mutter, "I'm the mayor of a fucking circus."

A nearby reporter and her cameraman gave each other a silent high five and ran off.

* * * * * * * * * *

The marked car carrying Stangler and Middleton passed the public parking area, heading for the rear entrance to the LEC. "See that?" said Middleton. Someone had written "Wash me" on every available surface of a dusty Lincoln.

"Yeah, funny," said Stangler, looking, but dealing with his own thoughts. "I'm damned if I know where we go next." He pulled off his hat and stared out the window. His hair was tied back at the nape of his neck with a small black ribbon. "And if I have to go to one more funeral, I'm going to shoot myself and fall in the hole with the casket."

"If you do, can I have your car?"

"Ah, Jeez!"

Holding his hat in one hand and pulling the snaps on the standing collar of his dress uniform, Stangler barged out of the elevator on the second floor, to see Emily in a face-off with Martin Driver and his entourage.

"No, seriously," said Emily, "you'll have to wait downstairs. You can't be up here unescorted."

"Here they are," said Kathy.

"Good," said Emily in frosty tones, and left.

Martin had hurried them down to the LEC so fast they had no time to change out of their usual street people garb. Stangler took a long look, and wondered if maybe Rask knew what he was talking about.

"We have to talk," said Martin.

Once in the conference room, Martin slapped a computer printout on the table and pointed to the fields. "These two men are over 60 years old and own a .25 caliber handgun. These three women have cosmetics backgrounds. These four doctors are tall."

"Yes, but so---" said Stangler.

"Wait," said Martin. "All of these people live in Riverbend, and they are the only people who fit the general descriptions of your killers and the only people who did not make any phone calls during the times of each and every one of the murders."

Stangler frowned at the printout.

Middleton moved over to study it. "You sorted out everyone who was using a phone when the murders were occurring."

"As close as we could call the time," said Martin.

"Cell or land line?"

"Both."

"That's technologically amazing," said Middleton. "Almost impossible."

"It was an accident," said Muggs. "My clients were looking for a good deal on a new cell phone and must have hit a strange combination of keys, and this popped up."

"Totally by chance," said Middleton.

"Absolutely," said Muggs.

Stangler thumped the printout several times with an index finger. "Let me make sure I understand this. There are only two short older guys---"

"Baby Jane," said Martin.

Stangler looked up sharply.

"Slip of the tongue!" said Muggs. "Just a random remark."

"I don't think it's important now," said Martin.

"The only two short older guys in all of Riverbend," said Stangler, "who own a .25 caliber handgun and who were not on the phone." He looked down at the printout. "Only four tall doctors not on the phone."

"Busy doing something else," said Martin.

"My god," said Stangler as he snatched up the paper and headed for the door. He stopped suddenly,

turned to Martin, and said, "Thanks." He smiled at
Muggs. "Like the outfit, Counselor." Then he and
Middleton were gone.

#   #   #   #   #   #

Chapter 44: Noon, Tuesday, August 10

The small trees in the boulevard created dappled shade for the patrons of the sidewalk cafe.

"What the hell's a trattoria?" grumbled Gregory Turner, carefully eating his ham and focaccia sandwich. He pronounced it "tra-TOR-ee-ah."

"It means a small Italian restaurant, and it's pronounced 'tra-te-REE-ah,'" said Audra Cantrell.

"This is America. If it's a restaurant, it should say restaurant."

"An outdoor cafe by any other name would be just as pleasant," said Wilfred Burkhalter.

"Let's get on with it; I've got to replace a hip at 2:00," said Lawrence Madden.

Three tables over, Brittany Olson sat in a sleeveless sun dress and espadrilles. Her long bare legs were crossed to show to best advantage, her bright blonde hair gleamed in the sun, a straw purse sat on the chair beside her. Looking like a movie starlet, except for the Glock and badge in the purse, she appeared to have no agenda other than to attract male stares.

Standing in the front window of a nearby antiques shop, a Vietnamese man in a bright floral Hawaiian shirt and a camera hanging around his neck, carefully examined a display of Venini blown glass. Looking through the window from time to time, Lu Nguyen could also see the quartet at the outdoor cafe.

Across the street, a scruffy man sat on the edge of a stone planter, smoking a cigarette and looking surly. Steve Wishink dropped his cigarette to the sidewalk, scuffed it out, and looked around in boredom.

Immediate surveillance had been placed on the nine people pinpointed by Martin Driver, and now here

were four of them, sitting over lunch together.
Watching from a third floor balcony of a nearby hotel,
Stangler said, "A developer, a banker, a fashion buyer,
and an orthopedic surgeon. And we know what they
have in common. God, Wiley, I'm so pumped I could
pee my pants."

"We're missing someone strong enough to garrote
Goetzman," said Middleton.

"We'll get him."

"The four of us shouldn't be seen together like
this," said Turner, glancing around the sunny street.

"Four city businessmen... business people,"
Burkhalter amended, glancing at Cantrell, "having
lunch together should cause no particular notice, even if
the local constabulary weren't spinning in one place,
asking which way was up."

"We could be really discreet and call each other
Owl and Snake," said Cantrell, laughing so hard she
slopped her cappuccino, which dropped through the
metal mesh of the table onto the hem of her skirt.
"Damn!" she said, dipping a corner of her napkin in her
water glass and dabbing at the stain.

"All right," said Burkhalter. "Audra, let's hear
about this Dagir fellow you three are hot about.
Personally, I have my doubts about hitting someone in a
wheelchair."

"He's a rotten piece of humanity," said Cantrell.
"Wild as a kid; in college he drove himself into a bridge
abutment and was ticketed for driving while
intoxicated. He was crippled, and his parents tried to
sue their insurance company, the car manufacturer, and
the highway department, but couldn't get anywhere
because of the DWI ticket." She paused to sip her
cappuccino. "Wild before and bitter now, he became an
attorney and handles only DWI cases. He's very good
at it, and has a reputation for getting the worst cases off

on technicalities. His TV commercials say, 'Let Hank Dagir slice through the bureaucratic bullpucky for you.'"

"I agree he's an unsavory human being, but he doesn't really fit our criteria," said Burkhalter.

"It gets better," said Cantrell. "He shoves his handicap down the throats of city businesses. Millions of dollars have been spent replacing and remodeling because of his complaints. He maliciously visits stores looking at aisles, displays, doors, automatic buttons, parking areas, concrete condition. Anything that's so much as a fraction of an inch shy of guidelines, he prosecutes. He close to bankrupts any business that's fractionally non-complying. You name it, he's looking for a way to get back at the world--and here's the bone in my throat--the government's Americans with Disabilities Act allows him to do it!"

"Gregory and I have been watching him," said Madden. "Every Saturday night he visits a new bar, buying drinks, talking about unreasonable penalties for DWI's, passing out cards, drumming up business."

"He has a set pattern," said Turner. "This Saturday he'll be at Brewster's."

"You think you can get at him?" said Burkhalter.

"Yes," said Madden. "Get him over to a table in a dark corner, slide a knife in him. He's in a wheelchair, for Christ's sake. He won't even call attention to himself by falling over."

"We're getting good," said Audra. "The last two with people all around. That's a big psychological thing. The panic will build when people realize they aren't even safe in a crowd."

"We've got to get serious about a manifesto," said Madden.

"Look at that," said Turner. "Jap with a camera taking pictures of every stupid building on the street. Damn tourists everywhere."

"How do you know he's Japanese?" said Cantrell.

"Jap, Chink, what's the difference?"

"All right," said Burkhalter. "It looks as though we're set on Dagir this Saturday."

Madden glanced at the showy blonde nearby, lowered his voice and leaned forward. "And our top cop," he said. "I wish I could see it happen." He stood. "You think you'll be okay, Audra?"

"You can bet on it," she said, pushing her chair back, lowering her voice as she, too, glanced at the airhead blonde two tables away. "This one is going to hit the news big time."

#   #   #   #   #   #

Chapter 45: Afternoon, Friday, August 13

"How ya doin' Mr. Chief of Police?" said Rask.

"After that funeral," said Pickett, "everything else is downhill all the way." He sat sideways in the detectives room so he could see them and the case board, where Middleton stood, ready to add information. "All right, tell me the good news."

"Wilfred Burkhalter, Dr. Lawrence Madden, Gregory Turner, Audra Cantrell," said Middleton as he taped up enlarged head shots from Nguyen's photos. "They're all clean as a whistle. Madden has a speeding ticket, Cantrell has a couple parking tickets. That's it."

"We think there's a fifth," said Stangler. "Someone with strength, but what do we look for? We're assuming we'll catch him in the same net."

"Or her," said Rivera.

"If you think there's a woman who could---"

"Amarantha could," said Middleton.

"You're right," said Stangler. "Someone go arrest Amarantha."

"We're just pointing out---" said Rivera.

"All right! Fine. We'll catch him *or her* in the same net."

"Moving on," said Pickett, "what hard evidence do we have?"

"Ah, man," said Stangler, "none or next to none. We know none of them was using his, *or her*, phone during any of the murder times. That information was obtained, uh, informally, and we could get it officially if we had enough probable cause to obtain a subpoena, which we don't."

"We observed them conspiring together, planning their next hit," said Olson.

"But a judge would say we could have observed nothing more than a downtown merchants planning committee."

"This Burkhalter had his own construction company way back when he was small peanuts," said Stummer, "before he started doing high-rise developments. He still owns a couple small warehouses where the van could be stashed. John and I checked them out, but we can't see in."

"And no probable cause for getting in," said Stangler.

Resting his chin on a closed fist, Pickett looked thoughtful. "So, despite the fact that we have no evidence whatsoever, we're positive that four prominent squeaky clean Riverbend citizens are serial killers?"

Everyone nodded solemnly.

Shaking his head and smiling ruefully, like someone about to invest in a dubious stock option, Pickett said, "All right, what does my crack team of detectives plan to do next?"

White board duties being zip, Middleton pulled up a chair and sat down.

"We're guessing our best bet is to figure out who they're targeting next and catch them in the act," said Stangler.

"Any *informal* predictions?" said Pickett, fully knowledgeable of the homeless connection.

"Not really. Someone 'socially distasteful' is the best they can do. If we had any televangelists in town, they would go with that, but we don't."

"Used car salesmen?" said Pedersen blushing at his own joke.

"Prostitutes?" said Rask.

"Male chauvinist pigs?" snapped Rivera.

"Yeah, yeah, can it," said Stangler. To Pickett. "We've been keeping an eye on these people and the only one who's done anything out of character is Dr. Madden. He spent his lunch hour today in Brewster's."

"Brewster's!" said Pickett. "And he got out alive? What was he doing in there?"

"We figure he was checking it out. It's where their next hit will happen."

"Can we talk to the bartenders beforehand? Get some clue about the regulars?"

"They'll warn everyone to stay away."

"So what's the plan?"

"We'll put Jim and Lu and Steve inside to catch the actual killer; we assume it will be Madden. They'll keep a close eye on whoever he homes in on. The rest of us will be outside and will round up the others."

Pickett looked at Pedersen and Nguyen in flat-out astonishment. "Jim and Lu are going to blend in in a redneck bar?"

"Steve says he can make it work. Our other choices are female, black, long-haired, and, uh, mean but slow."

"Hey!" said Rask.

* * * * * * * * * *

Martin drummed his fingers lightly on the keyboard of Laine's computer and sighed. "I feel like a mother hen whose chicks are big enough to fend for themselves, and I've got no more eggs to lay."

"'Mother hen' is redundant," said Muggs, half asleep on her air mattress.

"Put your eggs in the basket and turn out the light," said Kathy. "I swear I'm going back on the streets tomorrow; I don't care who picks me up."

"All right. Just one last check." He keyed a code and looked at the screen. "The police files have been updated," he said, his voice rising in excitement. "They've got a location and they're setting up a trap!"

In seconds he was surrounded by wide-awake people, crowding around to peer over his shoulders.

Muggs let out a low whistle. "Brewster's."

"I'm gonna be in there." said Laine.

"Me, too," said Kathy.

"No!" said Martin horrified. "You'd be raped and stomped into the floor in two minutes flat."

"I can take Big Erich."

"No. We three have to stay away. Erich can find an out-of-sight spot and keep an eye on things outside. Laine can go inside because he looks mean enough."

"Hey!" said Laine.

#   #   #   #   #   #

Chapter 46: Evening, Saturday, August 14

Brewster's had formerly been Art & Mel's. Before that, it was Pinky's Bright Spot, The Lounge Lizard, Rastelli's Dance Palace, O'Doule's Saloon and Grill, Gunnar's Saloon, back to its founding in the 1800's as the River Road Saloon. It had always sat right in the heart of downtown; or rather, it had always sat where it sat now. Streets had grown, names had changed, and where once it opened onto a rutted dirt horse track called River Road, its doors now opened onto the corner of River Street and First Avenue. Starting as a watering hole for rough men with rough language, it had passed through changing times, prohibition and gentrification to end full circle as a haven for rough men with rough language.

At 10:00 p.m. on a Saturday night, it was quiet outside on the street. The surrounding stores were closed, traffic was sparse. An older rusty van sat apparently empty in a parking lot across the street and half a block down. Rask and Stummer crouched and cursed in the back, peering through holes in the divider behind the front seats. Half a block and across an intersection in the other direction, Stangler and Middleton stood quietly in the deep shadows of a buttress on the third level of a parking ramp. Two blocks away, under the overhanging branches of a crabapple tree in the forecourt of a retirement high rise, Rivera and Olson waited in an unmarked car with Wisconsin plates. Twelve blocks away, parked behind an out-of-business drive-through restaurant, five patrol cars and ten officers sat waiting. They were all radio connected, but there was nothing to say. Patience was all.

Inside, Brewster's was packed with sweaty men, bellowing at each other like challenging moose over the deafening noise of a local guitar band with big speakers and a TV set blaring a wrestling match. Waitresses in white short shorts and deep-necked red T-shirts pushed through the wall of drinkers, casually ignoring the groping that came with the territory.

At one table slouched Wishink in a lavender silk suit and shirt, yellow tie, white panama hat, sun glasses, diamond stud earrings, six massive diamond rings, and what appeared to be a diamond imbedded in a front tooth, looking bored and irritated.

Brewster's regular patrons had eyed him with delight when her first walked in, wanting nothing more than to mop the floor with him. They were held off so far by the sight of his companions, but they still cast speculative looks from time to time.

To Wishink's right sat Pedersen in low-slung jeans, a heavy chain belt, and a dirty T-shirt that said, "Bite Me." His blond hair was greased in peaks, a red stained do-rag crossed his forehead, one hand had bandages crossing the knuckles and a small gold hoop appeared to be piercing an earlobe. His face was bruised on both sides, the purple makeup starting around his eyes and coming down to his cheekbones, blending with his constant blush. He clutched a beer bottle and scowled, trying not to look apprehensive. He wasn't afraid of the other customers; he was worried that he would drop character if he didn't concentrate. To Wishink's left sat Nguyen in a muscle shirt, arms crossed, looking placid. Somehow, his calm flat expression and the lack of any gang flags or flare looked doubly ominous.

"Nothing yet," said Middleton's voice in their ear buds.

Two customers came in. Maybe only in their early 20's, they already had that good ol' rowdy boy look to them of fight-ready grins, weight-lifting shoulders, and beer-lifting guts. Pushing carelessly through the throng, they greeted some pool players with heavy back slaps.

Next in was a smaller wiry guy in undershirt, jeans, tennis shoes and a spider web tattoo running up his neck. Looking around, he spotted the detectives, disappeared in the direction of the bar, reappeared again, holding a beer bottle. He made his way to their table, pulled an empty chair around to face the room, and sat next to Nguyen.

"Beat it; this is a private table," growled Wishink.

"Naah," said Laine. "I want ta watch the fun."

The door banged open and a man in an electric wheelchair maneuvered in. He was dressed in a suit and tie.

"Ah, shit," said Wishink, "what's he usin' for brains? We got a guy just came in here in a suit and wheelchair," he said disgustedly.

The man in the wheelchair rolled straight to the close end of the bar and caught the attention of one of the bartenders who leaned over the bar to hear what he was saying. Moments later the bartender flagged the waitresses and gave them instructions while pointing to the wheelchair man. After that, the women made many trips, filling their trays, delivering drinks to groups of men, each time pointing to the guy in the wheelchair. After a while, the wheelchair started nosing its way through the crowd, the guy in the suit stopping to talk to groups and hand out business cards.

Some time later, he rolled up to the detectives' table. "Good evening, gentlemen," he said, handing each of them a card. "I'm what you boys would call a goddamn shark." He chuckled genially. "Hank Dagir's the name. I specialize in DWI's. Keep the card." He leaned forward in his chair, all geniality gone. "You," he glanced again at Wishink, "or your lady friends, may need it come some day when the people of this state try to tell you how much you may or may not drink, when you may or may not drive your own goddamn vehicle, and when you have no choice but to have your own blood used against you--a medical breach of your rights as a citizen--to convict you of breaking laws that should not exist!" He sat back and assumed a sonorous tone. "If you are charged with a DWI, the government allows people to suck you dry of your rights, your freedom, and your money. And where does that money go? To line the pockets of the bureaucrats who are giving you the sucker punch. When that happens, you're going to want a shark, a killer shark with a big bite, who's going to stuff their laws up their asses, get *you* money in reparation, and put you back behind your wheel without all that anti-American crap about blood alcohol level. Remember the name. Hank Dagir. I'll slice through the bureaucratic bullshit for you."

The detectives and Laine nodded solemnly and stuck his business card in their pockets. Dagir rolled off to exhort another group.

"Dark van just pulled out of the alley behind the bar," said everyone's ear bud. "Turned south on River Street."

Everyone waited.

"It's coming back," said Middleton's voice. "Pulling up out front. Double-parking two spots back from the corner. Someone's getting out."

"You all set inside?" said Stangler's voice.

"We're set," said Wishink.

"Unmarked units move in slowly."

Stangler and Middleton quietly opened the door to the parking ramp stairwell and raced down the steps.

Rask and Stummer slipped noiselessly out the back of the van. While Stummer stayed put on the shadowed side, Rask loosened his tie, pulled his shirttail out and stumbled to the sidewalk, weaving slowly up the street, supporting himself from parking meter to parking meter, singing "Goodnight Irene" under his breath. Rivera and Olson slid slowly past, Olson holding an opened map of the city, the two of them pointing in different directions and appearing to argue.

Inside, a tall man with long blond hair hanging loose around his face walked into the bar and stood looking around. He was wearing a stained Vikings sweatshirt, despite the heat, ripped jeans, and motorcycle boots. His eyes stopped searching when they found Dagir. He made his way to the wheelchair occupant, and slouched in conversation.

One by one, the detectives got up from their table. Wishink gravitated to a pool table to watch the game, putting himself within 12 feet of the new man and Dagir. Nasty smiles bloomed among the pool players. So tempting. Should they go for it?

Pedersen headed for the men's room, a path that had him passing just the other side of the attorney and ending in the hall that led to the rear exit. Nguyen carried his bottle over and stood viewing the wrestling match on the ceiling TV, a move that put him on a collision course with anyone trying to leave fast. Not knowing the plan, Laine moved over to lean against a wall and appeared to be assessing the physical merits of the female servers.

The tall long-haired blond gestured to an empty table in a darker corner. Making their way to it, the man sat on the backside, leaving Dagir space to pull up to the other side, his back to the room. The man rose, smiling, made some friendly gestures and pushed through to the bar.

"He's setting it up," said Wishink, moving through the crowd. "It's gonna go down any minute, now."

"All units move in tight but quiet," said Stangler's voice. "We're going to take the van."

"Lu and Jim, pull in tighter, but be ready in case he runs," said Wishink.

The tall blond guy came back from the bar, set a bottle and a mixed drink down, and bent over the seated attorney as if to hear better. His right hand slid up, blocked from view by his body.

A hand shot out and grabbed his wrist. "I think not, Dr. Madden," said Wishink.

"Let go, you goddamned freak!" said Madden, twisting his hand free and lunging at Dagir with a long thin stiletto clutched in a latex-covered hand.

Wishink grabbed his arm in time to stop the lunge being lethal, although it did make a touch.

Dagir gaped at the weapon, shot his chair backwards from the table, and shrieked "He's trying to kill me!"

Pedersen and Nguyen pushed through the crowd toward Wishink.

Madden wrenched sideways, throwing himself and Wishink on top of the table. Momentarily loose, with the stiletto still in hand, he lunged around Wishink toward the attorney.

Dagir shrieked again. His chair was backed against a wall and he couldn't retreat farther. "Agghhhh! Agghhhh! Get away! Get away!"

Wishink again grabbed Madden by his knife wrist, and twisted.

Attracted by the struggle, men nearby began to slowly gravitate toward it.

Still hanging on to a flailing Madden, Wishink shouted, "Police! Don't interfere."

That did it. "A fuckin' pig in a purple suit!"
someone shouted, as a wall of half-drunk testosterone
headed for Wishink.

The stiletto landed on the floor with a clatter.
Wishink and Madden fell, struggling, the table crashing
down with them. Oncoming bodies collided with
Dagir's heavy wheelchair, bouncing it against a wall.

"Help! Somebody help me!" he screamed.

Sitting outside in the idling van with the windows
down, two figures in dark coveralls, transparent plastic
masks and green berets heard the shouts and tensed,
ready to speed off the second Madden ran out and
climbed in. They were looking to their right at the
entrance to Brewster's when a voice said, "Put your
hands where I can see them and step out of the van."
Jerking their heads left, they saw Stangler standing
outside the driver's door, a gun held inches from
Burkhalter's head. In the passenger seat, Turner
appeared to freeze, but his right hand slid
inconspicuously toward his door handle. "Uh-uh," said
Middleton, sliding into view by the passenger window,
gun in hand. "You bring both of your hands up; I'll
open the door."

"Lavorski, you and Wilson get inside and help
those guys," said Stangler. Four of you fan out to
perimeter stations. We still have a woman and another
big guy to find. You two stay here," he said, pointing
and searching his memory for names.

"Harders and Hanson," supplied Middleton.

While the two conspirators were being unmasked
and their wrists cuffed behind their backs, squad cars
rolled up and filled both streets. "Harders," said
Stangler, gesturing at Burkhalter and Turner, "you and
Hanson get these two locked up."

The two uniforms grabbed the prisoners by their
arms. Suddenly Turner went face-down hard. "Oops!,"

said Harders, "this cop-killer just accidentally tripped and fell."

"I think he's got a broken nose," said Hanson the rookie, grinning broadly while jerking Turner up.

"This is outrageous!" said Burkhalter. "Do you know who we are?"

"Yeah," said Rivera, "you're sick pieces of shit."

"See if they can make it to lockup without any more accidents," Stangler said.

Inside, Pedersen, Nguyen and Laine waded in to shield Wishink, who was trying to get cuffs on a wildly struggling Madden. The better fighter, Wishink was hampered by the suit. He had one cuff on and was going for the other.

Bellowing, a beefy drinker in an open shirt over a bare chest rushed with fists flailing at Pedersen, who turned sideways, bent from the hips, delivered a solid side-swinging kick to his opponent's kidneys, and let the drinker's momentum carry him in a somersault over the detective's back. A hard elbow to the guy's Adam's apple as he fell on the other side put him out.

A giant twice his size made a rushing grab at Nguyen's throat only to discover the Korean had spun aside at the last second, swept the giant's feet out from under him, and delivered a chop to the back of his neck on the way down that made lying numb on the floor an overpoweringly good idea.

Laine stood four-square while a large man wrapped oversized arms around him in what was intended to be a back-breaking bear hug. Once in close, Laine pistoned his fists several times into the man's large gut, butted his head straight up to hear the guy's jaw crack, and kicked him in the crotch for good measure.

More of the rowdy crowd stepped up and lost to the passive-aggressive, moves of Vovinam combat, while others succumbed to the no-nonsense brute force of Army training. There were still others shouting and pushing to get into the fray when Lavorski and Wilson ran through the door.

"Lights!" shouted Lavorski at the bartender. "Police!" he shouted again. "The next man who raises a fist is under arrest!"

"Help me! Help me! I've been stabbed! Call an ambulance!" shouted Dagir.

Bright overhead lights wiped out any atmosphere the room may have had. Sight of the uniforms recalled most of the combatants to some semblance of caution. Lavorski shouted, "Everyone find a chair and sit down!" He looked around. "Or stay on the floor," he said, biting a lip to keep from smiling. "You want to get your prisoner out of here, Detective Wishink?"

Wishink hauled Madden up, now fully cuffed, and pushed him toward the door.

Lavorski noticed Laine. "Down! Now!," he said. "Chair or floor!"

"He's with us," said Pedersen.

"I'm bleeding to death. I'm going to die," sobbed the attorney, looking at blood on his shirt front.

Lavorski glanced over, saw Nguyen was closest to the wounded man. "Can you check him out?" Nguyen popped the attorney's shirt open.

"Is he hit?" Lavorski said.

"Yes," said Nguyen.

"Does he need an ambulance?"

"Band-Aid," said Nguyen.

Wishink came out onto the street with his prisoner. "Good work, Steve," said Stangler. "Klindworth and Wilson, take him in." He stared at Wishink. "Isn't your pimp get-up just a little over-the-top?"

"Define over-the-top for a pimp."

"You look like a Chicago pimp, not a Riverbend pimp."

"Yeah, well, I didn't want to be recognized. Kill my whole fucking career if I had to switch over and dress like you guys. I'm getting out of here, okay?"

"Yeah, go." Looking over where the remaining four detectives stood, he said, "You guys want to go in and start getting names?" They moved towards the doors of the bar. Stangler turned to Middleton and said, "Two more to go. They can't get back to the van, so they're on foot. I'll take First. You want to go down River, hook up with those two uniforms and start looking?"

"Can do," said Middleton, pulling latex gloves from his pocket. "I'm going to give the interior of this van a quick eyeball first, just in case."

Stangler started walking along the First Avenue side of Brewster's. He could see a uniformed officer at the other end of the block. As he approached the alley entrance, a young female in goth get-up--black, studs, green and red spikes--ran out of it and caromed into him. "Oh god, oh god," she whimpered, clinging tightly to him. "In there. There's a... oh god."

"What?" he said, jerking her away from him.

"I think it's a policeman. Oh god, I think he's hurt." She started to sob.

"Ahh shit! said Stangler, pulling his gun and shoving the girl behind him. "Stay out of the way."

"I'm scared," she whined, clinging to his coat tails. "I don't want to be alone."

Middleton looked up when he heard Stangler's exclamation, saw him disappear into the alley with a female behind him.

"Lobo! Noooo!" he shouted and began to run.

"Behind that dumpster," quavered the girl following Stangler. "I think he's hurt." Her voice evened out and deepened, "And I think you're just as dumb as every other--- Ahh!"

Stangler spun to look behind him just as Middleton rounded the corner into the alley at breakneck speed. "Lobo!"

Between them stood Big Erich, his left arm wrapped around the waist of a woman in teen goth makeup, holding her with feet off the ground while she struggled fiercely. His right hand clamped firmly over the .25 caliber automatic she held.

#   #   #   #   #   #

Chapter 47: Afternoon, Wednesday, August 18

"I seriously missed this," said Muggs as she lay back on weed tufts and held her cigarette poised over the rusty tomato soup can balanced on her stomach. She crossed one leg over the other cocked knee and swung her foot in its torn tennis shoe in the air, careful not to nudge Big Erich, sleeping on a torn blanket. "Not that your place isn't nice for emergencies, Martin, but this, right here, is the life."

"I'm not arguing," said Martin, enjoying the deep shade under the bridge on a hot August afternoon.

"Yeah," said Laine, "this is the best. We might want to take a computer break every once in a while, though, what d'ya think, Martin?"

"I don't see anything," said a voice over their heads.

"Rask and Stummer were all hot under the collar about it. Threatened to take a lie detector test," said another voice. "Wait here, I'm going to take a look."

Stangler came off the bridge, down the bike path at the edge of the park, straddled the iron railing, and swore under his breath as he descended the riprap in his cowboy boots. Gaining level ground, he took his eyes off his feet, looked under the bridge and grinned.

Suddenly, running feet could be heard along the bike path, a flashing figure somersaulted through the air, and gasped "Cops!" as it landed.

Stangler laughed. "Too late." Turning to the group, he said, "Ms Collins, I was wondering if I might take you to lunch, see what you're like when you're not threatening to bite me."

Maintaining her position, Muggs took another drag on her cigarette, and said, "It would have to be a very fancy place."

"How fancy?"

"McDonald's."

"That could be arranged."

"And I never go anywhere without my clients."

"That also could be arranged."

"Yes!" said Kathy, "I want to hear all about everything!"

"Me too," said Laine, shaking Big Erich and standing up.

"Wiley!" called Stangler. "We got a date; bring up the van." To the group he said, "If you want information, we have to take my partner. He's the smart one; I'm the pretty one."

"So that's what that long hair covers," said Muggs, getting up, "a big head."

The group moved quickly up the riprap, except for Stangler, who was making slow going in his boot heels. Muggs paused and extended a hand to haul him up. "You might get around better if you didn't wear those stupid boots."

"You might get along better if you didn't have that smart mouth."

"It's part of my charm," she said as they gained the top.

"Yeah," he said, still holding her hand.

"'Yeah?'" she said. "'Yeah,' what?"

"Yeah, it's part of your charm."

The End #   #

8512296R0

Made in the USA
Charleston, SC
16 June 2011